Cotton Mather, Samuel Gardner Drake, Robert Calef

The Witchcraft Delusion in New England

Vol. 2

Cotton Mather, Samuel Gardner Drake, Robert Calef

The Witchcraft Delusion in New England
Vol. 2

ISBN/EAN: 9783337374877

Printed in Europe, USA, Canada, Australia, Japan

Cover: Foto ©Andreas Hilbeck / pixelio.de

More available books at **www.hansebooks.com**

Woodward's

Historical Series.

No. VI.

THE

𝕸𝖎𝖙𝖈𝖍𝖈𝖗𝖆𝖋𝖙 𝕯𝖊𝖑𝖚𝖘𝖎𝖔𝖓

IN

NEW ENGLAND:

ITS

RISE, PROGRESS, AND TERMINATION,

AS EXHIBITED BY

DR. COTTON MATHER,

IN

THE WONDERS OF THE INVISIBLE WORLD;

AND BY

MR. ROBERT CALEF,

IN HIS

MORE WONDERS OF THE INVISIBLE WORLD.

WITH A

Preface, Introduction, and Notes,

By SAMUEL G. DRAKE.

IN THREE VOLUMES.

VOL. II.

More Wonders of the Invisible World.

———————

PRINTED FOR W. ELLIOT WOODWARD,
ROXBURY, MASS.
MDCCCLXVI.

EDITION IN THIS SIZE 280 COPIES.

MUNSELL, PRINTER.

PREFATORY,

BY THE EDITOR.

 Y Object in this Edition of Mr. Calef's Work is fimilar to that in Dr. Mather's in the preceding Volume, namely, to give a perfectly accurate Reprint of the Work; fo that whoever has Occafion to ufe or confult it may do fo with entire Confidence. I have therefore reprinted the original Edition of 1700, with fuch Notes as was judged might be ufeful to a certain Clafs of Readers. And having mentioned the Notes, I will fay of them here all I have to fay about them. There may be thofe who have no need of fuch Additions. They can pafs them by unheeded;

but it was thought generally that a few Explanations and Additions would be a Help to the Party confulting the Work. They have been made as brief as was thought confiftent with the Subject.

With refpect to the original Text, it is given as exactly like the Original as a much better Type can be made to imitate an old Type of 166 Years ago. As to retaining all the Errors in the original Edition, it was thought incompatible with the general good Tafte of the Age. Some, of a peculiar Nature, if judged neceffary to fhow a Peculiarity of the Times, may have been retained, and noted for fuch Peculiarity; but a broken or imperfect Letter is difcarded as unworthy of Imitation; fo tranfpofed or inverted Letters are fet right, as any good proof Reader would have done, had he noticed them in the Original; but the Orthography of that Day is fcrupuloufly retained.

Why there was no Edition of the *More Wonders of the Invifible World,* for ninety-fix Years, will be found elfewhere explained. The Edition of 1796 is the firft American Edition. This bears the following Imprint: "Printed in London in the Year 1700. | *Reprinted in* SALEM, *Maffachufetts*, 1796, | By WILLIAM CARLTON. | *Sold at* Cushing & Carlton's *Book Store, at the Bible | and Heart, Effex-Street.*" The Volume is in Duodecimo, and contains 318 Pages. The fecond Salem Edition is in the lame Form, and contains 309 Pages, exclufive of the Article headed "Giles Cory," which occupies three Pages; hence Copies of this Edition contain 312 Pages. Its Imprint—all in fmall Capitals—is thus: "Printed in London, A. D. 1700. | Reprinted in Salem, by John D. and T. C. Cufhing, Jr. | for Cufhing and Appleton. 1823." The Publifhers of this Edition added the Article *Giles Cory*, at the Suggeftion of Mr. David Pulsifer, then employed in the Office where the *Witchcraft Records* were kept, as he many Years ago informed me.

The fecond Salem Edition appears to have been copied from the firft — that of 1796. In fome Inftances flight Departures are made from the Copy; and in all thefe, fuch Departures are alfo Departures from the Original. As late as 1796, it might be expected that fome Uniformity would have been obferved, as long as no Exactnefs was intended in refpect to the kind of Type ufed in reprinting an old Work — Uniformity in denoting Quotations; but there is no Exactnefs in this refpect in either Edition. In the firft, as will be feen, fometimes Brackets are ufed to diftinguifh Quotations, but generally italic Type is employed for that Purpofe. In the fecond, inverted Commas are generally ufed, fometimes Brackets. I have followed the Original, bracketing and italicifing as I find it. Inverted Commas to denote Extracts, Quotations and the poffeffive Cafe of Nouns have been introduced by Writers and Printers mainly, fince the Time of Mr. Calef.

Nothing appears in the Book to fhow whether the Author fuperintended the printing of it or otherwife. He may have refided in London at the Time of its Publication, although there are fome Confiderations that feem to lead to the Conclufion that it may have paffed through the Prefs without his Supervifion; but, as before obferved, Nothing is known in regard to it, and it is not very probable that Anything more will ever come to Light; yet equally ftrange Things as that would be, have happened.

Taking Liberties with old Authors is exceedingly diftafteful to me, even where well affured that an Author would have gladly made a Change himfelf, had a Defeft or Deformity been noticed by him; but I have not even affumed that Refponfibility in Mr. Calef's Work. I have done one Thing which the Student ought to thank me for, though he may not. I have placed the Headings of the different Sections at the Commencement of thofe Sections, throughout the Work.

B

In the original Edition thefe were omitted, probably on the fcore of Economy. They alfo ftand at the Commencement of the Book (as in the Original,) entitled " In- dex." The Benefit to the Reader, in reprinting the Captions or Contents of a Section or Chapter over fuch Section or Chapter will be too apparent to require Apology.

The Pagination of the Original is Ex- actly retained; being placed at the top inner Margin in Brackets, and in the Page where the original Page begins and ends, as was done in the previous Volume.

Robert Calef, probably from England, fe
Mass., previous to 1700; rented Lands in
is ftyled Clothier; died 13th April, 171
his Grave-ftone in the old Burying-grou

Jofeph, went to Ipf- — Mary; . . . fhe wich as early as m., 2dly, Tho- 1692; a Phyfician; mas Choate, of d. 28th Dec., 1707, Ipfwich. in his 36th Year.	John, liv- ing 1719	Jeremiah, liv- ing 1719.	ROBERT, (Author of *More Won- ders*, &c.); Merchant, of Bofton; died near the Clofe of 1722, or early in 1723, aged about 45. His Children all born in Bofton.

Robert, born 12th — Margaret, Dec., 1693, had a da. of Dea. Grant of Mill-pri- John Sta- vilege in Ipfwich, niford; d. 1715; died 12th 7th Octo- July, 1730. ber, 1727.	Jofeph, b. 20th May, 1695, in Ipfwich. Ad- miniftrator on Eftate of his Grandfather.	Samuel, b. 25th January, 1697; d. Sept. 1ft, 1720.	Ebenezer.	Peter,† (per- haps, Phyfician, of Charleftown,) d. 11th October, 1735.	— Sarah I ter, r July, 17

John, b. 1725; Phy- — Mary, dau. fician of great Re- of Nathan- fpectability; a Loyal- iel Rogers, ift in the Revolution; of Ipfwich. d. at St. Andrews, N. B., 1812.	Jofeph, living in 1754.	Jofeph, bapt. 3d of May, 1724; a Leather- dreffer.	Sarah, Mary, both d. early.	Peter, bapt. 26th Oct., 1729, died 1749.	Mary, bapt. 23d April, 1732, m. Stephen White, in Waltham, 5th June, 1758.	P: 1(ar m. w:

John, Capt. of a Vef- fel; drowned at Plum Ifland on his return Voyage from the W. Indies, 1782.	Margaret, born 15th October, 1748; m. Dr. Daniel Scott, of Bofton.	Mary, bapt. 24th March, 1750; m. Capt. John Dutch, of Ipfwich.	Thomas Green, Bethi living 1740. living

* This Pedigree is given with the Hope that it will tend to interest fome Defcendant to invefliga
of the Name, and has here thrown together fuch Facts as were among his Memoranda, chiefly made n
† Not much Confidence is felt that the Family given to this PETER is the correct one.
‡ This *James* may not be the one mentioned in *N. Eng. Hift. and Gen. Reg.*, xiv, 271; but is fupp

# of Calef.*

in Roxbury, ━ Mary . . . . died
efter, 1709;   November 12th, 1719.
d 71, as by
xbury.

---

irgaret, dau. of James   Martha, m. Solomon   Mary, m. Sam'l Ste-
rton, of Newton,   Hewes, 28th Septem-   vens, 9th of October,
d Dec., 1699. She   ber, 1700.   1712.
d before 17th Sept.,
44.

Mary.   James, b. 21ft Dec.,   Elizabeth, b. 7th   Anne, b.   Margaret, b.   James,‡ b. 7th ━ Abigail.
   1702, d. young.   May, 1704, liv-   7th July,   4th October,   Nov. 1714, li.
   —   ing in 1722.   1708, m.   1710, mar-   1744, but not
   James, b. 24th Feb.,   —   Green, li.   ried Star, li.   in the Province;
   1711-12, d. young.   Mary, born 25th   1722.   1722.   perhaps the Cap-
   —   Jan., 1712-13,   tive of 1757.
   Robert, b. 9th Mar.,   died young.
   17¾⁶⁄₇, d. young.

)apt.
bru-
4-5,
Ed-
ffin.

Samuel, a Cap-
tive among the
Indians with his
Father.

---

en,   John Green,   Mary Green,   Rebeckah Green,   Jafpar   Robert   Mary   Benjamin
   living 1740.   living 1740.   living 1740.   Star, li.   Star, li.   Star,   Star, li.
         1740.   1740.   living   1740.
             1740.

Subject, and to compose a Genealogy worthy of it. The Compiler of this is not acquainted with any
ears ago.

be he.

MEMOIR OF ROBERT CALEF.

HEN any Man has moral Courage enough to ſpeak plainly againſt any Vices, Follies, or Superſtitions ſurrounding him, he muſt not only be a bold Man, but he does ſo regardleſs of the Coſt; for all Experience teaches that whoever undertakes a Reformation of the Kind muſt experience a Fate not altogether unlike him who waged War with the Philiſtines.

If the Reformer eſcapes the Fury of the Deluded, and lives out his natural Time, he often loſes his ſocial ſtanding; is maligned, ſcoffed, and ſcorned by all whom he expoſed, and a Multitude of thoſe who follow them as their Leaders without knowing wherefore. It is much the ſame now. The Reformer or Corrector of Opinion is hiſſed and ſlandered in Proportion to the Effort he makes. That is to ſay, he is dealt with by Society leniently if he tells the Truth with a Sort of Proviſo; maintains his Poſition without Firmneſs, and gains but few Followers.

Little is known of Robert Calef, afide from his fingle Book, and what his Enemies have thought proper to fay about him in a bitter Spirit of Detraction. He was certainly a Man of good Education; but how he acquired it, where and when, no Mention is found. Dr. Mather, in his Rejoinder to the *More Wonders*, affails him at every Point; but his Attainments in Literature he probably viewed as not vulnerable, as he has made no Attack on that Quarter. It is true he accufes him of being affifted in his Labors, but gives no Clue by which fuch Affiftance may be known.

Notwithftanding Mr. Calef had, by his Independence in freely arraigning the abfurd Proceedings againft thofe charged with imaginary Crimes, he was not without fome Popularity in Bofton, his Place of Refidence, at the Period of thofe Profecutions; for in the Records of the Town are found the following Entries concerning him : April 16th, 1694, " Mr. Robert Calfe was chofen Hayward & Fence-viewer, in the Room of Mr. Edward Wyllys, who refufed to ferve." May 12th, 1702, he was added to the Number of the Overfeers of the Poor. On the 19th of April, 1704, Thanks were voted him for his Services in that Office. On March 12th, 1704–5, it was ordered that Mr. Calef be not charged with Intereft on Moneys remaining in his Hands. The next Year, March 10th, 1706–7, he was chofen one of the Affeffors, but declined the Service.

The Time of the Emigration of the Family of Calef, or Calfe, to this Country has not been afcertained, nor has there been publifhed any confiderable Memorial of it. The Name is an old Englifh one; and were Time beftowed upon it, many Items might doubtlefs be found in old Authors of Perfons who have borne it. At Prefent but a Reference or two muft fuffice. In the Time of Henry III (1216–1270,) a Sir John *Calfe* flourifhed, on whom a curious Epitaph may be feen in *Camden's Remains.* Another John Calfe has an Infcription to his Memory in St. Nicholas's Church, London, giving 1426 as the Year of his Deceafe.

It is not very remarkable that fo little is known of Robert Calef, when it is confidered that he had almoft the entire Community againft him. And lefs is learned about him than might be expected in the Perufal of his own Book. That his Character was above Reproach is evident from the Replies of Dr. Mather and his Friends, to his Queftions refpecting the Proofs of Witchcraft. It helps one's Caufe but very little, merely to call his Antagonift "a Lyar;" and this appears to have been the heavieft Argument brought againft Mr. Calef in Anfwer to his Statements.

In Dr. Mather's Account of the *Afflictions* of Margaret Rule, he thus refers to thofe who differ from him; undoubtedly having fpecial Reference to Mr. Calef: "Yea, to do like Satan himfelf, by fly, bafe unpretending Infinuations, as if I wore not

the Modefty and Gravity which became a Minifter
of the Gofpel, I could not but think myfelf unkindly dealt withal, and the Neglects of others to
do me Juftice in this Affair has caufed me to conclude this Narrative in *another hearing* of fuch
monftrous Injuries."

By "another hearing," is meant that he had or
would take legal Steps to filence his Opponent;
for about the fame Time the Doctor was fo an-
noyed by certain Queries fent him by Mr. Calef,
that he returned him Word by his (Mr. Calef's)
Bearer, that he would have him arrefted for Slander, as he was "one of the worft of Lyars." This
the Doctor proclaimed alfo in his Pulpit. Yet
Mr. Calef was always refpectful in his Language
in return, for anything that appears to the contrary.

On the 29th of September, 1693, Mr. Calef
addreffed Dr. Mather a Note, requefting that he
would meet him at either of the Bookfellers,
Richard Wilkins or Benjamin Harris. Mr. Calef
defired this Meeting that they might examine
together the Memoranda of what he had noted
after vifiting the "poffeffed" or bewitched Perfon,
Margaret Rule. At that Vifit were alfo both the
Doctors Mather, Father and Son. Meantime Mr.
Calef was complained of and taken into Cuftody,
on the Charge of having committed a fcandalous
Libel on Mr. Mather the younger; the Complaint being made by both. Mr. Calef ftates
that he did not remember that he had been

charged with Untruth in his Report of the Examination of Margaret; but it was afferted that
he had wronged Dr. Mather by his Omiffions.
To which Mr. Calef replied, that he had reported
only what *he* faw and heard himfelf.

As to the Profecution for Libel, Mr. Calef
fays he was taken to the Court of Seffions, and
after waiting a while for his Accufers, none appeared. He was therefore difmiffed. He had
had a Promife from Dr. Mather to meet him to
compare Notes, but it does not appear that any
Time was ftated; and after feveral Months had
elapfed Mr. Calef wrote, requefting him to fix
upon a Time and Place of Meeting. A Meeting
however never occurred, of the Kind defired;
but, as the only Means of getting the Doctor's
Views of what he had written, he fent him a
Copy of his Notes on Margaret Rule's Exhibitions, two of which he feems to have witneffed.
On the 15th of January, 1693–4, the Doctor
wrote him a long Letter, in which he fays: "I
have this to fay, as I have often already faid, that
do I fcarcely find any one Thing in the whole
Paper, whether refpecting my Father or felf, either
fairly or truly reprefented." The *Fairnefs* on
both Sides may be judged of, as both Papers will
be found in the enfuing Work, Pages 13–22.

The Doctor fent the Author, accompanying
his Letter, Copies of three Depofitions, or Statements from feveral Perfons, to the Effect that
what he had ftated regarding the ftrange Conduct

of Margaret Rule was true; efpecially as to the
Fact, that fhe was by invifible Hands raifed from
her Bed up to the Garret Floor, and that ftrong
Men, the Byftanders, could not hold her down.
The Height of the Room is not mentioned; but
one Witnefs, Samuel Aves, fays it was "a great
Way;" that fhe was lifted "towards the Top of
the Room." Three others faid, this was "in Subftance true." Alfo, Thomas Thornton, a Paver,
faid fhe was lifted up, "fo as to touch the Garret
Floor;" to which William Hudfon affented in
"Subftance." All of which Teftimonies, Mr.
Calef ventured to infinuate was about as true, as a
Report would be that Iron would fwim on Water; that if that Rifing in the Air without Hands
actually took place, it was a Miracle, and if a
Miracle it was wrought by the Devil. And yet
it feems that Mr. Calef believed none but God
himfelf could work Miracles.

Between the Date of his laft Letter and the
19th of February, 1693-4, inftead of anfwering
Mr. Calef's Letter, Dr. Mather fent him Word
that his Library was open to him, intimating that
he might find there Anfwers to any and all of his
Objections and Difficulties. But Mr. Calef did
not avail himfelf of the Kindnefs thus tendered,
though he thanked him by Letter, and at the
fame Time complained that he had not written
him, pointing out what he conceived to be Errors in his former Communications; adding, "if
you think Silence a Virtue in this Cafe, I fhall (I

suppose) so far comply with it as not to loose you
any more Time to look over my Papers." This
however did not end the Correspondence; for on
the 16th of April following he addressed a Letter
to the Doctor, calling his Attention to certain
Passages in the *Wonders of the Invisible World,* and
some other "late Books of his and his Relations."
After stating a few of the Author's strange Asser-
tions, such as that the Devil causes Wars, Plagues,
and other Calamities; that the Devil is a great
Linguist; that Suicides "are the Effects of a
cruel & bloody Witchcraft," and several other
similar Quotations. In closing this Letter, he
remarks that he is only performing what he believes to be his Duty; that he is far from doing
it to gain Applause, or from a Love of Contention; that, on the other Hand, he expected to
make many Enemies by it.

The next Letter which he wrote to Mr. Mather was dated March the 1st, 1694–5. In this
he says he had waited more than a Year "for the
Performance of a reiterated Promise" from him,
to reply to Arguments which he had sent for his
Refutation or Approval. Instead of that pro-
mised Answer, he had received, through the
Hand of a third Person, "four Sheets of recinded Papers." These were delivered under an
Injunction that no Copy was to be taken of them,
and he was allowed to keep them but a Fortnight. He has given some Account of those
"four Sheets," and observes that he does not won-
C

der at not being allowed to copy them, as they
contained fo much "crude Matter and impertinent
Abfurdities." Among other Things, he fent Mr.
Calef Baxter's *World of Spirits*, characterizing it
an *ungainfayable* Book; upon which Mr. Calef
remarks, as aptly as fignificantly, that he knows
of no "ungainfayable" Book but the Bible, and
thinks no other Man who had ever read it would
fo ftyle it except its Author. He is probably
correct when he attributes to Mr. Baxter the
Weaknefs incident to old Age, in allowing his
Name to appear as the Author of *The Certainty
of the World of Spirits.* But his own Words
are more to the Point: "As to the fometime
Reverend Author, let his Works praife the Remembrance of him; but for fuch as are either
Erroneous and foifted upon him, or the Effect of
an aged Imbecility, let them be detected that they
may proceed no further."

The Experience of Mr. Calef was fimilar,
probably, to that of moft Reformers, both before
and fince his Time. To combat fimilar Super-
ftitions at this Day would be nearly or quite as
hazardous as it was then. Indeed, there have
been Cafes within fome thirty Years in New
England, in which Individuals have fared much
worfe than Robert Calef did in Bofton more
than an hundred Years before, and for no offence
worthy of Notice; neither had an Eighth of the
Community a Voice in this Perfecution, while in
Mr. Calef's Cafe nine Tenths of the whole Peo-

ple probably were crying out againſt him. The Villainy of a ſingle Lawyer, and the Imbecility of a Judge may ſometimes ſucceed in ruining for a Time the Charaƈter of any Citizen.

Mr. Calef ſeems to have been almoſt alone in the Warfare he had undertaken. "How Few," he ſays, "are willing to be found oppoſing ſuch a Torrent, as knowing, that in ſo doing, they ſhall be ſure to meet with Oppoſition to the utmoſt, from the many, both of Magiſtrates, Miniſters and people; and the name of Sadducee, Atheiſt, and perhaps Witch too caſt upon them moſt liberally, by Men of the higheſt Profeſſion in Godlineſs."

Owing to the peculiar State of the Times when Mr. Calef wrote, he felt himſelf obliged to admit a great Deal that a Writer at a later Day would not have found it Neceſſary. This will account for ſome heavy Papers introduced into the Body of his Work. He had a moſt difficult Taſk to perform. Like the Mariner in a Tempeſt upon a Lee Shore, he needed an Eye on every Point of the Compaſs, and a deep Sea Lead ever in Hand.

What Overtures, if any, he made to Printers in Boſton to print his Books, are unknown. It is pretty certain, however, that no One would have dared to undertake it. And what Agency, if any, he employed to have it done Abroad, is equally unknown. But one Thing is known; no Book-ſeller had the Hardihood to offer it for Sale, or dared to give it Shop-room. He had a few

Friends who ftood by him, ready to fhield him, as far as was confiftent with their own Safety, but none had the Boldnefs to come out fo openly as he did. Some wrote ftrongly againft the Delu- fion, but not for Publication ; as Brattle of Cam- bridge, Cary of Charleftown, and Robert Paine. The Work of the laft named Gentleman has not been made public, and remains in private Hands. It is faid to be a moft mafterly Refutation of the Arguments made ufe of againft Witches, written in the Time of the Trials. But it feems, on a careful Perufal of Mr. Calef's *More Wonders,* that not much more can be faid (admitting or defer- ring to a Sort of Authority which cannot be argued from,) to fhow the utter Abfurdity of the Proceedings on the Witch Trials. He has, it muft be admitted, exhaufted the Subject. It is very eafy, it is true, to fay the fame Thing, ufing different and more elegant Language, according to the prefent Standard of Elegance ; but for clofe and fuccinct Argument, the Author has not been furpaffed by his Succeffors. His Statement of Apology for thofe poor People who had confeffed themfelves Witches, and accufed others, is highly fatisfactory.

Mr. Calef poffeffed more than ordinary At- tainments in Literature ; he was no Stranger to legal Forms ; and as to theological Learning, was, for Soundnefs of Argument, quite fuperior to thofe who were in the Field againft him. Thefe Facts excite a Defire to know more of his Hiftory ;

for all that has been learned about him, is that he was a " Merchant of Bofton," and that he was a Dealer in woolen Goods; and hence the Attempt of a narrow minded Oppofition to clafs him among the Ordinary and Illiterate of the Time They alfo defcended to vulgar Epithets, calling him a *Calf;* his Book they call a " Firebrand, thrown by a Mad-man;" and, "it was highly re-joycing to us, when we heard that our Book-fellers were fo well acquainted with the Integrity of our Paftors, as not one of them would admit of thofe Libels to be vended in their Shops.". This was the Language of the Men who pub-lifhed "Some few Remarks, upon a *Scandalous Book* .... written by one Robert Calef," with the Motto—"Truth will come off Conqueror." This Publication is dated " January 9th, 1700–1," and purports to have been drawn up by Obadiah Gill, John Barnard, John Goodwin, William Ro-bie, Timothy Wadfworth, Robert Cumbey, and George Robinfon; none of whom were Men of fpecial Note then or afterwards. It fhould be obferved, however, that they were Members of the Old North Church. Any further Notice of the Anfwer to the *More Wonders* is unneceffary here; but it will be ufed in the Notes occafion-ally, that the "*Slandered*" may fpeak for them-felves.

It was probably about the Time of the Iffue of the *Some Few Remarks* that the *More Wonders* was caufed to be burnt in the College Yard at

Cambridge, by Order of the Prefident, Dr. Increafe Mather. The Burning was doubtlefs performed with much of Ceremony and Formality,
but there does not appear to have been any Record
made of it upon the College Books; or if fo,
the Hiftorians of the Inftitution have not mentioned it. This Kind of *Argument* againft what
is fet forth in a Book, is about as effectual as that
employed againft the Tide of the Ocean by an
eaftern Monarch. That the Prefident of the
College had no great Faith in his *Argument*, is
pretty clear, or fo much Pains would not have
been taken by him in making another Book to
refute the Arguments contained in the one he
had burned.

The precife Date of Mr. Calef's Death is not
upon any Records which have been examined;
and the laft Time he appears to have tranfacted
any Bufinefs requiring his Signature, was at the
Regiftry of Deeds, then under the official Management of John Ballantine, Efq., when he
releafed a Mortgage which he held of certain
Lands in Roxbury; which Mortgage was given
by Jofeph Holland and his Wife Elizabeth, and
dated the 11th of March, 1720. [Of courfe,
1721, N. S.] The Releafe was figned by the
Mortgagor, April 11th, 1722. His Signature on
this Occafion has been copied, and is here prefented.

But a fhort Time previous to this Tranfaction he deeded certain Property to his Children. In this Inftrument, dated February 10th, 1721, [1722, N. S.,] he ftyles himfelf Clothier, and names Children, Elizabeth, Ann, Margaret and James. Two Houfes and Land; one in prefent Poffeffion of James Smith; the other in his own Poffeffion; bounded N. W. upon —— Street, N. E. upon Thomas Wheeler, S. E. upon William Gold, and S. W. upon Bond Street; alfo one Tract of Land in Brookline; alfo a Mortgage from James Barton, Ropemaker, referving to himfelf and his now married Wife the Ufe of the Premifes during their Lives.

The following is an Abftract of his Will:

"I Robert Calfe of Bofton, being now in found Body and Minde doe make this my laft Will [and] appoint my well beloved Wife Executrix. After funerall Charges and all Other my juft Debtts being paide, my Will is that my Wife [have] all my Eftate during her Widdowhood; and in Cafe fhe fee Caus to alter her Condition by Marraig, that then fhe fhall quitt her Adminifterfhip, and the Improvement of the Eftate, wholey to be for the Bennefitt of my Children; only two hundred Pounds I will unto her upon her Marraig, and the whoolly Remainder to be difpofte of as followe: Son James £100, when of Age more then any of the Reft of my Children: And allfo I give £200 ought of faid Eftate for defraying the Charges of bringing him up

to the Collig, if he inclines to Larning, but if
not then to be equaley divided among him and
the Reft of my Children, viz. Elizabeth, Ann
and Margaret, together with what Children it
fhall plees God to give me by my prefent Wife :
And it is my Will that my Daughters, Elizabeth,
Ann and Margaret have an equall Proportion of
all my Eftate, Perfonall and Reall, only what is
before excepted unto my Son James, and that
they be paid upon Marraig or at the Difcretion
of my Executrix, if fhe remain a Widow, and if
it pleafe God to take away my Children by Death
before of Age or without Iffue the whole of my
Eftate to return to my Wife or to her Difpofe.

2d of Jan., 1720.

"In Prefence of Sam^{ll} Wentworth, John Alden,
Jr. and John Tyler.

"Margaret Calfe prefented the within Will for
Probat and John Alden, Junr and John Tyler
made Oath, &c. and they together with Saml
Wentworth, who is now out of the Province fet
to their Hands as Witneffes in the Teftator's Prefence. Bofton, Feb. 18th, 1722–3.
            "SAMUEL SEWALL J Prob^t"

The Teftator was too ill, it is probable, to draw
up his Will himfelf, or one fo unclerical would
not have appeared. The Circumftances, how-

ever, under which it was made, are entirely con-
jectural. His Wife was living, a Widow, till
about 1744; as in September of that Year her
Will was proved. It was made four Years before, namely, September 17th, 1740. The Items
of Intereſt in it here follow:

"To Grandſon Thomas Green £60; to Mar-
garet Green £20, and a ſilver Porringer which
her Father now has. To Ann Green £30, and
a gold Necklace. To Bethiah Green £20. To
John Green £20. To Mary Green £20, and to
Rebeckah Green £30; all the Children of my
Daughter Ann Green deceaſed. To Daughter
Margaret Star's four Children, namely, to Joſeph,
£20; Robert, £20; Mary, £20; and Benjamin
Star, £20. Clothing to be divided between
Daughter Star, and Grand Daughter, Ann Green.
The Remainder of Eſtate to be divided between
Daughter Margaret Star and Son James Calf;
ſaid Son to be Executor if in the Province;
otherwiſe, Couſin Thomas Simpkins.

"*Dated*, January 2d, 1720. *Signed*,
                    "MARGARET CALF.

"Witneſſes — Abigail Weſt, Barnabas Gibbs,
John Swinnerton."

It was preſented for Probate by Thomas Simpkins; James Calf being out of the Province.

In the General Court Records Notice is given,
under Date June 25th, 1723, of a "Petition of
Margaret Calef, Widow, and ſole Executrix of

D

the laft Will of Robert Calef, late of Bofton, Merchant, deceafed," praying for Leave to fell a feventh Part of a Houfe and Land in Roxbury, of which faid Robert Calef died feized. The Father of Mr. Calef, alfo named Robert, had died inteftate, April 13th, 1719, and his Wife on the 12th of November following. In the Settlement of his Eftate, it is ftated that the "Houfing and Lands lying in Roxbury, cannot be divided without Prejudice and Injury;" hence the Petition before mentioned.

A few Items here follow, given for the Benefit of thofe who may hereafter defire to inveftigate the Hiftory of the Calef Family;

Dr. Jofeph Calef died at Ipfwich, Dec. 31ft, 1707, leaving a Wife, and Children, Robert, Jofeph, Samuel, Ebenezer, Peter and Mary. This was, doubtlefs the Emigrant to Ipfwich, where, in 1692, he had a Grant for a Fulling-mill. Jofeph Calef was a Scout in Capt. John Goff's Company in 1746. Mary, Widow of Jofeph Calef, married Thomas Choate of Ipfwich; Date of Marriage is not ftated. Jofeph Calef was of Bofton, 1746, in which Year he petitioned, with others, for the Paving of Atkinfon Street.

James Calef and his Son Samuel were Captives among the Indians and French; were taken at Fort William Henry, in Auguft, 1757. Abigail, the Wife of James and Mother of Samuel, made Application in their behalf to the Authorities of the Province. No Mention is made of

their place of Refidence. Dr. John Calef, of
Ipfwich, married Margaret, Daughter of Nathan-
iel and Mary (Leverett) Rogers, of the fame
Town. He was born 1725.

After the bloody Fight at Pequawket, Go-
vernor Dummer wrote to Eleazer Tyng: "Send
down to me forthwith by the Bearer hereof, Mr.
Calef, the moft intelligent Perfon among Lovell's
Men returned, that I may have a perfect Account
of that Action." What Mr. Calef this was, does
not with certainty appear.

A Mrs. Mary Calfe died at Concord, N. H.,
Auguft 10, 1817, aged ninety-eight Years. Her
firft Hufband was Samuel Bradley, who was killed
by the Indians, Auguft 11th, 1746. She after-
wards married Robert Calfe, Efq., of Chefter, in
the fame State. This is on the Authority of Mr.
Bouton, in his *Hiftory of Concord*, who, in another
Place, fays Calfe's Name was Richard. Whether
Richard or Robert, he was probably a Defcendant
of James, the only furviving Son of Robert, the
"Merchant of Bofton." The maiden Name of
Mrs. Calfe was Folfom.

When the Federal Conftitution of New Hamp-
fhire was adopted (1788,) John Calfe, Efq., was
chofen Secretary of the Convention. He was
alfo Secretary in 1791, when the Conftitution was
revifed. His Son Jofeph died at Hampftead, N.
H., Auguft 6, 1854, aged 79. A John Calef was
in the Old Mill Prifon, England, 1789. Jeremiah Calef, a Native of Exeter, N. H., died at

Northfield, 23d February, 1856, aged 73 Years,
10 Months. James, an only Brother of Jeremiah, died at Sanbornton, 30th March, 1856,
aged 71.

Robert Calef was an eminent Ship-mafter be-
tween Bofton and London before the Revolution.
His Arrival on one Occafion is thus noticed in
the *Gazette and News-Letter* of April 5th, 1764:
"In Captain Calef came Paffengers, the Captains,
Edward Wendell, John Marfhall, and Doctor
Marfhall of this Town. Mrs. McTaggart, and
her Son Gray of this Town, died of the Small-
pox in London." The Autographs of feveral of
the Name of Calef (always fo fpelt) are in the
Writer's Poffeffion from 1755 to 1780. In 1755,
Jofeph was engaged in fupplying Ships with
Water. In 1767, Jofeph Calef, probably the fame,
was largely in the leather Trade. He was a Tan-
ner, and his Tan-yard was in the Neighborhood
of the Old Bofton Theatre.

What Time the Family of Robert Calef came
to this Country has not been afcertained. It was
probably in the latter Half of the feventeenth
Century, and our Author may have had his Education before his Emigration. This View may
be confidered probable, from a Paffage in his
Preface to the *More Wonders*, &c.

After the Above was written, it came to my
Notice, that in a Volume iffued by the *Mafs.
Hift. Soc.*, were fome Extracts from the *Diary* of
Cotton Mather. Alfo the following, concerning

Robert Calef, in a Memorandum-book of Dr. Belknap: " Robert Calef, Author of *More Wonders of the Invifible World*, was a Native of England; a young Man of good Senfe, and free from Superftition; a Merchant in Bofton. He was furnifhed with Materials for his Work by Mr. Brattle, of Cambridge; and his Brother, of Bofton; and other Gentlemen, who were oppofed to the *Salem* Proceedings. E. P." [Ebenezer Pemberton?]

[1] The Epiſtle to the READER.

And more eſpecially to the Noble *Bereans*[1] of this *Age*, wherever
Reſiding.

Gentlemen,

*Y*OU *that are freed from the Slauery of a corrupt Education;
and that in ſpite of human Precepts, Examples and Precſidents,
can hearken to the Diſtates of Scripture and Reaſon:*

*For your ſakes I am content, that theſe Collections of mine, as alſo
my Sentiments ſhould be expoſed to publick view; In hopes that
having well conſidered, and compared them with Scripture, you will
ſee reaſon, as I do, to queſtion a belief ſo prevalent (as that here
treated of) as alſo the practice flowing from thence; they ſtanding
as nearly connext as cauſe and effect; it being found wholly imprac-
ticable, to extirpate the latter without firſt curing the former.*

*And if the Buffoon or Satyrical will be exerciſing their Talents,
or if the Bigots wilfully and blindly reject the Teſtimonies of their
own Reaſon, and more ſure word, it is no more than what I expected
from them.*

*But you Gentlemen, I doubt not are willing to Diſtinguiſh be-
tween Truth and Error, and if this may be any furtherance to you
herein, I ſhall not miſs my Aim.*

*But if you find the contrary, and that my belief herein is any way
Heterodox, I ſhall be thankful for the Information to any Learned
or Reverend Perſon, or others, that ſhall take that pains to inform*

---

[1] In both the ſecond and third
Editions this Name is printed *Ba-
rons.* The Printer probably not
knowing what elſe to make of it.
The Inhabitants of ancient *Berœa*
were called *Berœans.* The preſent
Aleppo occupies the Site. For the
Point, ſee *Acts,* xvii, 11.

*me better by Scripture, or found Reafon, which is what I have been
long feeking for in this Country* in vain.[2]

In a time when not only England *in particular, but almoft all*
Europe *had been labouring againft the Ufurpations of Tyranny
and Slavery. The* Englifh, America *has not been behind in a
fhare in the Common calamities; more efpecially* New-England,
*has met not only with fuch calamities as are common to the reft, but
with feveral aggravations enhanfing fuch Afflictions, by the Devaftations and Cruelties of the Barbarous* Indians *in their* Eaftern
borders, &c.

*But this is not all, they have been harraft (on many accounts) by
a more dreadful Enemy, as will herein appear to the confiderate.*

P. 66. Were it as we are told in *Wonders of the Invifible
World*, that the Devils were walking about our Streets with
lengthned Chains making a dreadful noife in our Ears, and Brimftone, even without a Metaphor, was making a horrid and a
hellifh ftench in our Noftrils.[3] P. 49.

And That the Devil exhibiting himfelf ordinarily as a black-
Man, had decoy'd a fearful knot of Proud, Froward, Ignorant,
Envious and Malitious Creatures, to lift themfelves in his horrid
Service, by entring their Names in a Book tendered unto them;
and that they have had their Meetings and Sacraments, and affo-
ciated themfelves to deftroy the Kingdom of our Lord Jefus

---

[2] This is the Remark that led me
to think the Author was not a Native of New England. An Extract
by Dr. Belknap, noted in the accompanying Memoir is corrobora-
tive of the Conjecture.

[3] See Vol. I, Pages 121-2. Co-
temporary with the Author, we find
that eminent Divine, Michael Wig-
glefworth, thus poetically impreffing
upon the Readers of his Poem the
Horrors fpoken of in the Text:

Whom having brought as they are taught,
  Unto the Brink of Hell,
(That Difmal Place far from Chrifts Face,
  Where Death and Darknefs dwell:
Where Gods fierce Ire kindleth the Fire,
  And Vengeance feeds the Flame
With Piles of Wood, and Brimftone Flood,
  That none can quench the fame.
    Day of Doom, Stanza 208.

Chrift, in thefe parts of the World ; having each of them their Spectres, or Devils Commiffionated by them, and [2] reprefenting of them to be the Engines of their Malice, by thefe wicked Spectres, fiezing poor People about the Country, with various and bloody Torments. And of thofe evidently preternatural Torments fome to have died. And that they have bewitched fome even fo far, as to make them felf deftroyers, and others in many Towns, here and there languifh'd under their evil hands. The People, thus afflicted, miferably fcratch'd and bitten ; and that the fame Invifible Furies did ftick Pins in them, and fcal'd them, diftort and disjoint them, with a Thoufand other Plagues ; and fometimes drag them out of their Chambers, and carry them over Trees, and Hills Miles together, many of them being tempted to fign the Devils Laws.

P. 7. *Thofe furies whereof feveral have killed more People perhaps than would ferve to make a Village. If this be the true ftate of the Afflictions of this Country, it is very deplorable, and beyond all other outward Calamities miferable. But if on the other fide, the Matter be as others do underftand it, That the Devil has been too hard for us by his Temptations, figns, and lying Wonders, with the help of pernicious notions, formerly imbibed and profeffed ; together with the Accufations of a parcel of poffeffed, diftracted, or lying Wenches, accufing their Innocent Neighbours, pretending they fee their Spectres* (i. e.) *Devils in their likenefs Afflicting of them, and that God in righteous Judgement, (after Men had afcribed his Power to Witches, of commiffionating Devils to do thefe things) may have given them over to ftrong delufions to believe lyes. &c And to let loofe the Devils of Envy, Hatred, Pride, Cruelty and Malice againft each other ; yet ftill difguifed under the Mafk of Zeal for God, and left them to the branding one another, with the odious Name of Witch ; and upon the Accufation of thofe*

above mentioned, Brother *to* Accuse *and* Prosecute Brother, *Children their* Parents, Pastors *and* Teachers *their immediate* Flock *unto
death;* Shepherds *becoming* Wolves, *Wise Men* Infatuated; *People
hauled to* Prisons, *with a bloody noise pursuing to, and insulting
over, the* (true) *Sufferers at* Execution, *while some are fleeing from
that called* Justice, Justice *itself fleeing before such* Accusations,
*when once it did but begin to refrain further proceedings; and to
question such* Practises, *some making their* Escape *out of* Prisons,
rather than by an obstinate Defence *of their* Innocency, *to run so
apparent hazard of their* Lives; Estates *seized,* Families *of* Children *and others left to the* Mercy *of the* Wilderness (*not to mention
here the* Numbers *prescribed, dead in* Prisons, *or* Executed, &c.)

All which Tragedies, *tho begun in one* Town, *or rather by one*
Parish, *has* Plague-like *spread more than through that* Country.
And by its Eccho *giving a brand of* Infamy *to this whole* Country,
throughout the World.

If this were the Miserable *case of this* Country *in the time
thereof, and that the* Devil *had so far prevailed upon us in our*
Sentiments *and* Actions, *as to draw us from so much as looking into
the* Scriptures *for our guidance in these pretended* Intricacies, *lead-
ing us to a trusting in blind guides, such as the corrupt practices of
some other* Countries *or the bloody* Experiments *of* Bodin,[4] [3] *and
such other* Authors. *Then tho our* Case *be most miserable, yet it
must be said of* New-England, *Thou hast destroyed thyself, and
brought this greatest of* Miseries *upon thee.*

---

[4] John Bodin was a Frenchman
of great Learning, born at Angers
1530. Some of his Historical Works
were formerly in great Repute in
England as well as in France. His
Work referred to above was published at Paris in 1579, under the
Title *La Démonomanie, ou Traite* *des Sorciers,* in 4to. It is full of all
those Superstitions for which the Age
in which the Author lived is cele-
brated. See Camerarius, *Living
Library,* Page 2, Edition 1625, *Fol.*
See also Mr. Fowler's interesting
Note to the last Salem Edition of
Salem Witchcraft, P. ix.

And now whether the Witches (such as have made a compact by Explicit Covenant with the Devil, having thereby obtained a power to Commissionate him) have been the cause of our miseries.

Or whether a Zeal governed by blindness and passion, and led by president, has not herein precipitated us into far greater wickedness (if not Witchcrafts) than any have been yet proved against those that suffered.

To be able to distinguish aright in this matter, to which of these two to refer our Miseries is the present Work. As to the former, I know of no sober Man, much less Reverend Christian, that being ask'd dares affirm and abide by it, that Witches have that power; viz. to Commissionate Devils to kill and destroy. And as to the latter, it were well if there were not too much of truth in it, which remains to be demonstrated.

But here it will be said, what need of Raking in the Coals that lay buried in oblivion. We cannot recal those to Life again that have suffered, supposing it were unjustly; it tends but to the exposing the Actors, as if they had proceeded irregularly.

Truly I take this to be just as the Devil would have it, so much to fear disobliging men, as not to endeavour to detect his Wiles, that so he may the sooner, and with the greater Advantages set the same on foot again (either here or elsewhere) so dragging us through the Pond twice by the same Cat.[5] And if Reports do not (herein) deceive us, much the same has been acting this present year in Scotland. And what Kingdom or Country is it, that has not had their bloody fits and turns at it. And if this is such a catching disease, and so universal, I presume I need make no Apology for my Endeavours to prevent, as far as in my power, any more such bloody Victims or

---

[5] That is by the same Cord, or Rope. In nautical Usage, a Rope to do or perform a certain Service. The Anchor was formerly hoisted to the Head of a certain bow Timber to which it was fastened by the Cat Rope; hence the Timber is called the *Cat-head*.

*Sacrifices ; tho indeed I had rather any other would have undertaken
fo offenfive, tho neceffary a tafk ; yet all things weighed, I had rather
thus Expofe myfelf to Cenfure, than that it fhould be wholly omitted.
Were the notions in queftion, innocent and harmlefs, refpecting the
glory of God, and well being of Men, I fhould not have engaged in
them, but finding them in my efteem, fo intollerably deftructive of both.
This together with my being by Warrant called before the Juftices,
in my own Juft Vindication, I took it to be a call from God, to my
Power, to Vindicate his Truths againft the* Pagan *and* Popifh
*Affertions, which are fo prevalent; for tho Chriftians in general do
own the Scriptures to be their only Rule of Faith and Doctrine, yet
thefe Notions will tell us, that the Scriptures have not fufficiently,
nor at all defcribed the crime of Witchcraft, whereby the culpable
might be detected, tho it be pofitive in the Command to punifh it by
Death ; hence the World has been from time to time perplext in the
profecution of the feveral Diabolical mediums of Heathenifh and
Popifh Invention, to detect an Imaginary Crime (not but that there
are* Witches, *fuch as the* Law *of* God [4] *defcribes)*[6] *which has
produced a deluge of Blood ; hereby rendering the Commands of God
not only void but dangerous.*

*So alfo they own Gods Providence and Government of the World,
and that Tempefts and Storms, Afflictions and Difeafes are of his
fending ; yet thefe Notions tell us, that the Devil has the power of
all thefe, and can perform them when commiffion'd by a Witch
thereto, and that he has a power at the Witches call to act and do,
without and againft the courfe of Nature, and all natural caufes,
in afflicting and killing of Innocents ; and this is that fo many have
died for.*

[6] It will elfewhere be feen that the Author makes it pretty clear, that to difcover Witches by that Law, or who they are, has never been done. It was therefore eafy to argue that Witches never would be difcovered by it. In other Words where nothing is looked for nothing will be found. This Subject will be found difcuffed elfewhere.

Alſo it is generally believed, that if any Man has ſtrength, it is from God the Almighty Being : but theſe notions will tell us, that the Devil can make one Man as ſtrong as many, which was one of the beſt proofs, as it was counted, againſt Mr. Burroughs *the Miniſter ; tho his contemporaries in the Schools during his Minority could have teſtified, that his ſtrength was then as much ſuperior to theirs as ever*[7] *(ſetting aſide incredible Romances) it was diſcovered to be ſince. Thus rendering the power of God, and his providence of none Effect.*

Theſe are ſome of the deſtructive notions of this Age, and however the aſſerters of them ſeem ſometimes to value themſelves much upon ſheltring their Neighbors from Spectral Accuſations. They may deſerve as much thanks as that Tyrant, that having induſtriouſly obtained an unintelligible charge againſt his Subjects, in matters wherein it was impoſſible they ſhould be Guilty, having thereby their lives in his power, yet ſuffers them of his meer Grace to live, and will be call'd gracious Lord.

It were too Icarian[8] *a taſk for one unfurniſh'd with neceſſary learning, and Library, to give any Juſt account, from whence ſo great deluſions have ſprung, and ſo long continued. Yet as an Eſſay from thoſe ſcraps of reading that I have had opportunity of; it will be no great venture to ſay, that Signs and Lying Wonders have been one principal cauſe.*

[7] Samuel Webber, aged about 36, teſtified that ſome ſeven or eight Years ago he lived at Caſco Bay, where Mr. B. was Miniſter. Having heard much of his great Strength, and coming to his Houſe, and in Diſcourſe about it, he told the ſaid Webber that he had put his Fingers into the Bung of a Barrel of " Malaſes " and lifted it up and carried it round him. See *Records of Sa-* *lem Witchcraft* (by Woodward) ii, 113. See alſo ſundry other Teſtimonies about Mr. Burroughs's great Strength, *ib.*, 123-5. Alſo (Vol. I, 153,) *The Wonders of the Inviſible World.*

[8] The Author's claſſical Learning was probably not very extenſive. The Uſe of this mythical Name however may have been according to its Acceptation in his Time.

It is written of Juftin Martyr,[9] *who lived in the fecond Century, that he was before his converfion a great Philofopher; firft in the way of the* Stoicks, *and after, of the* Peripateticks, *after that of the* Pythagorean, *and after that of the* Platonifts *fects; and after all proved of Eminent ufe in the Church of Chrift; yet a certain Author fpeaking of one* Apollonius Tyaneus[10] *has thefe words* [That the moft Orthodox themfelves began to deem him vefted with power fufficient for a Deity; which occafioned that fo ftrange a doubt from *Juftin Martyr,* as cited by the learned *Gregory,* Fol. 37. Ει Θεοςζοι &c. If God be the creator and Lord of the World, how comes it to pafs that *Apollonius* his *Telifms,* have fo much over-ruled the courfe of things! for we fee that they alfo have ftilled the Waves of the Sea; and the raging of the Winds, and prevailed againft the Noifome Flies, and Incurfions of wild Beafts,] &c. *If fo Eminent and Early a Chriftian were by thefe falfe fhews in fuch doubt, it is the lefs wonder in our depraved times, to meet with what is Equivalent thereto: Befides this a certain Author informs me, that* [Julian (*afterwards called the Apoftate) being inftructed in the Philofophy and Difciplines of the Heathen, by* Libarius *his Tutor, by this* [5] *means he came to love Philofophy better than the Gofpel, and fo by degrees turn'd from Chriftianity to Heathenifm.*]

[9] The Reader will not find, as he has a Right to expect, this Name in the common Biographical Works. In the large Work of *Chaudon et Delandine* is a fatisfactory Article under the Head Juſtın; who was a Martyr of the fecond Century; yet we meet with the Name conftantly in Hiftory, as *Juftin Martyr;* Martyr being added to his proper Name, to denote that he had fuffered Martyrdom. He is alfo ftyled *St. Juftin.*

[10] Apollonius *Thyaneus,* according to Lempriere. A Pythagorian Philofopher, well fkilled in the Arts of Magic; who, " one Day haranguing the Populace at Ephefus, he fuddenly exclaimed: 'Strike the Tyrant, ftrike him; the Blow is given, he is wounded and fallen!' At that very Moment the Emperor Domitian had been ftabbed at Rome. The Magician acquired much Reputation when the Circumftance was known."

This same Julian *did, when* Apoftate, *forbid that Chriftians should be inftructed in the Difcipline of the* Gentiles, *which (it seems)* Socrates *a Writer of the Ecclefiaftical Hiftory, does acknowledge to be by the fingular Providence of God; Chriftians having then begun to degenerate from the Gofpel, and to betake themfelves to Heathenifh learning. And in the* Mercury *for the Month of* February, 1695, *there is this Account* [That the Chriftian Doctors converfing much with the writings of the *Heathen,* for the gaining of Eloquence. A Counfel was held at *Carthage,* which forbad the reading of the Books of the *Gentiles.*]

From all which it may be eafily perceived, that in the Primitive times of Chriftianity, when not only many Heathen of the Vulgar; but alfo many learn'd Men and Philofophers had imbraced the Chriftian Faith; they ftill retained a love to their Heathen-learning, to which as one obferves being tranfplanted into a Chriftian foils, foon proved productive of pernicious weeds, which over-ran the face of the Church, hence it was fo deformed as the Reformation found it.

Among other pernicious Weeds arifing from this Root, the Doctrine of the power of Devils and Witchcraft as it is now, and long has been underftood, is not the leaft; the Fables of Homer, Virgil, Horace *and* Ovid, &c. *being for the Elegancy of their Language retained then (and fo are to this day) in the fchools; have not only introduced, but eftablifhed fuch Doctrines to the poifoning the Chriftian World.*[11]*. A certain Author expreffes it thus [that as the Chriftian Schools at firft brought Men from Heathenifm to the Gofpel, fo thefe Schools carry Men from the Gofpel to Heathenifm, as to their great perfection] and Mr.* I. M. *in his* Remarkable Providences, *gives an account that (as he calls it) an old Counfel*

---

[11] Although the Stories and Fables of former Ages may, and doubtlefs did, at the Period under Confideration, have a bad Influence upon the Minds of Scholars, they ought to have none in thefe Times. This, however, will depend on the Intelligence of Teachers.

F

did Anathematize all thofe that believed fuch power of the Devils, accounting it a Damnable Doctrine.[12] *But as other Evils did afterwards increafe in the Church (partly by fuch Education) fo this infenfibly grew up with them, tho not to that degree, as that any Counfel I have ever heard or Read of, has to this day taken off thofe* Anathema's; *yet after this the Church fo far declined, that Witchcraft became a Principal, Ecclefiaftical Engine (as alfo that of Herefy was) to root up all that ftood in their way; and befides the ways of Tryal, that we have ftill in practice, they invented fome, which were peculiar to themfelves; which whenever they were minded to improve againft any Orthodox believer, they could eafily make Effectual: That Deluge of Blood, which that* Scarlet Whore *has to anfwer for, fhed under this notion, how amazing is it.*

The firft in England *that I have read of, of any note fince the Reformation, that afferts this Doctrine, is the famous Mr.* Perkins, *he (as alfo Mr.* Gaul, *and Mr.* Bernard, *&c.) feems all of them to have undertaken one Tafk. They taking notice of the Multiplicity of irregular ways to try them by, invented by Heathen and Papifts, made it their bufinefs and main work herein to oppofe fuch as they faw to be pernicious. And if they did not look more narrowly into it, but followed the firft, viz. Mr.* Perkins *whofe Education (as theirs alfo) had foreftall'd him into fuch belief, whom they readily followed, it cannot be wondered at: And that they were men liable to Err, and fo not to be trufted to as perfect guides, will manifeftly appear to him that fhall fee their feveral receits laid down to detect them by their Prefumptive and Pofitive ones. And confider how few*

---

[12] It is only neceffary to obferve that the Title of Dr. I. Mather's Work is *An Effay for the Recording of Illuftrious Providences,* &c., which was printed in a 12mo. 1684. This Work was elegantly reprinted in a Crown 12mo or a 16mo. by John Ruffell Smith, London, 1856. This, I think, is the firft Time the Work was ever reprinted. It fhows the Author not lefs fuperftitious than his very credulous Son.

*of either have any foundation in Scripture or Reafon; and how
vaftly they differ from each other in both, each having his Art by
himfelf, which Forty or an Hundred more may as well imitate, and
give theirs,* ad infinitum, *being without all manner of proof.* [6]
*But tho this be their main defign to take off People from thofe Evil
and bloody ways of trial which they fpeak fo much againft.   Yet
this does not hinder to this day, but the fame evil ways or as bad are
ftill ufed to deteĒ them by, and that even among Proteftants ; and
is fo far juftified, that a Reverend Perfon has faid lately here, how
elfe fhall we deteĒ Witches ?*[13]   *And another being urged to prove
by Scripture fuch a fort of Witch as has power to fend Devils to·
kill men, replied that he did as firmly believe it as any article of his
Faith.   And that he* (the Inquirer) *did not go to the Scripture ; to
learn the Myfteries of his trade or Art.   What can be faid more to
Eftablifh there Heathenifh notions and to villifie the Scriptures, our
only Rule; and that after we have feen fuch dire effeĒts thereof, as
has threatned the utter Extirpation of this whole Country.*

    *And as to moft of the AĒtors in thefe Tragedies, tho they are fo
far from defending their AĒtions that they will readily own, that
undue fteps have been taken, &c. yet it feems they choofe that the
fame fhould be AĒted over again, inforced by their Example, rather
than that it fhould Remain as a Warning to Pofterity, as herein
they have mift it.   So far are they from giving Glory to God, and
taking the due fhame to themfelves.*

    *And now to fum up all in a few words, we have feen a Biggot-
ted Zeal, ftirring up a Blind, and moft Bloody rage, not againft
Enemies, or Irreligious proffligate Perfons.   But* (in *Judgment of
Charity, and to view*) *againft as Vertuous and Religious as any they*

---

[13] It would perhaps be fruitlefs to attempt a Conjeĕture as to who were the Perfons referred to, the Majority of the Community being of the fame Faith.

have left behind them in this Country, which have fuffered as Evil doers (with the utmoſt extent of rigour, not that ſo high a Character is due to all that Suffered) and this by the Teſtimony of Vile Varlets as not only were known before, but have been further apparent ſince by their Manifeſt Lives, whordoms, inceſt, &c. The accuſations of theſe, from their Spectral Sight, being the chief Evidence againſt thoſe that Suffered. In which Accuſations they were upheld by both Magiſtrates and Miniſters, ſo long as they Apprehended themſelves in no Danger.[14]

And then tho they could defend neither the Doctrine, nor the Practice, yet none of them have in ſuch a publick manner as the caſe Requires, teſtified againſt either; tho at the ſame time they could not but be ſenſible what a Stain and laſting Infamy they have brought upon the whole Country, to the indangering the future welfair not only of this but of other places, induced by their Example; if not, to an intailing the Guilt of all the Righteous Blood that has been by the ſame means Shed, by Heathen or Papiſts, &c. upon themſelves, whoſe deeds they have ſo far juſtified, occaſioning the great Diſhonour and Blaſphemy of the Name of God, Scandalizing the Heathen, hardning of Enemies; and as a Natural effect thereof, to the great Increaſe of Atheiſm.

I ſhall conclude only with acquainting the Reader, that of theſe Collections, the firſt containing more Wonders of the Inviſible World, I received of a Gentleman, who had it of the Author, and communicated it to uſe, with his expreſs conſent, of which this is a true Copy.[15] *As to the letters, they are for Subſtance the ſame I*

---

[14] It ſeems that for ſome Time it never occurred to the Rulers that *they* might be taken for Witches; or " cried out upon," as the Phraſe uſed to be.

[15] Who the Gentleman was that received the Paper from Dr. Mather does not appear. At the Time it was obtained, the Author (Dr. Mather) probably had no Apprehenſion that any Expoſition was to follow. The very vague Note in

sent, tho with some small Variation or Addition. Touching the two Letters from a Gentleman at his request, I have forborn naming him. It is great Pity the matters of Fast, and indeed the whole, had not been done by some abler hana better Accomplished and Advantages with both natural and acquired Judgments, but others not Appearing, I have inforc'd myself to do what is done, my other occasions Will not admit any further Scrutiny therein.

R. C.

Boston in New-England, Aug 11. 1697.

Proceedings Mass. Hist. Society for 1858, p. 288, enlightens the Reader but little. It is said in that Note — "He [Mr. Calef] was furnished with Materials for his Work by Mr. Brattle, of Cambridge; and his Brother of Boston; and other Gentlemen, who were opposed to the Salem Proceedings." This Extract is signed E. P.; but the Editor of the Article referred to makes no Conjecture as for whom the Initials stand. Perhaps they mean Ebenezer Pemberton, though that Gentleman was comparatively a young Man in 1697; old enough, however, to have been interested in these Affairs.

[7] The

INDEX.

PART I.

PART II.

PART III.

PART IV.

PART V.

G

[10] *SIR,*

I NOW *lay before you a very Entertaining Story*,[16] *a Story which relates yet more* Wonders of the Invifible World, *a Story which tells the Remarkable Afflictions and Deliverance of one that had been Prodigioufly handled by the* Evil Angels. *I was myfelf a daily* Eye Witnefs *to a large part of thefe Occurrences, and there may be produced Scores of Subftantial* Witneffes *to the moft of them; yea, I know not of any one Paffage of the Story but what may be fufficiently attefted. I do not Write it with a defign of throwing it prefently into the Prefs, but only to preferve the Memory of fuch Memorable things, the forgetting whereof would neither be* pleafing *to God, nor ufeful to Men; as alfo to give you, with fome others of peculiar and obliging Friends, a fight of fome* Curiofities, *and I hope this Apology will ferve to Excufe me, if I mention, as perhaps I may, when I come to a tenth Paragraph in my Writing, fome things which I would have omitted in a farther Publication.*

Cotton Mather.

---

[16] This fingular "Story" does not appear to have been publifhed by its Author, nor have I any other Hiftory of it than is found in thefe Pages. Nor do I find anything of a Family of the Name of Rule. Neither Farmer nor Savage have it in their genealogical Works. Yet there was a Family living for fome Time at the North End of the Name of *Rule*. They may not have been long refident. See Note 30.

[1] ANOTHER

B R A N D

Pluckt out of the

B U R N I N G,

Or, More Wonders of the Invifible World.

Part I. Section I.

The Afflictions of MARGARET RULE.

Within thefe few years there died in the *Southern Parts* a Chriftian *Indian*, who notwithftanding fome of his *Indian* Weaknefs, had fomething of a better Character of vertue and Goodnefs, than many of our People can allow to moft of their Country-men, that profefs the *Chriftian Religion.*[17] He had been a Zealous

---

[17] There were two noted Chriftian Indians on Martha's Vineyard a little previous to the Time the Above was written ; viz., *Hiacoomes* and *John Tokinofh*. It is to one of thefe, probably, that the Writer refers. See *Book of the Indians*, B. ii, 118; or p. 182, Edition 1851. See alfo Appendix to *Elect. Serm.* of 1698, p. 90, *et seq.*

Preacher of the Gofpel to his Neighbourhood, and a fort of *Overfeer*, or *Officer*, to whofe Conduct was owing very much of what good order was maintained among thofe Profelited *Savages*. This Man returning home from the Funeral of his Son, was complemented by an *Englifhman*, exprefling *Sorrow for his Lofs*; now, tho' the *Indians* ufe upon the Death of Relations, to be the moft Paffionate and Outragious Creatures in the World, yet this Converted *Indian* Handfomly and Chearfully replid, *Truly I am forry, and I am not forry; I am forry that I have Buried a dear Son; but I am not forry that the will of God is done. I know that without the will of God my fon could not have died, and I know that the will* [2] *of God is always juft and good, and fo I am fatisfied.* Immediately upon this, even within a few hours, he fell himfelf Sick of a Difeafe that quickly kill'd him; in the time of which Difeafe he called his Folks about him, earneftly perfwading them to be Sincere in their *Praying unto God*, and beware of the *Drunkennefs*, the *Idlenefs*, the *Lying*, whereby fo many of that Nation difgrac'd their Profeflion of Chriftianity; adding, that he was afhamed, when he thought how little Service he had hitherto done for God; and that if God would prolong his Life he would Labour to do better Service, but that he was fully fure he was now going to the Lord *Jefus Chrift*, who had bought him with his own Precious *Blood;* and for his part, he long'd to Die that he might be with his

Glorious Lord; and in the mid'ft of fuch paffages
he gave up the Ghoft, but in fuch repute, that
the *Englifh* People of good Fafhion did not think
much of Travelling a great way to his *Interment.*
Left my Reader do now wonder why I have related this piece of a Story, I will now haften to
abate that Wonder, by telling that whereto this
was intended, but for an *Introduction :* know then,
that this remarkable *Indian* being a little before
he Died at work in the Wood making of Tarr,
there appeared unto him a *Black Man,* of a Terrible afpect, and more than humane Dimenfions,
threatning bittterly to kill him if he would not
promife to leave off *Preaching* as he did to his
Countrey-Men, and promife particularly, *that if*
he preached any more, he would fay nothing of Jefus
Chrift unto them? The *Indian* amaz'd, yet had
the courage to anfwer, *I will in fpite of you go on*
to preach Chrift *more than ever I did, and the God*
whom I ferve will keep me that you fhall never hurt
me. Hereupon the Apparition abating fomewhat
of his fiercenefs, offered to the *Indian* a *Book* of a
confiderable thicknefs and a *Pen and Ink,* and
faid, that if he would now fet his hand unto that
Book, he would require nothing further of him ;
but the Man refufed the motion with indignation,
and fell down upon his knees into a Fervent and
Pious Prayer unto God, for help againft the
Tempter, whereupon the *Demon* Vanifh't.
    This is a Story which I would never have ten-
dered unto my Reader, if I had not Rcceiv'd it

from an honeſt and uſeful *Engliſh Man*,[18] who is
at this time a Preacher of the Goſpel to the *Indians ;* nor would the probable Truth of it have
encouraged me to have tendered it, if this alſo
had not been a fit introduction unto yet a further
Narrative.

Sect. 2. 'Twas not much above a year or two,
after this Accident (of which no manner of Noiſe
has been made) that there was a Prodigious de-
ſcent of *Devils* upon divers places near the Centre
of this Province; wherein ſome ſcores of *Miſerable People* were Troubled by horrible appearances
of a *Black-Man*, accompanied with *Spectres*,
wearing theſe and thoſe Humane Shapes, who offer'd them a *Book* to be by them ſign'd, in token
of their being Liſted for the Service of the *Devil*,
and upon their [3] denying to do it, they were
dragoon'd with a thouſand Preternatural Torments,
which gave no little terror to the beholders of
theſe unhappy *Energuments.* There was one in
the *North* part of *Boſton* ſeized by the *Evil Angels* many Months after the General Storm of the
late *Inchantments* was over, and when the Countrey had long lain pretty quiet, both as to Moleſ-
tations and Accuſations from the INVISIBLE
WORLD, her Name was *Margaret Rule*, a
Young Woman, She was born of ſober and honeſt
Parents, yet Living, but what her own Character
was before her Viſitation, I can ſpeak with the

18 Perhaps Capt. Thomas Tup- 1698, p. 95. There were alſo *El-*
per. See *Noyes's Election Sermon*, *dad* and Samuel T.—Sewall's *MSS.*

lefs confidence of exactnefs, becaufe I obferve that wherever the *Devils* have been let loofe to worry any Poor Creature amongft us, a great part of the Neighbourhood prefently fet themfelves to in-quire and relate all the little Vanities of their Childhood, with fuch unequal exaggerations, as to make them appear greater Sinners than any whom the Pilate of *Hell* has not yet Preyed upon: But it is affirm'd, that for about half a year before her Vifitation, fhe was obfervably im-proved in the hopeful fymptoms of a new Crea-ture; She was become furioufly concern'd for the everlafting *Salvation* of her Soul, and careful to avoid the fnares of *Evil Company*. This Young Woman had never feen the affliction of *Mercy Short*,[19] whereof a Narrative has been already given, and yet about half a year after the glorious and fignal deliverance of that poor Damfel, this *Margaret* fell into an affliction, marvellous, re-fembling hers in almoft all the circumftances of it, indeed the Afflictions were fo much alike, that the relation I have given of the one, would almoft ferve as the full Hiftory of the other, this was to that, *little more than the fecond part to the fame Tune;* indeed *Margarets* cafe was in feveral points lefs remarkable than *Mercies*, and in fome other things the Entertainment did a little vary.

Sect. 3. 'twas upon the *Lords Day* the 10th of *September*, in the Year 1693. that *Margaret Rule*,

---

[19] Nothing is learned of this Per-fon beyond what is to be found in this Work. There were Perfons early at Newbury of the fame Name.

after fome hours of previous difturbance in the
Publick Affembly, fell into odd *Fits*, which caufed
her Friends to carry her home, where her *Fits*
in a few hours grew into a Figure that fatisfied
the Speflators of their being preternatural; fome
of the Neighbours were forward enough to fuf-
pefl the rife of this Mifchief in an Houfe hard-
by, where lived a Miferable Woman, who had
been formerly Imprifoned on the fufpicion of
Witchcraft, and who had frequently Cured very
painfull Hurts by muttering over them certain
Charms, which I fhall not indanger the Poyfoning
of my Reader by repeating. This Woman had
the Evening before *Margaret* fell into her Calamities, very bitterly treated her, and threatn'd
her; but the hazard of hurting a poor Woman
that might be innocent, notwithftanding *Surmizes*
that might have been more ftrongly grounded
than thofe, cauf'd the pious People in the Vicinity
to try rather whether inceffant *Supplication* to
God [4] *alone*, might not procure a quicker and
fafer Eafe to the *Afflifled*, than hafty Profecution
of any fuppof'd Criminal, and accordingly that
unexceptionable courfe was all that was ever followed; yea, which I look'd on as a token for
good, the Afflifted Family was as averfe as any
of us all to entertain thoughts of any other
courfe.

Seff. 4. The Young Woman was affaulted by
Eight cruel *fpeflres*, whereof fhe imagin'd that
fhe knew *three* or *four*, but the reft came ftill

with their *Faces cover'd*, ſo that ſhe could never
have a diſtinguiſhing view of the countenance of
thoſe whom ſhe thought ſhe knew ; ſhe was very
careful of my reitterated charges *to forbear blazing
the names*, left any good Perſon ſhould come to
ſuffer any blaſt of Reputation thro' the cunning
Malice of the great Accuſer ; neverthelefs having
ſince privately named *them* to myſelf, I will venture to ſay *this* of them, that they are a ſort of
Wretches, who for theſe many years have gone
under as Violent *Preſumptions* of *Witchcraft*, as
perhaps any creatures yet living upon earth; altho' I am farr from thinking that the Viſions
of this Young Woman were Evidence enough
to prove them ſo. Theſe curſed *Spectres* now
brought unto her a *Book* about a *Cubet* long, a
Book Red and *thick*, but not very broad, and they
demanded of her that ſhe would ſet *her Hand* to
that *Book*, or touch it at leaſt with her *Hand*, as
a Sign of her becoming a Servant of the *Devil*,
upon her peremptory refuſal *to do* what they
aſked, they did not after renew the profers of the
Book unto her, but inſtead thereof, they fell to
Tormenting of her in a manner too Helliſh to
be ſufficiently deſcribed, in thoſe Torments con-
fining her to her *Bed*, for juſt *Six weeks* together.

Sect. 5. Sometimes, but not always together
with the *Spectres*, there looke't in upon the Young
Woman (according to her account) *a ſhort and a
Black Man*, whom they call'd their Maſter —
a Wight exactly of the ſame Dimenſions and

Complexion and voice, with the *Divel* that has
exhibited himfelf unto other infefted People, not
only in other parts of this Country but alfo in
other Countrys, even of the *European World*, as
the relation of the Enchantments there inform
us, they all profeft themfelves Vaffals of this
Devil, and in obedience unto him they addrefs
themfelves unto various ways of Torturing her;
accordingly fhe was cruelly *pinch'd with Invifible
hands*, very often in a Day, and the black and
blew marks of the pinches became immediately
vifible unto the ftanders by. Befides this, when
her attendants had left her without fo much as
one pin about her, that fo they might prevent
fome fear'd inconveniencies; yet fhe would ever
now and then be miferably hurt with Pins which
were found ftuck into her Neck, Back and Arms,
however the Wounds made by the Pins would in
a few minutes ordinarily be cured; fhe would
alfo be ftrangely diftorted in her Joynts, and
thrown into fuch exorbitant *Convulfions* as [5]
were aftonifhing unto the Spectators in General;
They that could behold the doleful condition of
the poor Family without fenfible compaffions,
might have Intrals indeed, but I am fure they
could have no true *Bowels* in them.

Sect. 6. It were a moft Unchriftian and uncivil,
yea a moft unreafonable thing to imagine that
the Fitt's of the Young Woman were but meer
Impoftures: And I believe fcarce any, but People of a particular *Dirtinefs*, will harbour fuch an

Uncharitable Cenſure,[20] however, becauſe I know
not how far the *Devil* may drive the Imagination
of poor Creatures when he has poſſeſſion of them,
that at another time when they are *themſelves*
would ſcorn to *Diſſemble* any thing. I ſhall now
confine my Narrative unto paſſages, wherein there
could be no room left for any Diſſimulation. Of
theſe the firſt that I'll mention ſhall be this;
From the time that *Margaret Rule* firſt found
herſelf to be formally beſieged by the *Spectres*
untill the Ninth Day following, namely from
the Tenth of *September* to the Eighteenth, ſhe
kept an entire Faſt, and yet ſhe was unto all appearance as Freſh, as Lively, as Hearty, at the Nine
Days End, as before they began ; in all this time,
tho' ſhe had a very eager *Hunger* upon her Stomach, yet if any refreſhment were brought unto
her, her Teeth would be ſet, and ſhe would be
thrown into many Miſeries, Indeed *once or twice
or ſo* in all this time, her Tormentors permitted
her to ſwallow a Mouthful of ſomewhat that
might increaſe her Miſeries, whereof a Spoonful
of *Rum* was the moſt conſiderable; but otherwiſe, as I ſaid, her *Faſt* unto the *Ninth day* was
very extream and rigid : However, afterwards
there ſcarce paſſed a day wherein ſhe had not
liberty to take ſomething or other for her *Suſten-
tation*, And I muſt add this further, that this

---

[20] If the learned Author were
living at this Day he would doubtleſs gladly blot out many Pages of
his own Matter, as being a more
dirty Work than any he then complained of.

bufinefs of her *Faſt* was carried fo, that it was
impoſſible to be diſſembled without a *Combination*
of Multitudes of People unacquainted with one
another to fupport the *Juggle*, but he that can
imagine fuch a thing of a Neighbourhood, fo
fill'd with Vertuous People is a *baſe man*, I cannot
call him any other.

Seƈt. 7. But if the Sufferings of this Young
Woman were not *Impoſture*, yet might they not
be pure Diſtemper? I will not here inquire
of our *Saducees* what fort of Diſtemper 'tis' ſhall
ſtick the Body full of *Pins*, without any Hand
that could be feen to ſtick them; or whether all
the *Pin-makers* in the World would be willing
to be Evaporated into certain ill habits of Body
producing a *Diſtemper*, but of the *Diſtemper* my
Reader ſhall be Judge when I have told him
fomething further of thofe unufual Sufferings. I
do believe that the *Evil Angels* do often take
Advantage from *Natural Diſtempers* in the Children of Men to annoy them with fuch further
Mifchiefs as we call *preternatural*. The Malignant *Vapours* and *Humours* of our Difeafed Bodies
may be ufed by *Devils* thereinto infinu[6]ating as
engine of the Execution of their Malice upon
thofe Bodies; and perhaps for this reafon one
Sex may fuffer more Troubles of fome kinds
from the *Invifible World* than the *other*, as well as
for *that reafon* for which the Old *Serpent* made
where he did his *firſt Adddreſs*. But I Pray
what will you fay to this, *Margaret Rule* would

fometimes have her Jaws forcibly pulled open,
whereupon fomething *Invifible* would be poured
down her throat; we all faw her fwallow, and
yet we faw her try all fhe could by Spitting,
Coughing and Shriking, that fhe might not
fwalow, but one time the ftanders by plainly faw
fomething of that odd *Liquor* itfelf on the outfide
of her *Neck;* She cried out of it as of *Scalding
Brimftone* poured into her, and the whole Houfe
would Immediately fcent fo hot of *Brimftone* that
we were fcarce able to endure it, whereof there
are fcores of Witneffes; but the Young Woman
herfelf would be fo monftroufly *Inflam'd* that it
would have broke a Heart of Stone to have feen
her Agonies, *this* was a thing that feveral times
happen'd and feveral times when her Mouth was
thus pull'd open, the ftanders by clapping their
Hands clofe thereupon the diftreffes that otherwife followed would be diverted.   Moreover there
was a *whitifh powder* to us *Invifible* fomtimes caft
upon the *Eyes* of this Young Woman, whereby
her *Eyes* would be extreamly incommoded, but
one time fome of this *Powder* was fallen actually
Vifible upon her Cheek, from whence the People
in the Room wiped it with their Handkerchiefs,
and fomtimes the Young Woman would alfo be
fo bitterly fcorched with the unfeen Sulphur
thrown upon her, that very fenfible *Blifters* would
be raifed upon her Skin, whereto her Friends
found it neceffary to apply the *Oyl's* proper for
common *Burning*, but the moft of thefe Hurts

would be cured in two or three days at fartheſt:
I think I may *without Vanity* pretend to have
read not a few of the beſt Syſtem's of *Phyſick*[21]
that have been yet ſeen in theſe *American* Regions,
but I muſt confeſs that I have never yet learned
the Name of the Natural Diſtemper, whereto
theſe odd ſymptoms do belong: However I might
ſuggeſt perhaps many a *Natural Medicine,* which
would be of ſingular uſe againſt many of them.

Sect. 8. But there fell out ſome *other matters*
far beyond the reach of *Natural Diſtemper:* This
Margaret Rule once in the middle of the Night
Lamented ſadly that the *Spectres* threat'ned the
Drowning of a Young Man in the Neighbourhood, whom ſhe named unto the Company: well
it was afterwards found that at that very time this
Young Man, having been preſt on Board *a Man
of War* then in the Harbour, was out of ſome
diſſatisfaction attempting to ſwim aſhoar, and he
had been *Drowned* in the attempt, if a Boat had
not ſeaſonably taken him up; it was by compu-
tation a minute or two after the Young Womans
diſcourſe of the *Drowning,* that the Young Man
took ·the Water; At another time ſhe told us
that [7] the *Spectres* bragg'd and laughed in her
hearing about an exploit they had lately done, by
ſtealing from a Gentleman his *Will* ſoon after he
had written it; and within a few hours after ſhe

---

[21] Jt would be curious, if not ad-
mirable, at this Day could we know
what medical Books the Doctor did
poſſeſs at that Time. Doubtleſs
Galen and Paracelſus were conſpi-
cuous on his Shelves.

had fpoken this there came to me a Gentleman
with a private complaint, that having written his
Will, it was unaccountably gone out of the way,
how or *where* he could not Imagine; and befides
all this, there were wonderful *Noifes* every now
and then made about the Room, which our People could Afcribe to no other Authors but the
Spectres, yea, the Watchers affirm that they heard
thofe fiends clapping of their hands together with
an *Audiblenefs*, wherein they could not be Im-
pofed upon: And once her Tormentors pull'd
her up to the *Cieling* of the Chamber, and held
her there before a very Numerous Company of
Spectators, who found it as much as they could
all do to pull her down again.²² There was alfo
another very furprifing circumftance about her,
agreeable to what we have not only *read* in feveral Hiftories concerning the *Imps* that have been
Imployed in *Witchcraft*; but alfo known in fome
of our own afflicted: *We once thought we perceived fomething ftir upon her pillow at a little diftance from her, whereupon one prefent laying his
hand there, he to his horror* apprehended that *he
felt*, tho' none could fee it, *a living Creature*, not
*altogether unlike a Rat, which nimbly efcap'd from
him:* and there were diverfe other Perfons who
were thrown into a great confternation by feeling,
as they Judg'd, at other times the fame *Invifible
Animal.*

²² Mr. Calef has not commented   as it merited, and as he might have
fo feverely on this Part of the Story   done with propriety.

I

Sect. 9. As it has been with a Thousand other *Inchanted* People, so it was with *Margaret Rule* in this particular, that there were several words which her *Tormentors* would not let her hear, especially the words Pray or Prayer, and yet she could so hear the letters of those words distinctly mentioned as to know what they ment. The standers by were forced sometimes thus in discourse to spell a word to her, but because there were some so ridiculous as to count it a sort of *Spell* or a *Charm* for any thus to accommodate themselves to the capacity of the Sufferer, little of this kind was done. But that which was more singular in this matter, was that she could not use these *words* in those penetrating discourses, wherewith she would sometimes address the *Spectres* that were about her. She would sometimes for a long while together apply herself to the *Spectres*, whom she supposed the *Witches*, with such *Exortations to Repentance* as would have melted an Heart of *Adamant* to have heard them ; her strains of Expression and Argument were truly Extraordinary ; A person perhaps of the best Education and Experience and of *Attainments* much beyond hers could not have exceeded them : nevertheless when she came to these Words *God, Lord, Christ, Good, Repent,* and some other such, her Mouth could not utter them, whereupon she would sometimes in an Angry *Parenthesis* complain of their Wickedness in stopping that *Word,* but she would then go [8] on with some other

Terms that would ferve to tell what fhe ment. And I believe that if the moft fufpicious Perfon in the world had beheld all the Circumftances of this matter, he would have faid it could not have been diffembled.

Sect. 10. Not only in the *Swedifh,* but alfo in the *Salem* Witchcraft the Inchanted People have talked much of a *White Spirit* from whence they received marvellous Affiftances in their Miferies; what lately befel *Mercy Short*[23] from the Com- munications of fuch a *Spirit,* hath been the juft Wonder of us all, but by fuch a *Spirit* was *Mar- garet Rule* now alfo vifited. She fays that fhe could never fee his *Face;* but that fhe had a fre- quent view of his bright, Shining and glorious Garments; he ftood by her *Bed-fide* continually heartning and comforting of her and counfelling her to maintain her Faith and hope in God, and never comply with the temptations of her Adver- faries; fhe fays he told her, that *God had permit- ted her afflictions to befall her for the everlafting and unfpeakable good of her own foul, and for the good of many others, and for his own Immortal Glory, and that fhe fhould therefore be of good Chear, and be affured of a fpeedy deliverance;* and the won- derful refolution of mind wherewith fhe encoun- tered her Afflictions were but agreeable to fuch expectations. Moreover a Minifter having one Day with fome Importunity Prayed for the de-

---

[23] Mr. Savage has found quite a Number of *Short* Families, but gives us no *Mercy* with them. See his *Genealogical Dictionary.*

liverance of this 'Young Woman, and pleaded that fhe belong'd to his Flock and charge; he had fo far a right unto her as that he was to do the part of a Minifter of our Lord for the bringing of her home unto God; only now the *Devil* hindred him in *doing* that which he had a *right* thus to do, and whereas He had a *better Title* unto her to bring her home to *God* than the *Divel* could have unto her to carry her away from the *Lord, he* therefore humbly applied him-felf unto *God*, who alone could right this matter, with a fuit that fhe might be refcued out of *Satans Hands;* Immediately upon this, tho' fhe heard nothing of this tranfaction fhe began to call that Minifter her *Father*, and that was the Name whereby fhe every day before all forts of People diftinguifhed him: the occafion of it fhe fays was *this,* the *white Spirit* prefently upon this tranfaction did after this manner fpeak to her, *Margaret, you now are to take notice that* (fuch a Man) *is your Father, God has given you to him, do you from this time look upon him as your Father, obey him, regard him as your Father, follow his Counfels and you fhall do well;* And tho' there was one paffage more, which I do as little know what to make of as any of the reft, I am now going to relate it; more than three times have I feen it fulfilled in the Deliverance of Inchanted and Poffeft Perfons, whom the Providence of God has caft into my way, that their Deliverance could not be obtained before the *third Faft* kept

for them, and the third day ˙ftill obtain'd the
Deliverance, altho' I have thought of *befeeching
of the Lord thrice, when buffered by Sa*[9]*tan*, yet
I muft earneftly Intreat all my Readers to beware
of any fuperftitious conceits upon the Number
Three, if our God will hear us upon once Praying
and Fafting before him 'tis well, and if he will
not vouchfafe his *Mercy* upon our *thrice* doing fo,
yet we muft not be fo difcouraged as to throw by
our Devotion but if the Soveraign *Grace* of our
God will in any particular Inftances count our
Patience enough tryed when we have Solemnly
waited upon him for any determinate Number of
times, who fhall fay to him, what doeft thou, and
if there fhall be any Number of Inftances, wherein this Grace of our God has exactly holden the
fame courfe, it may have a room in our humble
Obfervations, I hope, without any Superftition;
I fay then that after *Margaret Rule* had been
more than five weeks in her Miferies, this *White
Spirit* faid unto her, *Well this day fuch a Man*
(whom he named) *has kept a third day for your
deliverance, now be of good cheer you fhall fpeedily
be delivered.* I inquired whether what had been
faid of that Man were true, and I gained exact
and certain information that it was precifely fo,
but I doubt left in relating this Paffage that I
have ufed more opennefs than a Friend fhould be
treated with, and for that caufe I have concealed
feveral of the moft *memorable things* that have
occurred not only in this but in fome former

Hiftories, altho indeed I am not fo well fatisfied about the true nature of this *white Spirit*, as to count that I can do a Friend much Honour by reporting what notice this *white Spirit* may have thus taken of him.

Sect. 11. On the laft day of the Week her Tormentors as fhe thought and faid, approaching towards her, would be forced ftill to recoil and retire as unaccountably unable to meddle with her, and they would retire to the Fire fide with their Poppets; but going to ftick Pins into thofe Poppets, they could not (according to their vifions) make the Pins to enter, fhe infulted over them with a very Proper derifion, daring them now to do their worft, whilft fhe had the fatisfaction to fee their *Black Mafter* ftrike them and kick them, like an *Overfeer* of fo many *Negro's*, to make them to do their work, and renew the marks of his vengeance on them, when they failed of doing of it.[24] At laft being as it were tired with their ineffectual Attempts to mortifie her they furioufly faid, *Well you fhant be the laft.* And after a paufe they added, *Go, and the Devil go with you, we can do no more;* whereupon they flew out of the Room, and fhe returning perfectly to herfelf moft affectionately gave thanks to God for her deliverance; her Tormentors left her extream *weak and faint*, and overwhelmed with *Vapours*, which would not only caufe her fometimes to Swoon away, but

[24] This Relation is pretty nearly equal to anything told of the Swedifh Witches by Dr. Horneck. This Author will be further noticed.

alſo now and then for a little while diſcompoſe
the reaſonableneſs of her Thoughts; Neverthe-
leſs her former troubles returned not, but we are
now waiting to ſee the good effeɗs of thoſe
troubles upon the Souls of all concern'd, And
now I ſuppoſe that ſome of our Learned *wit-*[10]
lings of the *Coffee-Houſe*, for fear left theſe proofs
of an *Inviſible-world* ſhould ſpoil ſome of their
ſport, will endeavour to turn them all into ſport,
for which *Buffoonary* their only pretence will be,
*they cant underſtand how ſuch things as theſe could
be done* whereas indeed he that is but Philoſopher
enough to have read but one *Little Treatiſe*, Pub-
liſhed in the Year 1656, by no other Man than
the Chyrurgion of an *Army*, or but one Chap.
of *Helmont*,[25] which I will not quote at this time
too particularly, may give a far more intelligible
account of theſe *Appearances* than moſt of theſe
Blades can give *why* and how their *Tobacco* makes
'em Spit; or which way the flame of their Can-
dle becomes illuminating, as for that *cavil, the
world would be undone if the Devils could have ſuch
power as they ſeem to have in ſeveral of our ſtories*,[26] it may be Anſwered that as to many things

---

[25] Jean-Baptiſte Van-Helmont, a
Reſident of Bruſſels, born in 1577.
He was ſo noted a Phyſician and
Naturaliſt, that he was reputed a
Magician, for which he was thrown
into Priſon. He made his Eſcape
and fled into Holland, where he died
in 1644.

[26] The Writer nowhere informs

us how much Power the Devil has.
By ſome of his Aſſertions it ſeems
that it is unlimited. Indeed he (Dr.
Mather) has told us that this Con-
tinent in reality belonged to the
Devil. If that was aɗually the Caſe,
it certainly was an infringement on
his Rights for Europeans to intrude
themſelves here at all.

the *Lying Devils* have only known them to be done, and then pretended unto the doing of thofe things, but the true and beſt Anſwer is, that by thefe things we only fee what the *Devils* could have *powers* to do, if the great God ſhould give them thofe powers, whereas now our Hiſtories affords a *Glorious Evidence for the being of a God*, the World would indeed be *undone*, and horribly *undone*, if thefe Devils, who now and then get liberty to play ſome very miſchievous pranks, were not under a daily reſtraint of ſome *Almighty Superior* from doing more of ſuch Miſchiefs. Wherefore inſtead of all Apiſh *flouts* and *jeers* at Hiſtories, which have ſuch undoubted confirmation, as that no Man that has breeding enough to regard the Common Laws of *Humane Society*, will offer to doubt of 'em, it becomes us rather to adore the goodneſs of God, who does not permit ſuch things every day to befall us *all*, as he ſometimes did permit to befall ſome few of our miſerable Neighbours.

Sect. 12. And what after all my unwearied Cares and Pains, to refcue the *Miferable* from the Lions and Bears of *Hell*, which had ſiezed them, and after all my Studies to diſappoint the Devils in their defigns to confound my Neighbourhood, muſt I be driven to the neceſſity of an *Apology?* Truly the hard *reprefentations* wherewith *ſome Ill Men have reviled my conduct*, and the Countenance which other Men have given to thefe reprefentations, oblige me to give Mankind ſome account

of my Behaviour; No Chriftian can, I fay none
but evil workers can criminate my vifiting fuch
of my poor flock as have at any time fallen under
the terrible and fenfible moleftations of *Evil Angels;* let their Afflictions have been what they
will, I could not have anfwered it unto my
Glorious *Lord,* if I had withheld my juft *Counfels*
and *Comforts* from them; and if I have alfo
with fome exactnefs obferv'd the methods of the
Invifible World, when they have thus become
obfervable, I have been but a Servant of Mankind
in doing fo; yea no lefs a Perfon than the *Venerable Baxter,* has more than once or twice in the
moft Publick manner invited Mankind to thank
[11] me for that *Service.* I have not been infen-
fible of a greater danger attending me in this
fulfilment of my Miniftry, than if I had been to
take Ten Thoufand fteps over a Rocky Mountain
fill'd with *Rattle-Snakes;* but I have confider'd,
he that is wife will obferve things, and the *Sur-
prifing Explication* and confirmation of the *biggeft
part* of the *Bible,* which I *have feen* given in
thefe things, has *abundantly paid me* for obferving
them. Now in my vifiting of the Miferable, I
was always of this opinion, that we were Ignorant of what *Powers* the *Devils* might have to
do their mifchiefs in the fhapes of fome that had
never been explicitly engaged in *Diabolical Con-
federacies,* and that therefore tho' many *Witchcrafts* had been fairly detected *on Enquiries* provoked and begun by *Spectral Exhibitions,* yet we

K

could not eafily be too jealous of the *Snares* laid
for us in the *devices of Satan* ; the World knows
how many *Pages* I have Compofed and Publifhed,
and particular gentlement in the Government
know how many *Letters* I have written to prevent the exceffive Credit of *Spetteral Accufations*,
wherefore I have ftill charged the *Afflicted* that
they fhould *Cry* out of no body for Afflicting of
'em.   But that if this might be any Advantage
they might *privately* tell their minds to fome one
Perfon of *difcretion* enough to make no *ill ufe* of *
their communications, accordingly there has been
this effect of it, that the Name of *No one* good
Perfon in the World ever came under any blemifh
by means of any *Afflicted*, Perfon that fell under
my particular cognizance, yea no one Man, Woman
or Child ever came into any troube for the fake of
any that were *Afflicted* after I *had once begun* to
look after 'em ; how often have I had this thrown
into my difh, that many years ago I had an opportunity to have brought forth fuch People as have
in the late ftorm of *Witchcraft* been complain'd
of, but that I fmother'd all, and after that ftorm
was raif'd at *Salem*, I did myfelf offer to provide
Meat, Drink and Lodging for no lefs than Six of
the Afflicted, that fo an Experiment might be
made, whether *Prayer* with *Fafting* upon the
removal of the diftreffed might not put a Period
to the trouble then rifing, without giving the *Civil*
Authority the trouble of profecuting thofe things
which nothing but a Confcientious regard unto

the cries of Miferable Families, could have overcome the Reluctancies of the Honourable Judges
to meddle with ; [27] In fhort I do humbly but freely
affirm it, there is not that Man living in this
World who has been more defirous than the poor
Man I *to fhelter* my Neighbours from the Incon-
veniences of *Spectoral Outcries,* yea I am very
jealous I have done fo much *that way as to Sin*
in what I have done, fuch have been the Cow-
ardize and Fearfulnefs whereunto my regard unto
the diffatisfactions of other People has precipitated me. I know a Man in the World, who
has thought he has been able to Convict fome
fuch *Witches* as ought to Dye, but his refpect unto
the Publick *Peace* has caufed him rather to try
whether *He* [12] *could not renew them by repentance :* and as I have been Studious to defeat the
Devils of their expectations to fet people together
by the Ears, thus, I have alfo checked and quell'd
thofe forbidden curiofities, which would have
given the *Devil* an invitation to have tarried
amongft us, when I have feen wonderful *Snares*
laid for *Curious* People, by the fecret and future
things difcovered from the *Mouths of Damfels
poffeft with a Spirit of divination;* Indeed I can

---

[27] This will be found remarked
upon hereafter. The Author makes
a large Handle of Mr. Baxter's
Commendations of his Story of the
Goodwin Children ; which Story
he afterwards printed in the *Mag-
nalia,* Book vi, 71, &c.; and adds :
" When it was reprinted at London,
the famous Mr. Baxter prefixed a
Preface unto it, wherein he fays,
' *This great Inftance comes with fuch
convincing Evidence, that he muft be
a very obdurate* Sadducee, *that will
not believe it.*' "—*Ibid.,* 75.

recollect but one thing wherein there could be
given fo much as a Shadow of Reafon for *Excep-
tions*, and that is my allowing of fo many to come
and fee thofe that were *Afflicted*,[28] now for that I
have this to fay, that I have almoft *a Thoufand
times* intreated the Friends of the Miferable, that
they would not permit the Intrufion of any Company, but fuch as *by Prayers* or other ways might
be helpful to them; Neverthelefs I have not ab-
folutely forbid all Company from coming to your
Haunted Chambers, partly becaufe the Calamities
of the Families were fuch as required the Affiftance of *many friends;* partly becaufe I have been
willing that there fhould be *difinterefted Witneffes*
of all forts, to confute the Calumnies of fuch as
would fay *all was but Impofture;* and partly becaufe I faw God had Sanctified the Spectacle of
the Miferies on the Afflicted unto the Souls of
many that were Spectators, and it is a very Glorious thing that I have now to mention — The
Devils have with moft horrendous operations broke
in upon our Neighbourhood, and God has at fuch
a rate over-ruled all the Fury and Malice of thofe
Devils, that all the Afflicted have not only been
Delivered, but I hope alfo favingly brought home
unto God, and the Reputation of *no one* good
Perfon in the World, has been damaged, but

---

[28] It was befides hinted that there
were Times when the Numbers admitted to the Afflicted were not
above the *fingular* Number. But
this was doubtlefs a mifchievous Attempt of the *Sadducees* to implicate
fome one who might be rather zealous to detect *Witchcraft* when alone
with the Afflicted. The Doctor was
very indignant at this, as will appear.

inftead thereof the Souls of many, efpecially of
the rifing Generation, have been thereby awa-
ken'd unto fome acquaintance with *Religion,* our
young People who belonged unto the *Praying
Meetings* of both Sexes, a part would ordinarily
fpend whole *Nights* by whole Weeks together in
Prayers and Pfalms upon thefe occafions, in
which Devotions the Devils could get nothing
but like *Fools a Scourge for their own Backs,* and
fome fcores of other young People who were
ftrangers to real Piety, were now ftruck with the
lively demonftrations of *Hell* evidently fet forth
before their Eyes, when they faw Perfons cruelly
Frighted, wounded and Starved by Devils and
Scalded with burning *Brimftone,* and yet fo preferved in this tortured eftate as that at the end of
one Months wretchednefs they were as able ftill
to undergo another, fo that of thefe alfo it might
now be faid, Behold they Pray in the whole —
the Devil got juft nothing; but God got praifes,
Chrift got Subjects, the Holy Spirit got *Temples,*
the Church got *Addition,* and the Souls of Men
got everlafting *Benefits;* I am not fo vain as to fay
that any *Wifdome* or *Vertue* of mine did contribute unto this good order of things: But I am
fo juft, as to fay I did not hinder this Good.[13]
When therefore there have been thofe that pickt
up little incoherent fcraps and bits of my *Difcourfes* in this fruitful difcharge of my Miniftry,
and fo traverfted 'em in their abufive *Pamphlets,*
as to perfwade the Town that I was their *common*

Enemy in thofe very points, wherein, if in any one
thing whatfoever I have fenfibly approved myfelf
as true a Servant unto 'em as poffibly I could,
tho my Life and Soul had been at Stake for it.
Yea to do like *Satan* himfelf, by fly, bafe, unpretending *Infinuations*, as if I wore not the Modefty
and Gravity which became a Minifter of the
Gofpel, I could not but think myfelf unkindly
dealt withal, and the neglects of *others* to do me
juftice in this affair has caufed me to conclude
this Narrative with complaints in *another hearing*
of fuch Monftrous Injuries.[29]

PART II.

A Letter to Mr. C. M.

Bofton, Jan. 11*th*, 1693.

Mr. *Cotton Mather*,

REverend Sir, I finding it needful on many
accounts, I here prefent you with the Copy
of that Paper, which has been fo much Mifrep-
refented, to the End that what fhall be found
defective or not fairly Reprefented, if any fuch
fhall appear, they may be fet right, which Runs
thus.

[29] It would have been highly gra-
tifying had the Author informed his
Readers what he meant by "the
neglect of others." The "another
hearing" will be found explained by
and by.

September *the* 13*th*, 1693.

IN *the Evening when the Sun was withdrawn, giving place to Darkneſs to ſucceed, I with ſome others were drawn by curioſity to ſee* Margaret Rule, *and ſo much the rather becauſe it was reported* Mr. M—— *would be there that Night : Being come to her Fathers Houſe*[30] *into the Chamber wherein ſhe was in Bed, found her of a healthy countenance of about ſeventeen Years Old, lying very ſtill, and ſpeaking very little, what ſhe did ſay ſeem'd as if ſhe were Light-headed. Then* Mr. M— *Father and Son*[31] *came up and others with them, in the whole were about* 30 *or* 40 *Perſons, they being ſat, the Father on a Stool, and the Son upon the Bedſide by her, the Son began to queſtion her,* Margaret Rule, *how do you do?* then a pauſe without any anſwer. Queſtion. *What do there a great many Witches ſit upon you? Anſwer.* Yes. Q. *Do you not know that there is a hard Maſter?* Then ſhe was in a Fit; *He laid his hand upon her Face and Noſe, but, as he ſaid, without perceiving Breath; then he bruſh'd her on the Face with his Glove, and rubb'd her Stomach (her breaſt not covered with the Bedcloaths) and bid others do ſo too, and ſaid* [14] *it eaſed her, then ſhe revived.* Q. *Don't you know there is a hard Maſter?* A. *Yes.* Reply; *Don't*

---

[30] The Family of Rule appear to have reſided at the North End of the Town. Where they came from, or what became of them does not appear. They were, perhaps, tranſient Sojourners here. Mr. Mather ſays Margaret's Parents were ſober and honeſt, and living at the Time in Boſton. See *ante.*

[31] Increaſe and Cotton Mather.

ferve that hard Mafter, you know who. Q. *Do you believe?* *Then again fhe was in a Fit, and he again rub'd her Breaft,* &c. (*about this time* Margaret Perd [32] *an attendant affifted him in rubbing of her.* *The Afflicted fpake angerely to her faying don't you meddle with me, and haftily put away her hand*) *he wrought his Fingers before her Eyes and afked her if fhe faw the Witches?* A. *No.* Q. *Do you believe?* A. *Tes.* Q. *Do you believe in you know who?* A. *Tes.* Q. *Would you have other people do fo too, to believe in you know who?* A. *Tes.* Q. *Who is it that Afflicts you?* A. *I know not, there is a great many of them* (*about this time the Father queftion'd if fhe knew the Spectres?* *An attendant faid, if fhe did fhe would not tell; The Son proceeded.*) Q. *You have feen the Black-man, hant you?* A. *No.* Reply, *I hope you never fhall.* Q. *You have had a Book offered you, hant you?* A. *No.* Q. *The brufhing of you gives you eafe, don't it?* A. *Tes..* *She turn'd herfelfe and a little Groan'd.* Q. *Now the Witches Scratch you and Pinch you, and Bite you, don't they?* A. *Tes,* then *he put his hand upon her Breaft and Belly,* viz. *on the Cloaths over her, and felt a Living thing, as he faid, which moved the Father alfo to feel, and fome others.* Q. *Don't you feel the Live thing in the Bed?* A. *No.* Reply, *that is only Fancie.* Q. *the great company of People increafe your Torment, don't they?* A. *Tes.* *The People about were defired to withdraw.* *One Woman faid, I am fure I*

---

[32] A Name not met with beyond this Affair.

*am no Witch, I will not go; fo others, fo none with-
drew.* Q. *Shall we go to Prayers, Then fhe lay in
a Fit as before. But this time to revive her, they
waved a Hat and brufhed her Head and Pillow
therewith.* Q. *Shall we go to PRAY,* &c. *Spell-
ing the Word.* A. *Yes. The Father went to
Prayer for perhaps half an Hour,*[33] *chiefly againft
the Power of the Devil and Witchcraft, and that
God would bring out the Afflicters: during Prayer-
time, the Son flood by, and when they thought fhe
was ·in a Fit, rub'd her and brufh'd her as before,
and beckned to others to do the like, after Prayer
he proceeded;* Q. *You did not hear when we were
at Prayer, did you?* A. *Yes. You dont hear
always, you dont hear fometimes paft a Word or
two, do you?* A. *No. Then turning him about
faid, this is juft another* Mercy Short: Margaret Perd *reply'd, fhe was not like her in her
Fits.* Q. *What does fhe eat or drink?* A. Not
eat at all; but drink Rum. *Then he admonifhed
the young People to take warning,* &c. *Saying it
was a fad thing to be fo Tormented by the Devil
and his Inftruments:* A *Young-man prefent in the
habit of a Seaman, reply'd this is the Devil all
over, Than the Minifters withdrew. Soon after
they were gone the Afflicted defired the Women to
be gone, faying, that the Company of the Men was
not offenfive to her, and having hold of the hand of*

[33] The Doctor was greatly difturb- of the Prayer; averring that it was
ed at this Statement of the Length not above a quarter of an Hour.

L

a *Young-man, said to have been her Sweetheart formerly, who was withdrawing; she pull'd him again into his Seat, saying he should not go to Night.*

[15] September *the* 19th, 1693.

THIS *Night I renew'd my Visit, and found her rather of a fresher Countenance than before, about eight Persons present with her, she was in a Fit Screeming and making a Noise: Three or four Persons rub'd and brush'd her with their hands, they said that the brushing did put them away, if they brush'd or rub'd in the right place; therefore they brushed and rubbed in several places, and said that when they did it in the right place she could fetch her Breath, and by that they knew. She being come to herself was soon in a merry talking Fit. A Young-man came in and ask'd her how she did? She answered very bad, but at present a little better; he soon told her he must be gone and bid her good Night, at which she seem'd troubled, saying that she liked his Company; and said she would not have him go till she was well; adding, for I shall Die when you are gone. Then she complained they did not put her on a clean Cap, but let her ly so like a Beast, saying she should lose her Fellows. She said she wondered any People should be so Wicked as to think she was not Afflicted, but to think she Dissembled, A Young-woman answered Yes, if they were to see you in this merry Fit, they would say you Dissembled indeed; She reply'd, Mr. M— said this was her laughing time, she must laugh now: She said*

Mr. M —*had been there this Evening, and she en-quired, how long he had been gon? She said he stay'd alone with her in the room half an Hour, and said that he told her there were some that came for Spies, and to report about Town that she was not Afflicted. That during the said time she had no Fit, that he asked her if she knew how many times he had Prayed for her to day? And that she an-swered that she could not tell; and that he reply'd he had Prayed for her Nine times to Day; the At-tendants said that she was sometimes in a Fit that none could open her Joints,*[34] *and that there came an Old Iron-jaw'd Woman and try'd, but could not do it; they likewise said, that her Head could not be moved from the Pillow; I try'd to move her head, and found no more difficulty than another Bodies (and so did others) but was not willing to offend by lifting it up, one being reproved for endeavouring it, they saying Angrily you will break her Neck. The Attendants said Mr. M— would not go to Prayer with her when People were in the Room, as they did one Night that Night he felt the Live-Creature.* Margaret Perd *and another, said they smelt brim-stone;*[35] *I and others said we did not smell any; then they said they did not know what it was: This* Margaret *said, she wish'd she had been here when* Mr. M— *was here, another Attendant said, if you*

[34] The general Inference would naturally be that the Doctor's Pray-ers were not very effective.

[35] His Satanic Majesty was sup-posed to be very near, or the Scent of his Dominions would not have been perceptible. It may be that he did not make his Appearance, owing to the Presence of some ob-durate Unbelievers. See *Note* 3.

had been here you might not have been permitted in,
for her own Mother was not suffered to be present.

Sir, after the foreft Affliction and greateft blemifh to Religion that ever befel this Countrey, and
after moft Men began to Fear that fome undue
fteps had been taken, and after His Excellency
(with their Majeftyes Approbation as is faid) had
put a ftop to Executions, and Men began [16] to
hope there would never be a return of the like;
finding thefe Accounts to contain in them fomething extraordinary, I writ them down the fame
Nights in order to attain the certainty of them,
and foon found them fo confirmed that I have
(befides other Demonftrations) the whole, under
the Hands of two Perfons are ready to atteft
the Truth of it, but not fatisfied herewith; I
fhewed them to fome of your particular Friends,
that fo I might have the greater certainty: But
was much furprifed with the Meffage you fent
me, that I fhould be Arrefted for Slander, and at
your calling me one of the worft of Lyars, making
it Pulpit-news with the Name of *Pernicious Libels*, &c.   This occafion'd my firft Letter.

September *the* 29*th,* 1693.

Reverend SIR,

I *Having written from the Mouths of feveral*
Perfons, who affirm they were prefent with
Margaret Rule, *the* 13th *Inftant, her Anfwers and*
Behaviour, &c.   *And having fhewed it to feveral*
of my Friends, as alfo yours, and underftanding you

*are offended at it; This is to acquaint you that if
you and any one particular Friend, will pleafe to
meet me and fome other Indifferent Perfon with me,
at Mr.* Wilkinfs, *or at* Ben Harrifs,[36] *you intimating
the time, I fhall be ready there to read it to you, as
alfo a further Account of proceedings the* 19th
*Inftant, which may be needful to prevent Groundlefs
prejudices, and let deferved blame be caft where it
ought; From,*
  Sir, yours in what I may,   R. C.

The effects of which, Sir, (not to mention
that long Letter only once read to me) was, you
fent me word you would meet me at Mr. *Wilkins's* but before that Anfwer, at yours and your
Fathers complaint, I was brought before their
Majefties Juftice, by Warrant, as for Scandalous
Libels againft yourfelf, and was bound over to
Anfwer at Seffions; I do not remember you then
objected againft the Truth of what I had wrote,
but afferted it was wronged by omiffions, which
if it were fo was paft any Power of mine to
remedy, having given a faithful account of all
that came to my knowledge; And Sir, that you
might not be without fome Cognizance of the
reafons why I took fo much pains in it, as alfo
for my own Information, if it might have been,
I wrote to you my fecond Letter to this effect.

[36] Richard Wilkins and Benjamin Harris were Bookfellers and
Publifhers in Bofton at this Period.
They are duly noticed in the *Hiftory and Antiquities of Bofton,* out
of Dunton's *Life and Errors.* Harris printed *The Wonders of the Invifible World,* as will be feen on
reference to the Title-page. See
Thomas's *Hift. Printing,* ii, 412.

November *the* 24*th*, 1693.

Reverend SIR,

HAVING *expeĉted fome Weeks, your meeting me at Mr.* Wilkins *according to what you intimated to me,* J. M — *and the time drawing near for our meeting elfewhere, I thought it not amifs to give you a Summary of my thoughts in the great concern, which as you fay has been agitated with fo much* [17] *heat. That there are Witches is not the doubt, the Scriptures elfe were in vain, which affign their Punifhment to be by death; But what this Witchcraft is, or wherein it does confift, feems to be the whole difficulty: And as it may be eafily demonftrated, that all that bear that Name cannot be juftly fo accounted, fo that fome things and Aĉtions not fo efteemed by the moft, yet upon due examination will be found to merit no better Charaĉter.*

In your late Book you lay down a brief Synopfis of what has been written on that Subjeĉt, by a Triumvirate *of as Eminent Men as ever handled it* 37 (*as you are pleaf'd to call them*) viz. Mr. Perkins, Gaule, *and* Bernard *confifting of about* 30 *Tokens to know them by, many of them diftinĉt from, if not thwarting each other: Among all of which I can find but one decifive,* Viz. *That of Mr.* Gaule, *Head* IV. *and runs thus; Among the moft unhappy Circumftances to conviĉt a Witch, one is a maligning and oppugning the Word, Work, or Worfhip of God, and by any extraordinary Sign feeking to feduce any*

---

37 See Vol. i, Page 37.

from it, fee Deu. 13. 1, 2. Mat. 24. 24. Acts. 13.
8, 10. 2. Tim. 3. 8. *Do but mark well the places,
and for this very property of thus oppofing and perverting, they are all there concluded Arrant and
abfolute Witches.*

This Head as here laid down and inferted by you,
either is a Truth or not, if not, why is it here inferted from one of the Triumvirate *if it be a Truth.
as the Scriptures quoted will abundantly teftifie,
whence is it that it is fo little regarded, tho it be the
only Head well proved by Scripture, or that the reft
of the* Triumvirate *fhould fo far forget their Work
as not to mention it. It were to be unjuft to the
Memory of thofe otherwife Wife Men, to fuppofe
them to have any Sinifter defign ; But perhaps the
force of a prevailing opinion, together with an Education thereto Suited, might overfhadow their Judgments, as being wont to be but too prevalent in many
other cafes. But if the above be Truth, then the
Scripture is full and plain, What is Witchcraft?
And if fo, what need of his next Head of Hanging
of People without as full and clear Evidence as in
other Cafes? Or what need of the reft of the Re-
ceipts of the* Triumvirate? *what need of Praying
that the Afflicted may be able to difcover who 'tis
that Afflicts them? or what need of Searching for
Tet's for the Devil to Suck in his Old Age, or the
Experiment of faying the Lord's Prayer,* &c. *Which
a multitude more practifed in fome places Superfti-
tioufly inclin'd. Other Actions have been practifed
for eafing the Afflicted, lefs juftifiable, if not ftrongly*

favouring of Witchcraft itfelf, viz. *Fondly Ima-
gining by the Hand, &c. to drive off Speƈtres, or to
knock off Invifible Chains, or by ftriking in the Air
to Wound either the Affliƈted or others,* &c. *I write
not this to accufe any, but that all may beware believing, That the Devil's bounds are fet, which he
cannot pafs, That the Devils are fo full of Malice,
That it cannot be added to by Mankind, That where
he hath Power he neither can nor will omit Executing it, That 'tis only the Almighty that fets* [18]
*bounds to his rage, and that only can Commiffionate
him to hurt or deftroy any.*

Thefe *laft, Sir, are fuch Foundations of Truth,
in my efteem, that I cannot but own it to be my duty
to afcert them, when call'd, tho' with the hazard of
my All.*[38] *And confequently to deteƈt fuch as thefe,
That a Witch can Commiffionate Devils to Affliƈt
Mortals, That he can at his or the Witches pleafure
Affume any Shape, That Hanging or Drawing of
Witches can leffen his Power of Affliƈting, or reftore
thofe that were at a diftance Tormented, with many
others depending on thefe; all tending, in my efteem,
highly to the Dishonour of God, and the Indangering
the well-being of a People, and do further add, that
as the Scriptures are full that there is Witchcraft,
(ut fup.) fo 'tis as plain that there are Poffeffions,
and that the Bodies of the Poffeft have hence been
not only Affliƈted, but ftrangely agitated, if not their*

---

[38] The Author feemed to be fully aware of the Danger of afferting the plain Truth. It probably was a means of his ruin, as to any confiderable Fortune. See *Introductory Memoir.*

*tongues improved to foretell futurities, &c. and why
not to accufe the Innocent, as bewitching them;
having pretence to Divination to · gain credence.
This being reafonable to be expected, from him who
is the Father of Lies, to the end he may thereby in-
volve a Countrey in Blood, Mallice, and Evil, fur-
mifing which he greedily feeks after, and fo finally
lead them from their fear and dependance upon God
to fear him, and a fuppofed Witch thereby attaining
his end upon Mankind; and not only fo, but Natural
Diftemper, as has been frequently obferved by the
Judicious, have fo operated as to deceive, more than
the Vulgar, as is teftified by many Famous Phyfi-
cians, and others.   And as for that proof of Multitudes of Confeffions, this Countrey may be by this
time thought Competent Judges, what credence we
ought to give them, having had fuch numerous Inftances, as alfo how obtain'd.*

*And now Sir, if herein be any thing in your
efteem valuable, let me intreat you, not to account it
the worfe for coming from fo mean a hand; which
however you may have receiv'd Prejudices, &c. Am
ready to ferve you to my Power; but if you Judge
otherwife hereof, you may take your own Methods for
my better Information. Who am, Sir, yours to
command, in what I may,* P. C.[39]

In Anfwer to this laft, Sir, you replyed to the
Gentleman that prefented it, that you had nothing

---

[39] A mifprint. R. C. was in-   in the Salem Editions.
tended. The Correction is made

M

to Profecute againft me; and faid as to your Sentiments in your Books, you did not bind any to
believe them, and then again renew'd your promife of meeting me, as before, tho' not yet performed.   Accordingly, tho' I waited at Seffions,
there was none to objeﬆ ought againft me, upon
which I was difmiffed.   This gave me fome reafon
to believe that you intended all fhould have been
forgotten;   But inftead of that, I find the Coals
are frefh blown up, I being fuppofed to be reprefented, in a late Manufcript, *More Wonders of the,*
&c. as traverfing your Difcourfe in your Faithful
difcharge of your Duty, *&c.*   And fuch as fee not
with the Authors Eyes, rendred *Saducees* and
Witlins,[40] *&c.* and the Arguments that fquare not
with the Sentiments [19] therein contain'd, Buffoonary; rarely no doubt, agreeing with the Spirit
of Chrift, and his dealings with an unbelieving
Thomas, yet whofe infidelity was without compare
lefs excufable, but the Author having refolved
long fince, to have no more than one fingle Grain
of Patience, with them that deny, *&c* the Wonder is the lefs.   It muft needs be that offences
come, but wo to him by whom they come.   To
vindicate myfelf therefore from fuch falfe Impu-
tations, of *Satan-like* infinuations, and mifrepre-
fenting your Aﬆions, *&c.* and to vindicate yourfelf, Sir, as much as is in my power from thofe
fuggeftions, faid to be infinuated, as if you wore

---

[40] Epithets applied by Mr. Mather   "Flafhy and fleeting Witlings."—
to thofe who diffented from him.   *Remarkables* of Dr. I. M., 164.

not the Modeſty, and Gravity, that becomes a
Miniſter of the *Goſpel;* which it ſeems, ſome that
never ſaw the ſaid Narratives, report them to
contain; I ſay, Sir, for theſe reaſons, I here preſent you with the firſt Coppy that ever was taken,
&c. And purpoſe for a Weeks time to be ready,
if you ſhall intimate your pleaſure to wait upon
you, either at the place formerly appointed, or
any other that is indifferent to the End; that if
there ſhall appear any defeꞔts in that Narrative,
they may be amended.

Thus, Sir, I have given you a genuine account
of my Sentiments and Aꞔtions in this Affair; and
do requeſt and pray, that if I err, I may be
ſhewed it from *Scripture,* or found *Reaſon,* and
not by quotations out of *Virgil,* nor *Spaniſh
Rhetorick.*[41] For I find the *Witlings* mentioned,
are ſo far from anſwering your profound queſtions,
that they cannot ſo much as pretend to ſhew a
diſtinꞔtion between Witchcraft in the Common
notion of it, and Poſſeſſion; Nor ſo much as to
demonſtrate that ever the *Jews* or primitive
Chriſtians did believe, that a Witch could ſend a
Devil to Affliꞔt her Neighbours; but to all theſe,
Sir, (ye being the Salt of the Earth, *&c.*) I have
reaſon to hope for a Satisfaꞔtory Anſwer to him,
who is one that reverences your Perſon˙ and Of-

---

41 Whittier had, no doubt, been reading Calef recently, when he wrote:

"To garniſh the Story, with hear a ſtreak
Of Latin, and there another of Greek:
And the Tales he heard and the Notes he took
Behold are they not in his Wonder-Book?"

fice; And am, Sir, yours to Command in what I
may,   R. C.

Bofton, January the 15*th,* 169¾.

Mr. R. C.

WHEREAS you intimate your defires, that
what's not fairly (I take it for granted you
mean truly alfo,) reprefented in a Paper you lately
fent me, containing a pretended Narrative of a
Vifit by my Father and felf to an Afflicted Young
woman, whom we apprehended to be under a
Diabolical Poffeffion, might be rectified: I have
this to fay, as I have often already faid, that do I
fcarcely find any one thing in the whole Paper,
whether refpecting my Father or felf, either fairly
or truly reprefented. Nor can I think that any
that know my Parents Circumftances, but muft
think him deferving a better Character by far,
than this Narrative can be thought to give him.
When the main defign we managed in [20] Vifiting the poor Afflicted Creature, was to prevent
the Accufations of the Neighbourhood; can it
be fairly reprefented that our defign was to draw
out fuch Accufations, which is the reprefentation
of the Paper. We have Teftimonies of the beft
Witneffes and in Number not a few, That when
we afked *Rule* whether fhe thought fhe knew
who Tormented her? the Queftion was but an
Introduction to the Solemn charges which we
then largely gave, that fhe fhould rather Dye than
tell the Names of any whom fhe might Imagine

that fhe knew. Your Informers have reported
the Queftion, and report nothing of what follows, as effential to the giving of that Queftion :
And can this be termed a piece of fairnefs ? Fair
it cannot be, that when Minifters Faithfully and
Carefully difcharge their Duty to the Miferable
in their Flock, little bits, fcraps and fhreds of
their Difcourfes, fhould be tackt together to make
them contemtible, when there fhall be no notice
of all the Neceffary, Seafonable, and Profitable
things that occurr'd, in thofe Difcourfes; And
without which, the occafion of the leffer Paffages
cannot be underftood; and yet I am furnifhed
with abundant Evidences, ready to be Sworn, that
will poffitively prove this part of unfairnefs, by
the above mention'd Narrative, to be done both
to my Father and felf. Again, it feems not fair
or reafonable that I fhould be expof'd, for which
your felf (not to fay fome others) might have
expof'd me for, if I had not done, *viz.* for dif-
couraging fo much Company from flocking about
the Poffeft Maid, and yet, as I perfwade myfelf,
you cannot but think it to be good advice, to
keep much Company from fuch haunted Chambers; befides the unfairnefs doth more appear, in
that I find nothing repeated of what I faid about
the advantage, which the Devil takes from too
much Obfervation and Curiofity.[42]

[42] With this View of the Devil,
the Author was certainly, according
to his own Account, more in the
Way of becoming one of his deluded Followers than any other:
"Tis a moft commendable Cau-

In that feveral of the Queftions in the Paper are fo Worded, as to carry in them a prefuppofal of the things inquired after, to fay the beft of it is very unfair : But this is not all, the Narrative contains a number of Miftakes and Falfhoods; which were they wilful and defign'd, might juftly be termed grofs Lies. The reprefentations are far from true, when 'tis affirm'd my Father and felf being come into the Room, I began the Difcourfe; I hope I underftand breeding a little better than fo : For proof of this, did occafion ferve, fundry can depofe the contrary.

'Tis no lefs untrue, that either my Father or felf put the Queftion, how many Witches fit upon you? We always cautioufly avoided that expreffion; It being contrary to our inward belief : All the ftanders by will (I believe) fwear they did not hear us ufe it (your Witneffes excepted) and I tremble to think how hardy thofe woful Creatures muft be, to call the Almighty by an Oath, to fo falfe a thing. As falfe a reprefentation 'tis, that I rub'd *Rule's* Stomach, her Breaft not being covered. The Oath of the neareft Spectators, giving a true account of that matter [21] will prove this to be little lefs than a grofs (if not a doubled) Lie; and to be fomewhat plainer, it carries the Face of a Lie contrived on purpofe (by them at leaft, to whom you are be-

tioufnefs," he tells us elfewhere, "to be very fhy left the Devil get fo far into our Faith, as that for the fake of many Truths which we find he tells us, we come at length to believe any Lies, wherewith he may abufe us!" Faith can hardly remove fuch a Mountain.

holden for the Narrative) Wickedly and Bafely to
expofe me. For you cannot but know how
much this reprefentation hath contributed, to
make People believe a Smutty thing of me; I
am far from thinking, but that in your own Confcience you believe, that no indecent Action of
that Nature could then be done by me before
fuch obfervers, had I been fo Wicked as to have
been inclin'd to what is Bafe. It looks next to
impoffible that a reparation fhoud be made me
for the wrong done to, I hope, as to any Scandal
an unblemifh'd, tho' weak and fmall Servant of
the Church of God. Nor is what follows a lefs
untruth, that 'twas an Attendant and not myfelf
who faid, if *Rule* knows who Afflicts her, yet fhe
wont tell. I therefore fpoke it that I might en-
courage her to continue in that concealment of
all Names whatfoever; to this I am able to furnifh myfelf with the Atteftation of Sufficient
Oaths. 'Tis as far from true, that my apprehenfion of the Imp, about *Rule,* was on her Belly,
for the Oaths of the Spectators, and even of thofe
that thought they felt it, can teftify that 'twas
upon the Pillow, at a diftance from her Body.
As untrue a Reprefentation is that which follows,
Viz. That it was faid unto her, that her not
Apprehending of that odd palpable tho' not vifible, Mover was from her Fancy, for I endeavoured
to perfwade her that it might be but Fancy in
others, that there was any fuch thing at all.
Witneffes every way fufficient can be produced

for this alfo. 'tis falfely reprefented that my
Father felt on the Young-woman after the appearance mentioned, for his hand was never near
her; Oath can fufficiently vindicate him. 'Tis
very untrue, that my Father Prayed for perhaps
half an Hour, againft the power of the Devil
and Witchcraft, and that God would bring out
the Afflictors. Witneffes of the beft Credit, can
depofe, that his Prayer was not a quarter of an
Hour, and that there was no more than about one
claufe towards the clofe of the Prayer, which was
of this import; and this claufe alfo was guarded
with a fingular warinefs and modefty, *viz.* If
there were any evil Inftruments in this matter
God would pleafe to difcover them: And that
there was more than common reafon for that
petition I can fatisfie any one that will pleafe to
Inquire of me. And ftrange it is, that a Gentleman that from 18 to 54 hath been an Exemplary
Minifter of the Gofpel; and that befides a ftation
in the Church of God, as confiderable as any that
his own Country can afford, hath for divers years
come off with honour, in his Application to three
Crown'd Heads, and the chiefeft Nobility of three
Kingdoms, knows not yet how to make one fhort
Prayer of a quarter of an hour, but in *New-
England* he muft be Libell'd for it. There are
divers other down-right miftakes, which you [22]
have permitted yourfelf, I would hope, not know-
ingly, and with a Malicious defign, to be receiver
or Compiler of, which I fhall now forbear to

Animadvert upon. As for the Appendix of the
Narrative I do find myself therein Injurioufly
treated, for the utmoft of your proof for what
you fay of me, amounts to little more than, *viz.*
Some People told you, that others told them, that
fuch and fuch things did pafs, but you may affure
yourfelf, that I am not unfurnifh'd with Witneffes,
that can convict the fame. Whereas you would
give me to believe the bottom of thefe your
Methods, to be fome diffatisfaction about the
commonly receiv'd Power of *Devils* and *Witches ;*
I do not only with all freedom offer you the ufe
of any part of my Library, which you may fee
caufe to perufe on that Subject, but alfo if you
and any elfe, whom you pleafe, will vifit me
at my Study, yea, or meet me at any other place,
lefs inconvenient than thofe by you propof'd; I
will with all the fairnefs and calmnefs in the
World difpute the point. I beg of God that he
would beftow as many Bleffings on you, as ever
on myfelf, and out of a fincere wifh, that you
may be made yet more capable of thefe Bleffings,
I take this occafion to lay before you the faults
(not few nor fmall ones neither) which the Paper
contained, you lately fent me, in order to be Examined by me. In cafe you want a true and full
Narrative of my Vifit, whereof fuch an indecent
Traverfty (to fay the beft) hath been made, I am
not unwilling to communicate it, in mean time
muft take liberty to fay, 'Tis fcarcely confiftent with Common Civility, much lefs Chriftian
N

Charity, to offer the Narrative, now with you, for a true one, till you have a truer, or for a full one, till you have a fuller. Your Sincere (tho' Injur'd) Friend and Servant,

C. *MATHER.*

The Copy of a Paper Receiv'd with the above Letter.

I DO Teſtifie that I have ſeen *Margaret Rule* in her Afflictions from the Inviſible World, lifted up from her Bed, wholly by an Inviſible force, a great way towards the top of the Room where ſhe lay; in her being ſo lifted, ſhe had no Aſſiſtance from any uſe of her own Arms or Hands, or any other part of her Body, not ſo much as her Heels touching her Bed, or reſting on any ſupport whatſoever. And I have ſeen her thus lifted, when not only a ſtrong Perſon hath thrown his whole weight a croſs her to pull her down; but ſeveral other Perſons have endeavoured, with all their might, to hinder her from being ſo raiſed up, which I ſuppoſe that ſeveral others will teſtifie as well as myſelf, when call'd unto it. Witneſs my Hand,

SAMUEL AVES.[43]

[43] A Family of this Name is ſuppoſed to have lived at the Corner of Lynn Street and Henchman's Lane, as that Corner for a long Period was known as *Aves's Corner.* Savage had never read of *Samuel Aves.* Whether he was of the Family of *John Aves,* baniſhed for attempting to burn the Town in 1679, is not known.—*Hiſt. Boſton,* 431.

WE can alſo Teſtifie to the ſubſtance of what is above Written, and have ſeveral times ſeen [23] *Margaret Rule* ſo lifted up from her Bed, as that ſhe had no uſe of her own Lims to help her up, but it was the declared apprehenſion of us, as well as others that ſaw it, impoſſible for any hands, but ſome of the Inviſible World to lift her.

.Copia

ROBERT EARLE.[44]
JOHN WILKINS.
DAN. WILLIAMS.

WE, whoſe Names are under-writted do teſtifie, That one Evening when we were in the Chamber where *Margaret Rule* then lay, in her late Affliction, we obſerved her to be, by an Inviſible Force, lifted up from the Bed whereon ſhe lay, ſo as to touch the Garret Floor, while yet neither her Feet, nor any other part of her Body reſted either on the Bed, or any other ſupport, but were alſo by the ſame force, lifted up from all that was under her, and all this for a conſiderable while, we judg'd it ſeveral Minutes; and it was as much as ſeveral of us could do, with all our ſtrength to pull her down. All which happened when there was not only we two in the

Chamber, but we fuppofe ten or a dozen more, whofe Names we have forgotten,

Copia   *THOMAS THORNTON.*[45]

William Hudfon[46] *Teftifies to the fubftance of* Thorntons *Teftimony, to which he alfo hath fet his Hand.*

Bofton, January 18, 1693.

Mr. *Cotton Mather,*

Reverend SIR,

YOURS of the 15*th* Inftant, I receiv'd yefterday; and foon found I had promifed myfelf too much by it, *viz,* Either concurrence with, or a denial of thofe Fundamentals mentioned in mine, of *Novemb.* the 24*th.* finding this waved by an Invitation to your Library, *&c.* I thank God I have the Bible, and do Judge that fufficient to demonftrate that cited Head of Mr. *Gaule,* to be a Truth, as alfo thofe other Heads mentioned, as the Foundations of Religion. And in my apprehenfion, if it be afked any Chriftian, whether God governs the World, and whether it be he only can Commiffionate Devils, and fuch other Fundamentals, He ought to be as ready as in the Queftion, who made him? (a little Writing certainly might be of more ufe, to clear up the controverted points, than either looking over many

---

[45] Son of Timothy Thornton. His Occupation was that of a Paver.

[46] Perhaps Son of the firft William Hudfon, one of the firft Settlers of Bofton.

Books in a well furnifh'd Library, or than a difpute, if I were qualified for it; the Inconveniencies of Paffion being this way beft avoided) And
am not without hopes that you will yet oblige
me fo far, as to confider that Letter, and if I Err,
to let me fee it by Scripture, &c.

Yours, almoft the whole of it, is concerning
the Narrative I fent to you, and you feem to intimate as if I were giving Charaҫters, Reflecti-[24]
ons, and Libell's, &c. concerning yourfelf and
Relations; all which ·were as far from my
thoughts, as ever they were in writing after either
yourfelf, or any other Minifter. In the front you
declare your apprehenfion to be, that the Afflicted
was under a Diabolical Poffeffion, and if fo, I fee
not how it fhould be occafion'd by any Witchcraft (unlefs we afcribe that Power to a Witch,
which is only the Prerogative of the Almighty,
of Sending or Commiffionating the Devils to
Afflicҵ her.) But to your particular Objecҵions
againft the Narrative; and to the firft my intelligence not giving me any further, I could not
infert that I knew not. And it feems improbable
that a Queftion fhould be put, whether fhe knew
(or rather who they were) and at the fame time
to charge her, and that upon her Life, not to tell,
and if you had done fo, I fee but little good you
could promife yourfelf or others by it, fhe being
Poffeft, as alfo having it inculcated fo much to
her of Witchcraft. And as to the next Objecҵion
about company flocking, &c. I do profefs my

Ignorance, not knowing what you mean by it.
And Sir, that moft of the Queftions did carry
with them a prefuppofing the things inquired
after, is evident, if there were fuch as thofe
relating to the *Black-man* and a Book, and about
her hearing the Prayer, *&c.* (related in the faid
Narrative, which I find no Objection againft.)
As to that which is faid of mentioning yourfelf
firft difcourfings and your hopes that your breeding was better (I doubt it not) nor do I doubt
your Father might firft apply himfelf to others;
but my intelligence is, that you firft fpake to the
Afflicted or Poffeffed, for which you had the advantage of a nearer approach. The next two
Objections are founded upon miftakes: I find
not in the Narrative any fuch Queftion, as
how many Witches fit upon you? and that her
Breaft was not covered, in which thofe material
words, (with the Bed-Cloaths) are wholly omitted; I am not willing to retort here your own
Language upon you; but can tell you, that your
own difcourfe of it publickly, at Sir *W. P*'s Table,
has much more contributed to, *&c.* As to the
Reply, if fhe could fhe would not tell, whether
either or both fpake it it matters not much.
Neither does the Narrative fay you felt the live
thing on her Belly; tho I omit now to fay what
further demonftrations there are of it. As to
that Reply, that is only her fancy, I find the
word (her) added. And as to your Fathers feeling for the live Creature after you had felt it, if

it were on the Bed it was not fo very far from
her. And for the length of his Prayer, poffibly
your Witneffes might keep a more exact account
of the time than thofe others, and I ftand not for
a few Minutes. For the reft of the Objections
I fuppofe them of lefs moment, if lefs can be
(however fhall be ready to receive them, thofe
matters of greateft concern I find no Objections
againft) thefe being all that yet appear, it may be
thought that if the Narrative be not [25] fully
exact, it was as near as Memory could bear away;
but fhould be glad to fee one more perfect (which
yet is not to be expected, feeing none writ at the
time.) You mention the appendix, by which I
underftand the Second Vifit, and if you be by the
poffeffed belyed (as being half an hour with her
alone (excluding her own Mother) and as telling
her you had Prayed for her Nine times that day,
and that now was her Laughing time, fhe muft
Laugh now) I can fee no Wonder in it; what
can be expected lefs from the Father of Lies, by
whom, you Judge, fhe was poffeft.

And befides the above Letter, you were pleafed
to fend me another Paper containing feveral Teftimonies of the Poffeffed being lifted up, and
held a fpace of feveral Minutes to the Garret
floor, &c. but they omit giving the account,
whether after fhe was down they bound her
down: or kept holding her: And relate not
how many were to pull her down, which hinders
the knowledge what number they muft be to be

ſtronger than an Inviſible Force. Upon the whole, I ſuppoſe you expect I ſhould believe it; and if ſo, the only advantage gain'd, is that which has been ſo long controverted between Proteſtants and Papiſts, whether miracles are ceaſt, will hereby ſeem to be decided for the latter; it being, for ought I can ſee, if ſo, as true a Miracle as for Iron to ſwim, and that the Devil can work ſuch Miracles.

But Sir, leaving theſe little diſputable things, I do again pray that you would let me have the happineſs of your approbation or confutation of that Letter before referred to.

And now, Sir, that the God of all Grace may enable us Zealouſly to own his 'Truths, and to follow thoſe things that tend to Peace, and that yourſelf may be as an uſeful Inſtrument in his hand, effectually to ruin the remainders of Heatheniſh and Popiſh Superſtitions, is the earneſt deſire and prayer of yours to command, in what I may.   R. C.

Poſtſcript—Sir, I here ſend you the Coppy of a paper that lately came to my Hands, which tho' it contains no Wonders, yet is remarkable, and Runs thus.

An account of what an *Indian* told Captain *Hill*,[47] at *Saco-Fort*.

THE Indian *told him that the* French *Minifters were better than the* Englifh, *for before the* French *came among them there were a great many* Witches *among the* Indians, *but now there were none, and there were much* Witches *among the* Englifh *Minifters, as* Burroughs, *who was Hang'd for it.*

Were I difpofed to make reflections upon it, I fuppofe you will Judge the Field large, enough, but I forbear, as above.   R. C.

[26] *Bofton Feb. the* 19*th,* 1693.

Mr. *Cotton Mather,*

Reverend Sir, Having received as yet no Anfwer to mine of *Novemb.* the 24th. except an offer to perufe Books, *&c.* relating to the Doctrinals therein contain'd : Nor to my laft of *Jan-*

---

47 Captain *John Hill,* of whom Dr. Ufher Parfons has given an interefting and ample Account in the *N. E. Hift. and Gen. Reg.* for April and July, 1858.

As a Contraft to the next Sentence of the Text take this : "Some of the Indian Pawawes (*i. e.,* Wizzards) in this Country, have received the Gofpel, and given Good Evidence of a True Converfion to God in Chrift, have, with much Sorrow of Heart, declared how they had, whilft in their *Heathenifm* by the Hands of Evil Angels Murdered their Neighbors."—Dr. I. Mather, *to the Reader in Angelographia.* In the valuable Collection of Dr. J. S. H. Fogg, of S. Bofton, are many of the Papers of Capt. Hill, of much Intereft on the Period referred to.

O

uary the 18th. In which I did again pray that if
I err'd I might be fhewed it by Scripture, *Viz.* in
believing that the Devils bounds are fett, which
he cannot pafs; that the Devils are fo full of
Malice that it cant be added to by Mankind:
That where he hath power he neither can nor
will omit Executing it; That it's only the Al-
mighty that fets bounds to his rage, and that only
can commiffionate him to hurt or deftroy any;
And confequently to deteft as erroneous and dan-
gerous, the belief that a Witch can Commiffionate
Devils to Afflict Mortals; That he can at his or
the Witches pleafure affume any fhape: That
Hanging or Chaining of Witches can leffen his
Power of Afflicting, and reftore thofe that were,
at a diftance, Tormented by him.   And whether
Witchcraft ought to be underftood now in this
Age, to be the fame that it was when the Divine
Oracles were given forth, particularly, thofe quoted
by Mr. *Gaule* in that cited Head (*Wonders of the
Invifible World;* [48] Mr. *Gaules* IV. Head, to difcover Witches) which do fo plainly fhew a Witch,
in Scripture-fenfe to be one that maligne, *&c.*
And that pretend to give a Sign in order to feduce, *&c.* For I have never underftood in my
time, any fuch have Suffered as Witches, tho'
fufficiently known; But the only Witch now
inquired after, is one that is faid to become fo by
making an Explicit Covenant with the Devil, *i. e.*
the Devil appearing to them, and making a com-

[48] See Vol. I, Page 37, of thefe Volumes.

pact mutually, promifing each to other, teftified
by their figning his Book, a material Book, which
he is faid to keep and that thereby they are Intituled to a power, not only to Afflict others, but
fuch as is truly exorbitant, if not highly intrench-
ing upon the prerogative of him, who is the
Soveraign being; For who is he that faith, and
it cometh to pafs, when the Lord commandeth
it not.

Such explicit Covenant being as is faid in this
Age reckoned effential to compleat a Witch : Yet
I finding nothing of fuch covenant (or power
thereby obtain'd) in Scripture, and yet a Witch
therein fo fully defcrib'd, do pray that if there be
any fuch Scriptures I may be directed to them,
for as to the many Legends in this cafe I make
no account of them ; I Read indeed of a Covenant with Death and with Hell, but fuppofe that
to be in the Heart (or *Mental*) only, and fee not
what ufe fuch explicit one can be of between
Spirits, any further than as 'tis a Copy of that
Mental which is in the Heart.   The dire effects
and confequences of fuch notion may be found
written in indelible *Roman* Characters of Blood
in all Countryes where they have prevail'd, and
what can lefs be [27] expected when Men are
Indicted for that, which, as 'tis impoffible to
prove fo, for any to clear himfelf of, *Viz*, Such
explicit Covenant with the Devil, and then for
want of better Evidence, muft take up with fuch as
the Nature of fuch fecret Covenant can bear, as Mr.

Gaule hath it, *i. e.* Diftracted Stories, and ftrange and Foreign Events, *&c.* Thereby endeavouring to find it, though by it's but fuppofed effects; By the fame Rules that one is put to purge himfelf of fuch Compact, by the fame may all Mankind.[49]

This then being fo Important a cafe, it concerns all to know what Foundations in Scripture is laid for fuch a Structure; For if they are deficient of that Warrant, the more Eminent the Architects are the more dangerous are they thereby rendered, *&c.* Thefe are fuch confiderations as I think will vindicate me in the efteem of all Lovers of Humanity, in my endeavours to get them cleared. And to that End, do once more pray; that you would fo farr oblige me as to give your Approbation or Confutation of the above Doctrinals; But if you think filence a Vertue in this cafe, I fhall (I fuppofe) fo far comply with it as not to loofe you any more time to look over my papers. And if any others will fo far oblige me, I fhall not be ungrateful to them; Praying God to guide and profper you, I am, Sir, yours to my power,

R. C.

(He that doth Truth, cometh to the Light.)

[49] The Abfurdity of the Practice of the Courts then in Ufe, in their fhocking Abufes of accufed Perfons, will be found in all its Deformity, on perufing the Trials of thofe Days. The Practice of infulting and browbeating thofe on Trial was according to the Cuftom of the Englifh Courts of thofe Days, and for a long Time after.

Bofton April *the* 16*th*, 1694.

Mr. *Cotton Mather.*

Reverend Sir,

HAVING as yet Received no Anfwer to my laft, touching the Doctrinals therein referred to, tho' at the delivery of it, you were pleafed to promife the Gentleman that prefented it, that I fhould have it, and after that you acqainted the fame Gentleman that you were about it. The length of time fince thofe promifes, makes me fuppofe you are preparing fomething for the Prefs (for I would not queftion your veracity) do think it may not be amifs, when you do any thing of that Nature for the publick view, that you alfo explain fome paffages of fome late Books of yours and your Relations, which are hard to be underftood, to Inftance in a few of many Wonders of the *Invifible World*, pag. 17. [Plagues *are fome of thefe woes with which the Devil caufes our Trouble*, pag. 18. *Hence come fuch Plagues as that befom of deftruction which within our Memory fwept away fuch a throng of People from one* Englifh *city, in one Vifitation.* Wars *are fome of thofe woes with which the Devil caufes our Trouble*, pag. 16. *Hence 'tis that the Devil like a Dragon keeping a Guard upon fuch Fruits as would refrefh a Languifhing World, has hindered Mankind for many Ages from hitting upon thofe ufefull Inventions. The benighted World muft Jogg on for thoufands of Years, without the knowledge of the Load-ſtone, Printing and Spectacles,* pag. 10, *It is* [28] *not likely that every Devil does know every Language.* 'Tis poſſible the Experience, or if I may call it ſo, the Education of all Devils is not alike; Caſes of conſcience, page 63. The Devil has inflicted on many the Diſeaſe call'd Lycanthropia.⁵⁰

Memor. provid. Relat. to Witch. Diſc. on Wit. pag. 24. ` I am alſo apt to think that the Devils are ſeldom able to hurt us in any of our exteriour concerns, without a Commiſſion from ſome of our fellow Worms. When foul Mouth'd Men ſhall wiſh harm to their Neighbours, they give a Commiſſion to the Devil to perform what they deſire, and if God ſhould not Mercifully prevent, they would go thro' with it; Hear this you that in wilde Paſſion will give every thing to the Devil; Hear it you that beſpeak a Rot, a Pox, or a Plague, on all that ſhall provoke you ; I here Indict you as Guilty of Helliſh Witchcraft in the Sight of God.* More Wonders of the Inviſible World, *pag.* 49. *They each of them have their Spectres or Devils Commiſſioned by them and repreſenting of them,* pag. 14. *But ſuch a permiſſion from God for the Devil to come down and break in upon Mankind muſt often times be accompanied with a Commiſſion from ſome of Mankind itſelf,* Inchantments Encountered. *Theſe Witches*

---

⁵⁰ Nothing was more common among thoſe who imagined themſelves bewitched, than the Notion that they were transformed into Cats, and other Animals; and that in thoſe Shapes they attended Witch Meetings. At ſuch Meetings the Devil was always preſent, and acted as Maſter of Ceremonies. A very ſure Evidence of Inſanity.

have driven a Trade of Commiſſionating their con-
federate Spirits, to do all ſorts of Miſchiefs to their
Neighbours, pag. 50. *They have bewitched ſome*
even ſo farr, as to make them Self-deſtroyers, pag.
144. As I am abundantly ſatisfied, that many of
the Self-murders committed here, have been the ef-
fects of a cruel and Bloody Witchcraft, letting fly
Dæmons *upon the Miſerable Seneca's, pag.* 51. *We*
have ſeen ſome of their Children ſo Dedicated to the
Devil, that in their Infancy the Imps have ſucked
them. Caſes of conſcience, *pag.* 24. *They be-*
queath their Dæmons to their Children as a Legacy,
by whom they are often aſſiſted to ſee and do things
beyond the Power of Nature, pag. 21. *There are*
in Spain *a ſort of People call'd* Zahurs,[51] *that can*
ſee into the Bowels of the Earth. ⌊*On* Tueſdays
and Fridays,⌉ (and to add) that in pag. 49. The
words are ⌊*For the Law of God allows of no Reve-*
lation from any other Spirit but himſelf, Iſa. viii.
19. *It is a Sin againſt God to make uſe of the*
Devils help, to know that which cannot be otherways
known; and I teſtify againſt it as a great tranſ-
greſſion, which may Juſtly provoke the Holy one of
Iſrael, *to let looſe Devils on the whole Land.*⌉ Altho the Devils Accuſation may be ſo far regarded,
as to cauſe an inquiry into the Truth of things,
Job. i. 11, 12, and ii, 5, 6. *Yet not ſo as to be an*

---

[51] Called in Captain John Ste-
vens's *Spaniſh and Engliſh Diction-*
ary, Cabori, which is defined, "one
that pretends to ſee into the Bowels
of the Earth, through Stone Walls,
or into a Man's Body; a Cheat put
upon the Ignorant." There is ſomething very ſimilar in our Times,
even leaving out the Founder of the
Mormon Sect.

Evidence or Ground of Conviction, for the Devils Testimony ought not to be taken in WHOLE Nor In PART.] It is a known Truth, that some unwary expreſſions of the primative Fathers, were afterwards improved for the Introducing and eſtabliſhing of Error, as their calling the Virgin *Mary,* the Mother of God, *&c.* Hence occaſion and Advantage was taken to propagate the Idolizing of her (the like might be ſaid of the *Eucha*[29]*riſt,* theſe aſſertions, above rehearſed, being apparently liable to a like Male Conſtruction, and no leſs dangerous, are therefore as I ſaid highly needful to be explain'd, and that in a moſt publick manner. For were they to be underſtood Litterally and as they are ſpoken, it muſt ſeem as if the Authors were Introducing among Chriſtians very dangerous Doctrines, ſuch, as were they aſſerted by the beſt of Men, yet ought to be rejected by all, *&c. Viz.* That 'tis the Devil that brings the moſt of Evils upon Mankind, by way of Infliction, that do befall them ; And that the Witch can commiſſionate him to the performance of theſe, with many others as dangerous Doctrines, and ſuch as ſeem in their tendency to look favourably upon the Antient *Pagan* Doctrine of this countrey, who did believe that God did hurt to none, but Good to all, but that the Devil muſt be pleaſ'd by Worſhipping, *&c.* From whom came all their Miſeries, as they believed. For what were all this but to Rob God of his Glory in the higheſt manner, and giving it to a Devil

and a Witch ; Is it not he that has faid fhall there
be Evil in a City and the Lord hath not done it ?
But if any are fond of their own notions becaufe
fome Eminent Men have before now afferted
them ; they may do well to compare them with
that excellent faying, *Wonders of the Invifible
World*, pag. 7. [*About this Devil there are many
things, whereof we may reafonably and profitably
be inquifitive, fuch things I mean as are in our Bi-
bles reveal'd to us ; according to which if we do not
fpeak on fo dark a Subject, but according to our
own uncertain and perhaps Humourfom Conjectures,
there is no Light in us.* Or that other, pag. 75.
*At every other Weapon the Devil will be too hard
for us.*] For 'tis moft certain that other Notions,
Weapons and Practices have been taken up with ;
And that the event has been anfwerable, the
Devil has been too hard for fuch as have fo done.
I fhall forbear to inftance from the Dogmatical
part, and fhall mention fome practices that as
much need explaining. *Mem. provid. Relat. to
Witch. pag.* 29, 30, 31.[52] Where account is given
that it was Pray'd for that the afflicted might be
able to declare, whom fhe apprehended herfelf
Afflicted by, together with the Immediate anfwer
of fuch Prayer. To this you once Reply'd when
it was mentioned to you, that you did not then
underftand the wiles of *Satan.*

---

[52] This Work, here often refer- *Providences relating to Witchcraft
red to, was printed in 1689. Its and Poffeffions,* in a 16mo. But
more extended Title is, *Memorable* few Copies are known to exift.

P

To which I have nothing to object, but it
might be a good Acknowledgment; But con-
fidering that the Book is gone forth into all the
World, cannot but think the Salve ought to be
proportion'd to the Sore, and the notice of the
Devils wiles as Univerſal, as the means recom-
mending them.　Another Practice is *pag.* 20, 21.
[*There was one fingular paſſion that frequently attended her, an Inviſible Chain would be clapt about
her, and ſhe in much pain and fear cry out when
they began to put it on, once I did with my own hand
knock it off as it began to be faſtened about her.*] [30]
If this were done by the power or Vertue of any
ord'nance of Divine Inſtitution, it is well, but
would have been much better if the Inſtitution
had been demonſtrated, or was there any Phyſical
Vertue in that particular Hand.　But ſuppoſing
that neither of theſe will be aſſerted by the Author, I do think it very requiſite, that the World
may be acquainted with the Operation, and to
what Art or Craft to refer their Power of Knock-
ing off *Inviſible Chains.*

And thus, Sir, I have Faithfully diſcharged
(what in this I took to be my Duty) and am ſo
far from doing it to gain applauſe, or from a
Spirit of Contradiction, that I expect to procure
me many Enemies thereby, (but as in caſe of a
Fire) where the Glory of God, and the Good
and Wellfare of Mankind are ſo nearly concern'd,
I thought it my duty to be no longer an Idle
Spectator; And can, and do ſay, to the Glory of

God, in this whole Affair, I have endeavoured a
Confcience voide of offence, both towards God
and towards Man; And therein at the leaft have
the advantage of fuch as are very Jealous they
have done fo much herein, as to Sin in what they
have done, *viz.* In fheltring the Accufed, fuch
have been the Cowardice and Fearfulnefs, whereunto the regard to the Diffatisfaction of other
People have precipitated them; Which by the
way muft needs acquaint all, that for the future
other meafures are refolved upon (by fuch) which
how Bloody they may prove when opportunity
fhall offer, is with him who orders all things,
according to the counfel of his own Will: And
now that the Song of Angels may be the Emula-
tion of Men, is the earneft Defire, and Prayer, of
Sir, Yours to Command in what I may,

R. C.

*Glory to God in the Higheft, and on Earth
Peace and good Will towards Men.*

Bofton, March the 1ft. 1694.

Mr. B.[53] *Worthy Sir,*

AFTER more than a Years waiting for the
performance of a reiterated promife from
one under fingular obligations, and a multitude

---

[53] I fuppofe Mr. Thomas Brattle, the then Treafurer of Harvard College. He was a principal Founder of the Church in Brattle Square, known by his Name. He wrote an Account of the Witchcraft of 1692, which laid in Manufcript about one hundred Years, when Dr. Belknap caufed it to be printed in Part, in the *Colls. Ms. H. So-*

of advantages to have done it fooner, The utmoft
compliance I have mett with, is (by your Hands)
the fight of four Sheets of recinded Papers, but I
muft firft be obliged to return them in a Fortnight, and not Copied, which I have now com-
plied with : And having read them am not at all
Surprized at the Authors Caution in it, not to
admit of fuch crude matter and impertinent abfurdities, as are to be found in it to fpread. He
feems concern'd that I take no notice of his
feveral Books, wherein, as he faith, he has unan-
fwerably proved things to which I might reply,
that I have fent him letters of quotations out of
thofe Books, to know how much of them he will
abide by, for I thought it hard to affix their [31]
Natural confequences till he had opportunity to
explain them.   And faith that he had fent me
(Mr. Baxters *World of Spirits*) an ungainfayable
Book, *&c.* (tho I know no ungainfayable Book,
but the Bible) which Book I think no Man that
has read it, will give fuch a Title to but the Author, he fpeaks of my reproaching his publick
Sermons, of which I am not confcious to myfelf,
unlefs it be about his interpretation of a *Thunder
Storm* (that broke into his Houfe) which favoured
fo much of Enthufiafm.[54]

ciety, v, 61-80. Mr. Brattle was a
Scholar, a Graduate of Harvard
College, and, like Mr. Calef, a
Merchant of Bofton.   His Com-
munications to the Royal Society of
London procured him the Title of
F. R. S.

It is poffible that the Initial (Mr.
B—) may ftand for Gov. Brad-
ftreet; but I prefume Mr. Brattle is
meant.

[54] It muft have been difficult for
a common-fenfe Man, as Mr. Calef
was, to hear fuch Matters treated

As to thofe papers, I have (as I read them) noted in the Margin where, in a hafty reading, I thought it needful, of which it were unreafonable for him to complain; feeing I might not take a Copy, thereby to have been inabled, more at leafure to digeft what were needfull to be faid on fo many Heads; and as I have not flatter'd him, fo for telling what was fo needful, with the hazard of making fo many Enemies by it, I have approved myfelf one of his beft Friends: And befides his own fenfe of the weaknefs of his Anfwer, teftified by the prohibition above, he has wholly declined anfwering to moft of thofe things that I had his promife for, and what he pretends to fpeak to, after mentioning, without the needful Anfwer or Proof drops it.

His firft main Work is after his definition of a Witch, which he never proves (without faying any thing to Mr. *Gauls* Scriptural defcription, tho' fo often urged to it, and tho' himfelf has in his Book recommended and quoted it) is to magnifie the Devils Power, and that as I think beyond

---

ferioufly in the Pulpit, and keep his Rifibility under complete Controll. If Thunder and Lightning were the Work of the Devil, as it feems Mr. Mather believed, it is not very ftrange that he fhould difcover fome very odd Pranks in their Operations. The Father (Dr. I. Mather) relates, among his *Philofophical Meditations*, that as "a Man was walking, in Auguft, 1682, in the Field, near Darking in England, he was ftruck with a Clap of Thunder; on being taken up, his dead Body was found exceeding hot, and withall fmelling ftrong of Sulphur, infomuch that they were forced to drop him, and let him ly a confiderable Time ere he could be removed. It is reported that fometimes Thunder and Lightning has been generated out of the fulphurous and bituminous Matter which the firey Mountain Ætna hath caft forth."

and againſt the Scripture, this takes him up about
11 *Pages,* and yet in *Page* 22 again returns to it,
and as *I* underſtand it, takes part with the *Phariſees* againſt our Saviour in the Argument, for
they charge him that he caſt out Devils thro'
Beelzebub, Our Saviours Anſwer is, *Mat.* xii. 25.
*Every Kingdom divided againſt itſelf is brought to
deſolation; and every City or Houſe divided againſt
itſelf, ſhall not ſtand, and if Satan caſt out Satan,
he is divided againſt himſelf, how ſhall then his Kingdom ſtand:* And yet notwithſtanding this Anſwer
together with what follows, for further Illuſtra-
tion, our Author is it ſeems reſolved to aſſert that
our Saviour did not in this Anſwer deny that
many did ſo, (*viz.*) caſt out Devils by *Beelzebub,*
and *Page* 23 grants that the Devils have a Miraculous Power, but yet muſt not be call'd miracles,
and yet can be diſtinguiſhed, as he intimates, only
by the Conſcience or Light within, to the no
ſmall ſcandal of the Chriſtian Religion.

Tho' our Saviour and his Apoſtles accounts this
the chief or principal proof of his Godhead,
John xx. 30, 31. *John* x. 37, 38. *John* v. 30.
Mark xvi. 17, 18. *Acts* ii. 22. and iv. 30. with
many others and that Miracles belong only to
God, who alſo Governs the World, *Pſal.* cxxxvi.
4. *Jer.* xiv. 22. *Iſa.* xxxviii. 8. *Pſal.* lxii. 11.
Lam. iii. 37. *Amos* iii. 6. [32] But to forbear
quoting that which the Scripture is moſt full in,
do only ſay that he that dares aſſert the Devil to
have ſuch a Miraculous Power had need have

other Scriptures than ever I have feen. In *Page*
12. our Author proceeds and ftates a queftion to
this effect, If the Devil has fuch Powers, and cant
exert them without permiffion from God, what
can the Witch contribute thereunto? Inftead of
an Anfwer, to this weighty objection, our Author
firft concedes that the Devil's do ordinarily exert
their Powers, without the Witches contributing
to it, but yet that to the end to increafe their
guilt he may cheat a Witch, by making her believe herfelf the Author of them.[55] His next
is, if Witchcraft be, as I fuppofe it is, the fkill of
applying the Plaftic Spirit of the World, *&c.* then
the confent of the Witch doth naturally contribute to that mifchiefs that the Devil does. And
his laft anfwer runs to this effect, Is it not the
Ordination of God, that where the Devil can get
the confent of a Witch for the hurting of others,
the hurt fhall as certainly be as if they had fet
Maftiff Dogs upon them, or had given them
Poyfon into their Bowels; and Gods Providence
muft be as great in delivering from one as from
the other, and this it feems is not only his Belief,
but the moft Orthodox and moft learned anfwer
that our Author could pitch upon. If Witchcraft be as I fuppofe it is, *&c.* and is it not the

[55] There feems always to have been great Confufion, and no lefs Perplexity, among Believers in Witchcraft refpecting the Parts to be affigned to the Devil and the Witch refpectively. Sometimes they af- fure us that the Devil commiffions the Witch, and fometimes that the Witch governs the Devil. Hence, even Believers are very much puz- zled to know *what to believe.* See Vol. I, *Introd.*, Pages xviii, xix.

Ordination of God, that, *&c.* What is all this but precarious, and begging the queſtion, and a plain dropping the Argument he cannot manage; however, to amuſe the Ignorant, and to confound the Learned, he hooks in a cramp word, if not a nonentity, (*viz.*) *Plaſtic* Spirit of the World, for who is it either knows that there is a *Plaſtic Spirit*, or what it is, or how this can any way ſerve his purpoſe.[56]

He then proceeds to *Scripture* Inſtances of Witches, *&c.* and where I thought it needful, I have, as I ſaid, ſhewed my diſſent from his Judgment: He accounts it unreaſonable to be held to the proof of his definition of a Witch, which he makes to conſiſt in a Covenant with the Devil, and chuſes rather a tedious proceſs about a Piſtol to defend him from it, which indeed is one particular way whereby Murder has been Committed, and ſo the Dore becomes Culpable; But his definition of a *Witch*, which as I ſaid, ſtill remains to be proved, is to this effect, That a *Witch* is one that Covenants with, and Commiſſions *Devils* to

---

[56] It would no doubt puzzle the Devil himſelf to explain that Term, *Plaſtic Spirit*. It appears to have been made uſe of for the ſame Reaſon that a certain Fiſh diſcolors the Water when purſued by an Enemy.

The following Ideas reſpecting the Devil then entertained may not be out of Place in this Connection: " The Devil is the oldeſt Sinner, and the moſt curſed Creature in all the World. It is ſaid, Iſa. 65, 20. *That the Sinner of an hundred Years ſhall be accurſed.* But then what ſhall the Sinner be that is more than 5000 Years old? The Devil and all the Angels that ſinned with him, are Sinners of above 5000 Years old, and will therefore become the moſt accurſed and damned Creatures in the whole Univerſe at the Great Day."—Dr. I. Mather, *Angelographia,* 120.

do mifchiefs, that fhe is one in Covenant, or that by Vertue of fuch Covenant fhe can Commiffion-ate him to Kill. The not bringing Scripture to prove thefe two, is a fufficient demonftration there is none; and fo that our Author leaves off juft where he began, *viz.* in a bare Affertion, together with his own Biggoted experiences, hinting alfo at multitudes of Hiftories to confirm him in the belief of his definition. Here being all that I take notice of to be confiderable.

[33] And now, Sir, if you think fit to improve your Friendfhip with the Author for the Glory of God, the Sovereign Being, the good and wel-fare of *Mankind*, and for his real and true Intereft, as you fee it convenient, put him in mind, That the Glory of God is the end why *Mankind* was made, and why *He* hath fo many Advantages to it. That the Flames we have feen threatning the utter extirpation of the Country, muft own their Original to thefe dangerous Errors (if not herefies) which if they remain Unextinguifhed, may and moft likely will be acted over again.

That 'tis more Honour to own an Error in time, than tenacioufly after full Conviction to re-tain it. But if our Author will again Vindicate fuch matters, pleafe to acquaint him, that I fhall not any more receive his Papers, if I may not Copy and ufe them; and that when he does, inftead of fuch abftrufe matters, I ftill pray his determination in thofe things I have his promife for. And thus begging Pardon for thus long detaining of you, I am, Sir, your to Command,

. R. C.

Bofton, March 18, 1694.

To the Minifters, whether Englifh, French, or Dutch,

I Having had not only occafion, but renewed provocation to take a view of the Myfterious Doctrines, which have of late been fo much contefted among us, could not meet with any that had fpoken more, or more plainly the fenfe of thofe Doctrines (relating to the *Witchcraft*) than the Reverend Mr. *C. M.* but how clearly and confiftent, either with himfelf or the truth, I medle not now to fay, but cannot but fuppofe his ftrenuous and Zealous afferting his opinions, has been one caufe of the difmal Convulfions we have here lately fallen into; Suppofing that his Books of *Memorable Providences,* relating to Witchcraft, as alfo his *Wonders of the Invifible World,* did contain in them things not warrantable, and very dangerous, I fent to him a Letter of Quotations out of thofe Books, *&c.*

That fo, if it might have been, I might underftand what tollerable Senfe he would put upon his own words, which I took to be a better way of Proceeding, than to have affixed what I thought to be their natural confequences, and left I might be Judged a Sceptic I gave him a full and free account of my belief relating to thoſe Doctrines, together with the grounds thereof; And prayed him that if I err'd I might be ſhewed it by Scripture, and this I had his reiterated promiſe for. But after more than a Years waiting for the performance thereof, all that is done in compliance therewith, is that in *Feb.* laſt, he ſent me four ſheets of his writing as his belief, but before I might receive it I muſt engage to deliver it back in a Fortnight and not Copy'd.[57] A Summary account [34] of which I ſhall give you, when I have firſt acquainted you what the Doctrines were which I ſent to him for his concurrence with, or confutation of, and to which I had his promiſe, as above.

Theſe by way of Queſtion, (*Viz.*) whether that fourth Head cited and recommended by himſelf (In *Wonders of the Inviſible World,* of Mr. *Gauls*) ought to be believed as a truth, which runs thus; Among the moſt unhappy circumſtances to Convict a Witch, one is a Maligning and Oppugning the Word, Work, and Worſhip of God, and ſeeking by any Extraordinary ſign to ſeduce any from it, *Deut.* xiii. 1, 2. *Mat.* xxiv. 24. *Acts* xiii. 8, 10. 2 *Tim.* iii. 8. do but mark well the

---

[57] In Anſwer to this, the Dr. ſays: "The Reaſon that made me unwilling to truſt any of my Writings in the Hands of this Man, was becauſe I ſaw the *Weaver* (though he preſumes to call himſelf a *Merchant*) was a Stranger to all the Rules of Civility." This is the Kind of Anſwer which every impartial Reader will decide, redounds entirely to the Credit of Mr. Calef, and that *Civility* is alſo altogether on his Side. Yet, in an Air of Triumph the Doc·tor adds: "The *Antiſcriptural Doctrines* eſpouſed by this Man do alſo call for no further Anſwer."

places, and for this very property of thus oppugning and perverting, they are all there concluded arrant and abſolute Witches.

And if in Witchcraft the Devil by means of a
Witch does the Miſchief, how 'tis poſſible to
diſtinguiſh it from Poſſeſſion, both being ſaid to
be performed by the Devil, and yet without an
Infallible diſtinction there can be no certainty in
Judgment. And whether it can be proved that
the *Jewiſh* Church in any Age before, or in our
Saviours time, even in the time of their greateſt
Apoſtacy did believe that a Witch had power to
Commiſſionate Devils to do Miſchief.

So much to the Queſtions. Theſe were ſent
as my belief: That the devils bounds are ſett,
that he cant paſs; That the devils are ſo full of
Malice, that it cant be added to by Mankind;
That where he hath power he neither can nor
will omit executing it; That 'tis only the Almighty that ſets bounds to his rage, and that only
can Commiſſionate him to hurt or deſtroy. And
now I ſhall give you the Summary account of his
four ſheets above mentioned, as near as memory
could recollect, in Ten Particulars.

I. That the Devils have in their Natures a
power to work Wonders and Miracles; particularly that the *Phariſees* were not miſtaken in
aſſerting that the Devils might be caſt out by
Beelzebub; and that our Saviours Anſwer does not
oppoſe that aſſertion; and that he hath the Power
of Death, that he can make the moſt Solid things

Inviſible; and can Inviſibly bring poyſon and force it down Peoples Throats.[58]

2. That to aſſert this Natural, wonderful Power of the Devil, makes moſt for the Glory of God, in preſerving Man from its effects,

3. Yet this Power is reſtrained by the Almighty, as pleaſeth him.

4. That a Witch is one that makes a Covenant with the Devil.

5. That by vertue of ſuch a Covenant, ſhe arrives at a Power to Commiſſionate him.

6. That God has ordain'd, that when the Devil is call'd upon by the Witch, tho' he were before reſtrained by the Almighty, the deſired miſchiefs

---

[58] In this Connection it may be intereſting to have the Views of Dr. Increaſe Mather reſpecting the Attributes of the Devil.

" There were many of them [the Devils Angels] that were concerned in that firſt Tranſgreſſion and Rebellion againſt the Lord. It is ſaid, Epheſ. 2. 3. That the Devil is *the Prince of the Power of the Air.* So that there is a *Power,* an *Hoſt,* a vaſt *Army* of thoſe Evil Spirits, that did joyn with the Devil, in ſetting themſelves againſt the Great God. How many, is not for us to ſay, the Written Word of God not ſpeaking anything as to the Quantity of their Number; only it is manifeſt from the Scripture, that there are far more Angels that have ſinned, far more Devils than there are Men in all the World. There is not a Man in the whole World but there are Devils to tempt him continually. And if ſo, they muſt needs be more in Number than Men are. We read in the Goſpel of no leſs than a Legion of Devils in one poor miſerable Man. Luk. 8, 30. You read there of a poſſeſed Man, and Chriſt demanded of the Evil Spirit what his Name was: The chief Devil among them made Anſwer, *It is Legion for we are many.* A Legion is ſix Thouſand ſix Hundred and Sixty-ſix. Now then, if the Devil has ſuch vaſt Numbers of Infernal Spirits under him; if he has ſuch Troops of them, as that he can ſpare no leſs than a Legion to afflict, and as it were to keep Garriſon in one poor miſerable Man: what prodigious Numbers of Evil Angels muſt there needs be."—*Angelographia,* 111-112. See alſo *The Devil Diſcovered*, Vol. I, 217-247.

ordinarily ſhall as certainly be performed, as if the Witch had [35] lodged poyſon in the Bowels of her Neighbour, or had ſet Maſtiff Dogs on them.

7. That the Witche's Art of applying the *Plaſtic Spirit of the World* to unlawful purpoſes, does Naturally contribute to the miſchiefs done by the Devil.

8. That that God which reſtrain'd an *Abime-lich* and a *Laban* from hurting, does alſo reſtrain the Witch from Calling upon or Improving the Devil, when he will not have his Power ſo exerted.

9. That to have a Familiar Spirit, is to be able to cauſe a Devil to take bodily ſhapes, whereby either to give reſponſes, or to receive orders for doing miſchief.

10. That this is the Judgment of moſt of the Divines in the Countrey, whether *Engliſh, Dutch* or *French.*[59]

[59] Dr. Mather's Animadverſions on theſe *" Ten Articles"* ſhould be read in Connexion: *"* When he ſent about unto all the Miniſters a *Libellous Letter* againſt myſelf, falſely charging me with writing in a Manuſcript of mine *Ten Articles* (which are of his own drawing up) whereof the chief are of his *own pure Invention,* there was not one of all thoſe reverend Perſons, who thought him worthy of an Anſwer. And now his Book is come abroad, I cannot hear (and many obſerve the Like) of ſo much as one ver- tuous and ſenſible Man, but let their Opinions about the *Salem* Troubles be what they will, they deteſt it, as, a *Vile Book;* as being an intire Libel upon the whole *Government* and *Miniſtry* in the Land; yea, they think it beneath a Miniſter of the Goſpel to beſtow the Pains of an *Anſwer* upon it. The Book ſerves but as an Engine to diſcover (by their approbation of it) a few Perſons in the Land that will diſtinguiſh themſelves by an exalted *Malignity."* *Some Few Remarks on a Scandalous Book,* 34·5.

This as I ſaid, I took to be moſt material in the four ſheets ſent to me as his belief, and is alſo all the performance he has yet made of his ſeveral promiſes; which ten Articles being done only by memory, left thro' miſtake or want of the Original, I might have committed any errors, I ſent them to him that, if there were any, they might be rectified :   But inſtead of ſuch an Anſwer, as might be expected from a Miniſter and a learn'd Gentleman, one Mr. *W*— ſhewed me a Letter writ by Mr. *C. M*— to himſelf, which I might read, but neither borrow nor Copy, and ſo, if I were minded, could give but a ſhort account of it.

And paſſing over his hard Language, which, as I am conſcious to myſelf; I never deſerv'd, (relating to my writing in the margin of the four ſheets; and to theſe ten Articles) ſo I hope I underſtand my Duty, better than to imitate him in retorting the like.   Among his many words in his ſaid Letters, I meet with two ſmall Objections; one is againſt the word (*Miracle*) in the firſt Article, the word, I ſay, not the matter, for the works he attributes to the Devil are the ſame in their being above or againſt the Courſe of Nature and all Natural cauſes, yet he will not admit of theſe to be call'd Miracles.   And hence he reckon's it the greateſt difficulty he meets with in this whole affair, to diſtinguiſh the works of the Devil from Miracles.   And hence alſo he concedes to the Devil the Power to make the

moft Solid things Invifible, and Invifibly to bring
Poyfon and force it down Peoples Throats, &c.
Which I look upon to be as true Miracles as
that. 2 *Kings* vi. 18. and this is the fenfe I
underftand the word in, and in this fenfe, he
himfelf in the four fheets admits it; for he has
an objeƈtion to this effeƈt, *Viz.* [If the Devils
have fuch power, &c. then miracles are not
ceaf'd; and where are we then? (his Anfwer is)
Where! even juft where we were before, fay I]
fo that it feems the only offence here is at my
ufing his words.   His fecond objeƈtion (for
weight) is againft the whole ninth Article, and
wonders [36] how 'tis poffible for one Man fo
much to mifunderftand another; Yet as I remember, he fpeaking of the Witch of *Endor* in
the faid four fheets fays, fhe had a familiar Spirit,
and that [a Spirit belonging to the Invifible
World, upon her calling appear'd to *Saul*] &c.
and if fo 'tis certain he gave refponfes, he alfo
tells of *Balaam,* that it was known that he could
fet Devils on People to deftroy them, and therefore how this objeƈtion fhould bear any Force I
fee not; The reft of the objeƈtions are of fo
fmall weight that once reading may be fufficient
to clear them up, and if this be not fo, he can,
when he pleafes, by making it Publick together
with the Margins I writ, Convince all People of
the truth of what he afferts; But here 'tis to be
noted, that the 2*d.* 3*rd.* 4*th.* and 5*th* Articles he
concedes to, as having nothing to objeƈt againft

them, but that they are his belief; and that the
6*th*. and 7*th*. he puts for Anfwer to an objection
which he thus frames, *Viz.* If the Devil have
fuch powers but cannot exert them but by permiffion from God, what can the Witch contribute thereto.   And thus I have faithfully
performed what I undertook, and do folemnly
declare, I have not intentionally in the leaft
wronged the Gentleman concern'd, nor defign'd
the leaft blemifh to his Reputation; but if it
ftands in competition with the Glory of God,
the only Almighty Being, his truths and his
Peoples welfare, I fuppofe thefe too valuable to
be trampled on for his fake, tho' in other things
I am ready to my power (tho' with denying fome
part of my own intereft) to ferve him.   Had
this Gentleman declin'd or detracted his four
fheets, I fee not but he might have done it, and
which I think there was caufe enough for him
to have done, but to own the four fheets, and at
the fame time to difown the Doctrine contain'd
in them, and this knowing that I have no Copy,
renders the whole of the worfe afpect.

And now I fhall give you a further account of
my Belief, when I have firft premifed, that 'tis a
prevailing Belief in this Countrey, and elfewhere,
that the Scriptures are not full in the Defcription
of, and in the way and means how to detect a
Witch, tho' pofitive in their Punifhment to be
by Death; and that hence they have thought
themfelves under a neceffity of taking up with

R

the Sentiments of fuch Men or Places that are
thought worthy to give rules to detect them by :
And have accordingly practifed, *viz.* In fearching
for Tets for the Devil to fuck ; Trying whether
the fufpected can fay the Lords Prayer ; And
whether the Afflicted falls at the fight, and rifes
at the touch of the fuppofed Witch ; As alfo by
the Afflicted or Poffeffed giving account who is
the Witch.

Touching thefe my belief is, that 'tis highly
Derogatory to the wifdom of the Wife Lawgiver,
to afcert, That he has given a Law by *Mofes,* the
Penalty whereof is Death ; and yet no direction to
his People, whereby to know and detect the culpable, till our *Triumvirate* Mr. [37] *Perkins, Gaul*
and *Bernard,* had given us their receits, and that
that fourth Head of Mr. *Gauls,* being fo well
prov'd by Scripture is a truth, and contains a full
and clear Teftimony, who are Witches culpable
of Death, and that plainly and from Scripture,
yet not excluding any other branch, when as
well proved by that infallible rule. And that
the going to the Afflicted or Poffeffed, to have
them Divine who are Witches by their Specteral
fight, is a great wickednefs, even the Sin of *Saul*
(for which he alfo Died) but with this difference,
the one did it for Augury, or to know future
Events, the other in order to take away Life ;
and that the fearching for Tets, the experiment
of their faying the Lords Prayer ; the falling at
the fight and rifing at the touch of the fuppofed

Criminal, being all of them foreign from Scripture, as well as reafon, are abominations to be
abhor'd and repented of. And that our *Salem*
Witchcraft, either refpecting the Judges and Juries, their tendernefs of Life, or the Multitude
and pertinency of witneffes, both Afflicted and
Confeffors, or the Integrity of the Hiftorians,
are as Authentic, and made as certain as any ever
of that kind in the World; and yet who is it
that now fees not through it, and that thefe were
the Sentiments that have procured the foreft
Afflicttion, and moft lafting infamy that ever
befel this Country, and moft like fo to do again,
if the fame notions be ftill entertain'd and finally
that thefe are thofe laft times, of which the Spirit
fpeaks expreffly, *Tim.* iv. 1. *And now ye that*
are Fathers in the Churches, Guides to the People,
and the Salt of the Earth.

I befeech you confider thefe things ; and if you
find the Glory of God diminifht by afcribing
fuch power to Witches and Devils; His truths
oppof'd by thefe notions ; and his People afperfed
in their Doctrines and Reputations, and indan-
gered in their Lives; I dare not dictate to you,
you know your duty as Watchmen, and the Lord
be with you.

But if you find my belief contrary to found
Doctrine, I intreat you to fhew it me by the
Scripture ; And in the mean time blame me not
if I cannot believe that there are feveral Al-
mighties ; for to do all forts of wonders, beyond

and above the Courfe of Nature, is certainly the
work of *Omnipotency*. So alfo, he that fhall
Commiffionate or Impower to thefe, muft alfo
be Almighty; and I think it not a fufficient
falvo, to fay they may be reftrain'd by the moft
High; and hope you will not put any hard Conftruction on thefe my Endeavours to get information (all other ways failing) in things fo needful
to be known; praying the Almightys Guidance
and protection, I am

   Yours to the utmoft of my Power,

        R. C.

   [38] Bofton, *Sept. the* 20*th*, 1695.
Mr. *Samuel Willard.*

 Reverend Sir,

MY former of *March* the 18th. directed to
the Minifters (and which was lodg'd with
yourfelf) containing feveral Articles, which I
fent as my belief, praying them if I erred to
fhew it me by Scripture, I have as yet had no
Anfwer to, either by word or writing, which
makes me gather that they are approved of as
Orthodox, or at leaft that they have fuch Foundations, as that none are willing to manifeft any
oppofition to them : And therefore with fubmif-
fion, *&c.* I think that that late feafonable and
well-defign'd Dialogue intituled, *Some mifcella-
ny Obfervations*,[60] *&c.* of which yourfelf is the

  60 The Suppofition was correct. referred to, printed in Philadelphia in
There was an Edition of the Work 1692, in a fmall Quarto of 16 Pages.

fuppof'd Author (and which was fo ferviceable in
the time of it) is yet liable to a male conftruction,
even to the endangering to revive what it moft
oppofes, and to bring thofe practices again on
Foot, which in the day thereof were fo terrible
to this whole Countrey: The words which I
fuppofe fo liable to Mifconftruction, are *pag.* 14.
B. *Who informed them?* S. *the Spectre.* B. *very
good, and that's the Devil turned Informer. How
are good Men like to fare againft whom he hath
particular Malice!*

*It is but a Prefumption, and Wife Men will weigh
Prefumptions againft Prefumptions. There is to be
no Examination without grounds of Sufpicion. Some
Perfons Credit ought to be accounted too good to be
undermined fo far as to be fufpected on fo flight a
ground: and it is an Injury done them to bring
them upon Examination, which renders them openly
Sufpected. I will not deny but for Perfons already
fufpected and of Ill fame, it may occafion their*

Upon this Letter and the Work of
Mr. Willard Dr. Mather remarks,
evidently under great Excitement
und Indignation as refpects the Former: "I remember that when this
miferable Man fent unto an eminent
Minifter in the Town, a *Libellous
Letter*, reflecting both on a Judicious Difcourfe written by *him*, and
on the Holy Propofals made by the
Præfident and Fellows of *Harvard-
College*, about *recording of Remarkable Providences*, and when he demanded and expected an Anfwer
to his Follies, that Reverend Perfon
only faid *Go tell him That the Anfwer to him and his Letter is in the
Twenty Sixth of the* Proverbs, *and
the Fourth.*"

Mr. Willard's Silence was undoubtedly owing to a very different
Caufe than that given by Dr. Mather. It is fairly inferable that Mr.
Willard was too good a Logician
not to fee that Mr. Calef's Argument did not admit of Refutation,
and that his own Reputation would
be beft conferved by Silence.

being examin'd. In which thefe words ('tis but a prefumption, *&c.*) (and fome Perfons credit, *&c.*) (and I will not deny but for Perfons already fuf-pected, *&c.*) this I take to be waving to difcufs thofe points, the fpeaking to which might at that time have hindered the ufefulnefs and fuccefs of that Book, rather than any declaring the Senti-ments of the Author. But notwithftanding many Perfons will be ready to underftand this, as if the Author did wholly leave it with the Juftice, to Judge who are Ill Perfons, fuch as the Devils Accufations may faften upon ; And that the Devils Accufation of a Perfon, is a Prefumption againft them of their guilt ; and that upon fuch prefump-tions, they may be had to Examination, if the Juftice counts them Perfons of ill fame (for the Author I fuppofe knows that the bear Examina-tion will leave fuch a ftain upon them, and well if their Pofterity efcape it !) as the length of a Holy and unblameable Life will be found too fhort to Extirpate. And if the Juftice may go thus far with the Devils Evidence, then the addi-tion of a ftory or two of fome Cart overfet, or perfon taken Sick after a quarrel, might as well be thought fufficient for their Commitment, in order to [39] their Tryal as 'tis call'd (tho' this too often has been more like a Stage Play, or a *Tragicomical Scene*) and fo that other ways ufeful Book, may prove the greateft Snare to revive the fame practices again.

  Thefe things being fo liable, as I faid, to fuch

male-conſtruction, it were needful that Men
might be undeceiv'd, and the matter more fully
demonſtrated, (*Viz.*) That the Devils Accuſation
is not ſo much as any preſumption againſt the
Life or Reputation of any perſon, for how are
good Men like to fare, if his malicious accuſations may be taken as a preſumption of their
Guilt; and that his accuſations as they are no
preſumption againſt perſons of unſpotted Fame,
ſo neither are to be heard, or any ways regarded
againſt perſons tho' otherways of ill Life, much
leſs for their having long ſince had their Names
abuſed by his outcries, or by the Malice of Ill
Neighbours; and that Juſtice knows no difference
of Perſons; that if this Evidence be ſufficient to
bring one perſon 'tis ſo to bring any other to
Examination, and conſequently to the utmoſt
extent of odium, which ſuch Examination will
certainly expoſe them to, for who can know any
other, but that as the one may be Maliciouſly
accuſed by Devils and a Deviliſh report gone before it; ſo that another who has not been ſo
much as accuſed before, being more Cunning or
more ſeeming Religious, might yet be more
guilty; the whole depending upon Inviſible Evidence, of which Inviſible ſtuff, tho' we have had
more than ſufficient, yet I find (among other
Reverend Perſons) your Names to a certain Printed
Paper, which runs thus.

Certain Propofals⁶¹ *made by the Prefident and Fellows of* Harvard *College, to the Reverend Minifters of the Gofpel, in the feveral Churches of* New-England.

Firft. *To obferve and record the more Illuftrious Difcoveries of the Divine Providence in the Government of the World, is a defign fo holy, fo ufeful, fo juftly approved, that the too general neglect of it in the Churches of God, is as juftly to be Lamented.*

    2. *For the redrefs of that neglect, altho' all Chriftians have a Duty incumbent on them, yet it is in a peculiar manner to be recommended unto the Minifters of the* Gofpel, *to improve the fpecial advantages which are in their Hands, to obtain and preferve the knowledge of fuch notable occurrences as are fought out by all that have pleafure in the great Works of the Lord.*

    3. *The things to be efteemed Memorable, are fpecially all unufual accidents in the Heaven, or Earth,*

---

61 Concerning this curious Paper, Quincy, in *Hift. Harvard College*, remarks: "As the Belief in the Agency of the Invifible World began to leffen, and fome of thofe, who were the chief Actors in the Tragedy, to feel the Weight of public Indignation preffing upon them, they being Members of the Corporation, brought this Body into the Field for the Purpofe of giving Countenance to that Belief, and of fuftaining this decaying Faith." This was "prepared by both the Mathers, and figned by the whole Board, and circulated throughout New England."—Vol. I, *Page* 62. The Signers will all be found duly noticed in Dr. Allen's *Biographical Dictionary.*

*or Water, All wonderful Deliverances of the Dif-
treffed, Mercies to the Godly, Judgments on the
Wicked, and more Glorious fulfilments of either the
Promifes or Threatnings in the Scriptures of Truth,
with Apparitions, Poffeffions, Enchantments, and all
extraordinary things, wherein the Exiftence and
Agency of the Invifible World is more fenfibly demonftrated.*

[40] 4. *It is therefore Propofed, That the Minifters throughout this Land, would manifeft their
regards unto the Works of the Lord, and the Oppe-
ration of his hands, by reviving their cares to take
Written Accounts of fuch* Remarkables: *But ftill
well Attefted with credibled and fufficient Witnefs.*

5. *It is defired that the Accounts, thus taken of
thefe Remarkables, may he fent in unto the* Prefident,[62]
or the Fellows *of the Colledge, by whome they fhall be
carefully referved for fuch a ufe to be made of them,
as may by fome fit Affembly of Minifters be Judged
moft conducing to the Glory of God, and the Service
of his People.*

6. *Tho' we doubt not, that love to the Name of
God will be motive enough unto all good Men, to
Contribute what Affiftance they can unto this Under-
taking; yet for further Incouragement, fome fingu-
lar Marks of Refpects fhall be ftudied for fuch good
Men, as will actually affift it, by taking pains to*

[62] It will be remembered that the Prefident (Mather) had publifhed a Volume of *Remarkable Provi-* dences, which, doubtlefs, met with a ready Sale, and induced a Defire for another.

S

Communicate any Important Paſſages proper to be inſerted in this Collection.

Increaſe Mather, Preſident.

James Allen,
Char. Morton,
Sam. Willard,
Cotton Mather,   } Fellows.
John Leverett,
Will. Brattle,
Neh. Walter,

Cambr. March 5, 169¾

Here being an Encouragement to all good Men, to ſend in ſuch remarkables as are therein expreſſed, I have ſent the following, not that I think them a more ſenſible demonſtration of the being of a future State (with Rewards and Puniſhments) or of Angels good and bad, &c. than the Scriptures of truth hold forth, &c. Or than any of thoſe other demonſtrations God hath given us; for this were Treacherouſly and Perfidiouſly to quit the Poſt to the Enemy, the *Sadducee, Deiſt,* and *Atheiſt* would hereby be put in a condition ſo Triumphantly to deny the Exiſtence and Agency thereof. As that a few Stories told (which at beſt muſt be owned to be fallible and liable to miſrepreſentations) could not be thought Infallibly ſufficient to demonſtrate the truth againſt them. I have heard that in Logick a falſe Argument is reckon'd much worſe than none : Yet ſuppoſing that a Collection of In-

ftances may be many ways ufeful, not only to the
prefent but fucceeding Ages, I have fent you the
following remarkables, which have lately occurred,
the certainty of which, if any fcruple it, will be
found no hard matter to get fatisfaction therein :
But here, not to infift on thofe lefs occurrents, as
the fudden Death of one of our late Juftices,[63]
and a like Mortallity that fell upon the two Sons
of another of them, with the Fall of a Man that
was making provifion to raife the New Northern
Bell, which, when it was up, the firft perfon,
whofe death it was to fignifie, was faid to be a
Child of him, who by Printing and fpeaking,
had had as great hand in procur[41]ing the late
Actions as any, if not the greateft ; and the Split-
ting the Gun at *Salem,* where that furious Mar-
·fhal, and his Father, *&c.* was rent to pieces,[64] *&c.*
As to all thefe it muft be owned, that no man
knows love or hatred by all that is before him,
much lefs can they be more fenfible demonftrations of the Exiftence or Agency of the *Invifible
World,* than the fcriptures of Truth afford, *&c.*

[63] To which of the Juftices the
Author refers is not certain, as Mr.
Danforth and Mr. Saltonftall, two
of them, were dead when he wrote.
The Latter died in 1694, and the
Former in 1699.

[64] "That furious Marfhal" was
George Herrick, who, in October,
1692, ftated, that "for nine Months
his whole Time had been confumed
as Marfhal and Deputy Sheriff, in

Cafes of Witchcraft."—Felt, *An-
nals of Salem,* ii, 480.   The Death
of George Herrick is noticed in
the Herrick Genealogy, as having
occurred in 1695, but nothing is
faid of any Cafualty.   Mr. Savage
fuppofes Him to be the fame who
came over in 1685, in the Ship
with John Dunton, who, John fays
faved his Life at Sea.—*Life and
Errors,* 126-7.

tho' the Rich Man in the Parable might think
otherwife, &c. who was feeking to fend fome
more fenfible Demonftrations thereof to his
Brethren, &c. In that Tremendous Judgment
of God upon this Countrey, by the late amazing
Profecution of the People here, under the Notion
of Witches; whereby 20 Suffered as Evil doers
(befides thofe that died in Prifon) about ten more
Condemned, and a hundred Imprifoned, and
about two hundred more Accufed, and the Countrey generally in fears, when it would come to
their turn to be Accufed; and the Profecution and
manner of Tryal fuch, that moft would have chofen to have fallen into the hands of the Barbarous Enemy, rather than (under that notion) into
the hands of their Brethren in Church Fellow-
fhip; and in fhort, was fuch an Affliction as far
exceeded all that ever this Countrey hath laboured
under.

Yet in this Mount, God is feen; when it was
thus bad with this diftreffed People, a full and a
fudden ftop is put, not only without, but againft
the Inclination of many, for out of the Eater
came forth Meat: Thofe very Accufers which
had been improved as Witneffes againft fo many,
by the Providence of the moft High, and perhaps
blinded with Malice, are left to accufe thofe in
moft High efteem, both Magiftrates and Minifters, as guilty of Witchcraft, which fhewed our
Rulers, that neceffity lay upon them, to confound
that which had fo long confounded the Countrey,

as being unwilling themfelves to run the fame
Rifque, this that was in the Event of it to this
Countrey, as Life from the Dead, is moft eafie
with him, in whofe Hands are the Hearts of all
Men, and was a very fignal deliverance to this
whole Countrey. No lefs Obfervable was it, that
tho' at the time when the Devils Teftimony, by
the Afflicted, was firft laid afide, there were great
Numbers of (real or pretended) Afflicted : Yet
when this was once not Judged of Validity
enough to be any longer brought into the Court
againft the Accufed as Evidence, the Affliction
generally ceafed, and only fome remainders of it
in fuch places, where more Encouragement was
given to the Actors, God feeming thereby plainly
to Decipher that Sin of going to the Devil, *&c.*
as the rife and foundation of thofe Punifhments.

And thus, Reverend Sir, I have, as I underftand it, performed my Duty herein, for the
Glory of God, and the well-being of Men.
And for my Freedome ufed in this, and former
Writings, relating to the Actors in this Tragedy,
I fhall not Apologize, but give you the words
of one to [42] whom fome can afford the
title of Venerable (when he is arguing for that
which they have undertaken to afcert, tho' at
other times, more Diminutive Epithete, muft
serve) it is the Reverend Mr. R. *Baxter* in his
Book, *the Cure of Church Divifions*, p. 257, 258.
But (I pray you mark it) *the way of God is to
fhame the Sinner, how good foever in other refpects,*

That the sin may have the greater shame, and Reli-
gion may not be shamed, as if it allowed men to sin;
Nor God the Author of Religion he Dishonoured;
Nor others be without the Warning; But the way
of the Devil is, to hide or justifie the sin, as if it
were for fear of Disparaging the goodness of the
Persons that committed it; that so he may hereby
Dishonour Religion and Godliness itself, and make
men believe it is but a Cover for any Wickedness,
and as consistent with it, as a looser Life is, and
that he may keep the Sinner from Repenting, and
blot out the Memory of that warning, which should
have preserved After-Ages from the like falls.
Scripture shameth the Professors, (*tho'* a David, *a*
Solomon, Peter, Noah, *or* Lot) *that the Religion*
profest may not be shamed but vindicated: Satan
would preserve the Honour of Professors, that the
Religion professed may bear the shame; and so it may
fall on God himself.

And now that all that have had a hand in any
horrid and bloody practices may be brought to
give glory to God, and take the due shame to
themselves; and that our Watchmen may no
longer seek to palliate (much less give thanks for)
such, &c. (thereby making them their own) and
that the people may no longer perish for want of
knowledge in the midst of such means of light;
Nor God be any longer dishonoured by false sentiments in these matters, is the earnest desire and
prayer of, Sir, yours to my power.

R. C.

Mr. Cotton Mather.

Reverend Sir,

HAVING long fince fent you fome doctrinals as to my belief, together with my requeft to you, that if I erred you would be pleafed to fhew it me by fcripture, *viz.* That the Devils bounds are fet which he cannot pafs; That the Devils are fo full of malice that it cannot be added to by mankind; That where he hath power he neither can nor will omit executing it; That 'tis only the Almighty that fets bounds to his rage, and that only can commiffionate him to hurt and deftroy, *&c.* But inftead of fuch an Anfwer as was promifed, and juftly expected, you were pleafed to fend me a Book, which you fince call'd an ungainfayable one; which Book till lately I have not had opportunity fo fully to confider. And to the end you may fee I have now done it, I have fent to you fome of the remarkables contained in the faid Book, Intituled,

[43] *The Certainty of the World of Spirits, written by Mr.* R. B.[65] London, *Printed.* 1691.

IT *is therein conceded* (Preface) That to fee Devils and Spirits ordinarily would not be enough to convince Atheifts. Page 88. Atheifts are not to

---

[65] Richard Baxter. William Bates, D.D., preached an excellent Sermon on the Death of the great Divine, and gives an Account of

be convinced by ftories, their own fenfes are not enough to convince them any more than fenfe will convince a Papift from Tranfubftantiation. (*D. Laderd.*) P. 4. No Spirit can do any thing but by God's will and permiffion. (*Preface*) 'Tis the free will of Man that gives the Devils their hurting power :   And without our own confent they cannot hurt us. (*It is afferted.* P. 222, 223,) That it is a perverfe oppofition of Popery which caufes many Proteftants not to regard the benefits we receive by Angels.   And Minifters are faulty, that do not pray and give thanks to God for their Miniftry; and that neglect to teach Believers, what love and what thanks they owe to Angels. P. 225. Moft good people look fo much to God and to Minifters, that they take little notice of Angels, which are God's great Minifters.   P. 234. The Author dares not, as fome have done, judge the Catholick Church to become Anti-Chriftian Idolaters, as foon as they gave too much Worfhip to Saints and Angels.   P. 7.   The Bleffed Souls fhall be like the Angels, therefore may appear

---

his Books, but fays nothing of that whofe Title is given above; doubt-lefs for the fame Reafon mentioned by our Author, namely : that it was written or affented to by him in his Dotage.   Dr. Bates was a Friend and Acquaintance of Dr. Increafe Mather.   In his Sermon, above cited, he fays : "I went to Mr. Baxter with a very worthy Friend, Mr. Mather, of New Eng-land, the Day before he died; and, fpeaking fome comforting Words to him, he replied, 'I have Pain; there is no arguing againft Senfe; but I have Peace.'   To Mr. Ma-ther, he faid, 'I blefs God that you have accomplifht your Bufinefs, the Lord prolong your Life.' "—*Page* 129-30.   See Page 11 of this Vol-ume for the Author's fenfible Re-marks on Mr. Baxter's Book.

here, P. 3, 4. 'Tis hard to know whether it be
a Devil or a human Soul that appears, or whether
the Soul of a good or a bad perſon. P. 61. or the
Soul of ſome dead friend that ſuffers, and yet
retains love, &c. P. 222. No doubt the Souls of
the wicked carry with them their former incli-
nations of Covetouſneſs, Revenge, &c. P. 7. When
Revengeful things are done, as on Murderers, De-
frauders, &c. it ſeems to be from the revengeful
wrath of ſome bad Soul, if it be about Money or
Lands, then from a Worldly minded one; ſome
ſignifications of God's mercy to wicked Souls
after this Life. P. 4. 'Tis a doubt whether beſides the Angels (good and bad) and the Souls of
men, there is not a third ſort, call'd Faries and
Goblins. It is unſearchable to us how far God
leaves Spirits to freewill in ſmall things, ſuſpend-
ing his predetermining motion.

P. 246. The Devils have a Marvellous power,
if but a ſilly wretched Witch conſent. P. 10.
202. The ſtories of Witches and Spirits are many
ways uſeful, particularly to convince Atheiſts, and
confirm Believers, and to prove the Operation of
Spirits. P. 232. To help men to underſtand that
Devils make no ſmall number of Laws, and Rulers
in the World, and are Authors of moſt of the
Wars, and of many Sermons, and of Books that
adorn the Liberaries of learned men. P. 6. 102.
The Devil's lying with the Witch is not to be
denied, and is more to Exerciſe the Luſt of the
Witch than of the Devil, who can alſo bring in

T

another Witch with[44]out opening the door, and fo perform it by one Witch with another. P. 105. Witches can raife Storms, fell Winds, &c. as is commonly affirmed. P. 107. In *America* 'tis a common thing to fee Spirits day and night. P. 95, 96, 97, 110. Stories of a Child that could not be cured of Witchcraft, becaufe the *Ember*[66]-weeks were paft, Vomited a Knife a fpan long, Cart Nails, &c. neither eat nor drank fifteen days and nights together; a long piece of Wood, four Knives, and two 'fharp pieces of Iron, ev'ry one above a fpan long, taken out of the Stomach, &c. Hair, Stones, Bones, Vomited, &c. 1000 l. of Blood loft by one perfon in a years time.

P. 250. A ftory that makes the Author think it poffible that fuch great things (as he mentions) fhould be gotten down and up Peoples Throats.

P. 164. Partial credibility fpoils many a good ftory.

P. 125. The Devil's fubftance enters into the poffeffed.

P. 174. Diftracted are poffeffed.

---

[66] The Days of certain Weeks fet apart by the Roman Catholic Church for Fafting and Prayer, in the four Seafons of the Year. Wednefday, Friday and Saturday after the firft Sunday in Lent, the Feaft of Whitfuntide, the 14th of September, and the 13th of December, are the *Ember-days;* and the Weeks in which they occur are *Ember-weeks.* "Ember-days were fo called, from the Word Ember, *i. e.*, Afhes; becaufe in old Times the Fathers uf'd to fprinkle themfelves with Afhes; or from the Cuftom of eating nothing on thofe Days till Night, and then only a Cake, baked under the *Embers,* which was thence called *Ember-bread.*"—*Phillips and Kerfey.*

P. 149. A fick Woman while fhe lay in bed went to fee her Children.

P. 153. A Dog appeared like a Fly or a Flea.

P. 165. Some knowing Agents directs Thunder ftorms, tho' the Author knows not who, and that they fo often fall on Churches he knows not why.

P. 2, 80. Mr. *J. M.* and Mr. *C. M.* Recommended together with *Bodin, &c.*

P. 237. A *Crifpian,* if through Ignorance he believes not what he faith, may be a Chriftian.

In this, Sir, I fuppofe that if I have not wronged the fenfe of the Author in the places quoted (which I truft you fhall not find I have done) I can't be thought accountable for the Errors or Contradictions to himfelf or to the truth, if any fuch be found, particularly what he grants in the Preface (of the freewill of Man, giving the Devil his hurting power.) This being not only more than thofe call'd Witch-Advocates would defire to be conceded to them : But is a palpable and manifeft overturning the Authors defign in all his Witch ftories. For who would confent to have the Devil afflict himfelf? As alfo his conceffion [that no Spirit can do any thing but by God's will and permiffion,] I cannot perfwade myfelf but you muft be fenfible of their apparent contradictorinefs to the reft. Others there are of a very ill afpect, as *p.* 234. the Catholicks are much encouraged in their Adoration of Angels and Saints. If that were fo Innocent as not to render them Anti-chriftian Idolaters; and that *p.* 4. if

admitted, will ſeem to lay an ungainſayable foundation for the *Pagan, Indian,* and *Diaboliſts* Faith;
by telling us it is beyond our ſearch to know how
far God leaves the Devils to free-will, to do what
they pleaſe, in this World, with a ſuſpenſion of
God's Predetermination; which if it [45] were
a truth, what were more rational than to oblige
him that has ſuch power over us. The Atheiſts
alſo would take encouragement if it were granted
that we cannot know how far God ſuſpends his
predetermining motion, he would thence affirm,
we as little know that there is a predetermining
motion, and conſequently whether there be a
God, and *p.* 165. would abundantly ſtrengthen
them, when ſuch a Learned, experienced, and
highly eſteemed Chriſtian ſhall own that he
knows not who 'tis that governs the Thunder-
ſtorms; for it might as well diſcover ignorance,
who 'tis that diſpoſes of Earthquakes, Gun-ſhot,
and afflictions that befall any, with the reſt of
Mundane Events. I deſign not to remark all that
in the Book is remarkable, ſuch as the departed
Souls wandering again hither to put men upon
revenge, *&c.* favouring ſo much of *Pithagoras*
his Tranſmigration of Souls, and the Separation
of the Soul from the Body without death, as in
the caſe of her that went to ſee her Children,
while yet ſhe did not ſtir out of her Bed, which
ſeems to be a new ſpeculation; unleſs it determins
in favour of Tranſubſtantiation, that a Body may
be at the ſame time in ſeveral places. Upon the

whole it is ungainſayable, That that Book, though
ſo highly extol'd, may be juſtly expected to occaſion the ſtaggering of the weak, and the harden-
ing of unbelievers in their Infidelity.   And it
ſeems amazing, that you ſhould not only give it
ſuch a recommend, but that you ſhould ſend it to
me, in order (as I take it) to pervert me from the
belief of thoſe fundamental Doctrinals (above re-
cited) Though I account them more firm than
Heaven and Earth.   But that which is yet more
ſtrange to me, is that Mr. *B* his Friends did not
adviſe him better, than in his declined Age to
emit ſuch crude matter to the public.   As to the
ſometime Reverend Author, let his works praiſe
the Remembrance of him; but for ſuch as are
either Erroneous and foiſted upon him, or the
effect of an aged Imbecillity, let them be detected
that they may proceed no further.[67]

I am not ignorant that the manner of Education of Youth in, I think, almoſt all Chriſtian
Schools hath a natural tendency to propagate
thoſe Doctrines of Devils heretofore (ſolely) pro-
feſt among *Ethnicks*,[68] and particularly in matters
of Witchcraft, *&c.*   For notwithſtanding the
Council of *Carthage* their taking notice that the
Chriſtian Doctors did converſe much with the
writings of the Heathens for the gaining of Eloquence, forbad the reading of the Books of the

[67] See Note 61.
[68] The *Ethnics* or *Ethnicks*. The
Gentiles of ancient Times were
denominated *Ethnics*.   All Unbelievers in the Religion of the Jews
and Chriſtians.

Gentiles; yet it feems this was only a Bill without a penalty, which their fucceffors did not look upon to be binding. He that fhould in this age take a view of the Schools, might be induced to believe that the ages fince have thought, that without fuch Heathen Learning a man cannot be fo accomplifh'd, as to have any pretence to Academick Literature : and that the vulgar might not be without the benefit of fuch Learning, fome of their Dif[46]ciples have taught them to fpeak *Englifh,* which has given me the opportunity to fend you thefe following Verfes.

Virg. Buco- licks. Eclog. 13.— Eclog. 8.—	*Sure love is not the caufe their bones appear.* *Some eyes bewitch my tender Lambs I fear.* *For me thefe Herbs in* Pontus Maris *chofe.* *There ev'ry powerful Drug in plenty grows ;* *Transform'd to a Wolf, I often* Mæris *faw,* *Then into fhady Woods himfelf withdraw :* *Oft he from deepeft Sepulchers would Charm* *Departed Souls. And from anothers Farm,* *Into his own ground Corn yet ftanding take.* *Now from the Town my Charms bring* Daphnis *back.* *Vanquifht with charms from Heaven the Moon Defcends.* *Circe with charms transform'd* Ulyffes *friends :* *Charms in the Field will burft a Poyfonous Snake,* *Now from the Town,* &c.
Ovid's Meta- morphofis. Lib. 7.	*Her Arms thrice turns about, thrice wets her crown* *With gather'd dew, thrice yawns, and kneeling down ;* *Oh Night ! thou friend to fecrets you clear fires,* *That with the Moon fucceed when day retires.* *Great* Hecate, *thou know'ft and aid Imparts,*

To our defign, your Charms and Magick Arts:
And thou, oh Earth, that to Magicians yields
Thy powerful fimples: Airs, Winds, Mountains, Fields,
Soft murmuring Springs, ftill Lakes and Rivers clear,
You Gods of Woods, you Gods of night appear;
By you at will, I make fwift Streams retire,
To their firft Fountain, while their Banks admire.
Seas tofs and fmooth; clear Clouds with Clouds deform,
Storms turn to Calms, and make a Calm a Storm.
With Spells and Charms, I break the Vipers Jaws,
Cleave folid Rocks, Oaks from their fifures draw;
Whole Woods remove, the Airy Mountains fhake;
Earth forc'd to groan, and Ghofts from Graves awake.
              —— *her Journey takes,*

Lib. 14.   *To* Rhegium *oppofite to* Zanle's *fhore,*
             And treads the troubled Waves, that loudly roar;
             Running with unwet Feet on that profound,
             As if Sh' had trod upon the folid ground.

     [47] *This with portentous poyfon fhe pollutes,*
          Befprinkled with the juice of wicked roots,
          In words dark, and perplext nine times thrice,
          Inchantments mutters with her wicked voice, &c.

'Thefe Fables of the Heathens (tho' in themfelves of no more validity than the idle Tales of
an *Indian,* or the Difcourfes of a known Roman-
cer) are become the School-learning, not to fay
the Faith of Chriftians, and are the Scriptures
brought (inftead of that moft fure Word) if not
to prove Doctrine, yet as illuftrations thereof.
Cafes of Confcience concerning Witch *pag.* 25.
Remarkable Providences *pag.* 250. (This per-

haps might be the caufe that in *England* a people
otherways fober and Religious) have for fome Ages
(in a manner wholly) refufed admitting thofe fo
educated to the work of the Miniftry. Such
education and practice, have fo far prevailed that
it has been a means of corrupting the Chriftian
world, almoft to that degree as to be ungainfayable; for tho' there is Reafon to hope that thefe
Diabolical principles have not fo prevail'd (with
multitudes of Chriftians) as that they afcribe to a
Witch and a Devil the Attributes peculiar to the
Almighty; yet how few are willing to be found
oppofing fuch a torrent, as knowing that in fo
doing they fhall be fure to meet with oppofition
to the utmoft, from the many, both of Magiftrates, Minifters and People; and the name of
Sadducee, Atheift, and perhaps Witch too caft
upon them moft liberally, by men of the higheft
profeffion in Godlinefs. And if not fo learned
as fome of themfelves, then accounted only fit to
be trampled on, and their Arguments (tho both
Rational and Scriptural) as fit only for contempt.
But tho this be the deplorable Dilemma; yet
fome have dared from time to time (for the glory
of God, and the good and fafety of Mens lives,
&c.) to run all thefe Rifques. And that God
who has faid, *My glory I will not give to another,*
is able to protect thofe that are found doing their
duty herein againft all oppofers; and however
other ways contemptible can make them ufeful
in his own hand, who has fometimes chofen the

weakeſt Inſtruments, that his power may be the
more Illuſtrious.

*And now, Reverend Sir, if you are conſcious to
yourſelf, that you have in your principles, or practices been abetting to ſuch grand Errors, I cannot ſee
how it can conſiſt with ſincerity to be ſo convinc'd in
matters ſo nearly relating to the glory of God, and
lives of Innocents ; and at the ſame time ſo much to
fear diſparagement among Men, as to ſtifle Conſcience, and diſſemble an approving of former ſenti-
ments ; you know that word,* he that honoureth me
I will honour, and he that deſpiſeth me ſhall be
lightly eſteemed. *But if you think that in theſe
matters you have done your duty, and taught people
theirs ; and that the Doctrines cited from the mentioned* [48] *Book are ungainſayable: I ſhall conclude in almoſt his words, He that teaches ſuch Doctrine, if through Ignorance he believes not what he
ſaith, may be a Chriſtian : But if he believes them, he
is in the broad path to Heatheniſm, Deviliſm, Popery
or Atheiſm. It is a ſolemn caution, Gal.* i. 8. But
tho we or an Angel from Heaven preach any
other Goſpel unto you than that which we have
preached unto you, let him be accurſed. *I hope
you will not miſconſtrue my Intentions herein, who
am, Reverend Sir, Yours to command, in what I
may,*   R. C.

V

To the Minifters in and near *Bofton*, *January* 12, 1696.

CHRISTIANITY *had been but a fhort time in the World, when there was raifed againft it, not only open profeft Enemies; but fecret and imbred underminers, who fought thereby to effect that which open force had been fo often baffled in.*

And notwithftanding that primitive purity and fincerity, which in fome good meafure was ftill retained; yet the cunning deceivers and Apoftate Hereticks found opportunity to beguile the unwary, and this in fundamentals.

Among others which then fprung up, with but too much advantage in the third Century, the Maniche[68] *did fpread his Peftiferous fentiments, and taught the Exiftence of two Beings, or Caufes of all things, viz. a good and a bad: but thefe were foon filenced by the more Orthodox Doctors, and Anathematized by General Councels. And at this day the American Indians, another fort of* Maniche, *entertaining (thus far) the fame belief, hold it their prudence and intereft to pleafe that evil Being, as well by perpetrating other Murders, as by their Bloody Sacrifices, that fo he may not harm them. The Iron teeth of time have now almoft devoured the name of*

---

[68] A Sect of Philofophers who took their Name from a Perfon named *Manichæus*, or Manes. Manes flourifhed about A. D. 277, and his Doctrine or Philofophy fpread chiefly in Arabia, Egypt and Africa. He taught that Light was the Origin of all Good, and that in Darknefs originated all Evil. *Maniche* is not unlike *God* among the Indians.

the former, and as to the latter, it is to he hoped that as Chriftianity prevails among them, they will abhor fuch abominable belief.[69]

And as thofe primitive times, were not priviledged againft the fpreading of dangerous Herefie, fo neither can any now pretend to any fuch Immunity, tho' profeffing the enjoyment of a primitive purity.

Might a Judgment be made from the Books of the modern learned Divines, or from the practice of Courts, or from the Faith of many, who call themfelves Chriftians, it might be modeftly, tho' fadly concluded, that the Doctrine of the Maniche, *at leaft great part of it, is fo far from being forgotten that 'tis almoft every where profeft.   We in thefe ends of the Earth need not feek far for Inftances, in each refpect to demonftrate this*.   *The Books here Printed, and recommended not only by the refpective Authors, but by many of their Brethren, do fet forth that the Devil inflicts Plagues,*[a] Wars,[b] Difeafes,[c] Tempefts[d] and can render the moft folid things invifible,[e] and can do things above and againft the courfe of Nature, and all natural caufes.

[49] *Are thefe the Expreffions of Orthodox believers ? or are they not rather expreffions becoming a* Maniche, *or a* Heathen, *as agreeing far better*

[69] Had the Author lived to this Time he would have feen that his Hopes were much further from being realized than he could have anticipated.   Many Years ago, a noted Indian Chief, on being importuned refpecting Chriftianity, and urged to adopt it in his Tribe, replied that "It might do for White People, but it did not fuit Indians."
   [a] Wonders of the Invifible World, p. 17, 18.   [b] p. 18.   [c] Cafes of Confcience, p. 63.   [d] Remarkable providences, p. 124.   [e] Wonders of the Invifible World, p. 141.— *Notes in the Original.*

with thefe than with the facred Oracles our only rule; the whole current whereof is fo Diametrically oppofite thereto, that it were almoft endlefs to mention all the Divine cautions againft fuch abominable belief; he that runs may read, Pfal. lxii. 11, *and* cxxxvi. 4. Lam. iii. 37. Amos iii. 6. Jer. iv. 22. Pfal. lxxviii. 26, *and* clxviii. 6. 8. Job xxxviii. 22. to the 34 v.

Thefe places with a multitude more, do abundantly teftifie that the Affertors of fuch power to be in the evil Being, do fpeak in a dialect different from the fcriptures, (laying a firm foundation for the Indians adorations, which agrees well with what A. Rofs[70] *fets forth, in his Miftag. Poetic, p.* 116, *that their ancients did Ufurp the furies and their God* Averinci, *that they might forbear to hurt them.)*

And have not the Courts in fome parts of the World by their practice teftified their concurrence with fuch belief, profecuting to Death many people upon that notion, of their improving fuch power of the Evil one, to the raifing of Storms; afflicting and

---

[70] Alexander Rofs, a Scotchman, a very voluminous Author, though a Prelate and poffeffed of much and varied Learning, is meagrely noticed in Biographical Works. He continued Sir Walter Ralegh's Hiftory of the World, in a large folio; wrote "a View of the Religions of the World;" "Virgilii Evangelifantis Chriftiados, Librii xiii," &c. little known. The Work referred to in the Text is entitled "Myftagogus Poet-icus, or the Mufe's Interpreter: Explaining the Hiftorical Myftteries, and Myftical Hiftories of the Ancient Greek and Latin Poets," &c. a fifth Edition of which was publifhed in 1672. Notwithftanding his immenfe literary Labours, he is unknown to Thoufands of the prefent Day, beyond thofe *anachronifmical* Lines in Hudibras:

"There was an ancient fage Philofopher
That had read Alexander Rofs over."

*killing of others, tho at great diſtance from them;
doing things in their own perſons above humane
ſtrength, deſtroying of Cattle, flying in the Air,
turning themſelves into Cats or Dogs,* &c. *Which
by the way muſt needs imply ſome thing of goodneſs
to be in that evil Being, who, tho he has ſuch power,
would not exert it, were it not for this people, or elſe
that they can ſome way add to this mighty power.*[71]

*And are the people a whit behind in their beliefs?
is there any thing (abovementioned,) their ſtrong Faith
looks upon to be too hard for this evil Being to effect?*

*Here it will be anſwered, God permits it. Which
anſwer is ſo far an owning the Doctrine, that the
Devil has in his nature a power to do all theſe
things, and can exert this power, except when he is
reſtrained, which is in effect to ſay that God has
made Nature to fight againſt itſelf. That he has
made a Creature, who has it in the power of his
Nature to overthrow Nature, and to act above and*

[71] Some Perſon once put into the Hands of the ſince famous James Howell a Manuſcript, attempting to diſprove the Exiſtence of Witches. In writing to his Friend, Sir Edward Spencer, ſoon after, Howell ſaid: "I will not ſay that this Gentleman is ſo perverſe; but to deny there are any Witches, to deny that there are not ill Spirits which ſeduce, tamper and converſe in divers Shapes with human Creatures, and impel them to Actions of Malice, I ſay, that he who denies there are ſuch buſy Spirits, and ſuch poor paſſive Creatures upon whom they work, which commonly are called Witches; I ſay again, that he who denies there are ſuch Spirits, ſhews that he himſelf hath a Spirit of Contradiction in him, oppoſing the current and conſentient Opinion of all Antiquity." James wrote this Nonſenſe in 1647. Moſt certainly if our Affairs are to be meaſured by the Laws and Uſages of Antiquity, all Advancement in Knowledge is a Crime; and inſtead of being tolerated, ſhould be prevented by the ſame ſanguinary Laws then in uſe. Fortunately ſome Improvement is diſcernible.

against it. Which he that can believe may as well believe the greatest contradiction. That Being which can do this in the smallest thing, can do it in the greatest. If Moses *with a bare permission might stretch forth his Rod, yet he was not able to bring Plagues upon the* Egyptians, *or to divide the Waters, without a Commission from the most high; so neither can that evil Being perform any of this without a Commission from the same power. The Scripture recites more Miracles wrought by Men than by Angels good and bad; Tho this Doctrine be so dishonourable to the only Almighty Being, as to ascribe such Attributes to the Evil one, as are the Incommunicable prerogative of him, who is the alone Sovereign Being; yet here is not all: But as he that Steers by a false Compass, the further he Sails the more he is out of his way; so though there is in some things a variation* [50] *from, there is in others a further progression in, or building upon the said Doctrine of the* Maniche.

Men in this Age are not content barely to believe such an exorbitant power to be in the nature of this evil Being; but have imagined that he prevails with many to sign a Book, or make a contract with him, whereby they are inabled to perform all the things abovementioned. Another Account is given hereof, viz. that by vertue of such a Covenant they attain power to Commissionate him. And though the two parties are not agreed which to put it upon, whether the Devil *impowers the* Witch, *or the* Witch *commissionate him; yet both parties are agreed in*

this, That one way or other the mifchief is effected,
and fo the Criminal becomes culpable of Death.   In
the fearch after fuch a fort of Criminals, how many
Countries have fallen into fuch Convulfions.   That
the Devaftations made by a Conquering Enemy, nor
the Plague itfelf, has not been fo formidable.

That not only good perfons have thus been
blemifh'd in their Reputations, but much innocent Blood hath been fhed, is teftified even by
thofe very Books, Cafes of Confcience, *p.* 33.
Remarkable provid. *p.* 179.   Memor. provid.
p. 28.

And (to add) what lefs can be expected, when
Men having taken up fuch a belief, of a covenanting, afflicting and killing Witch ; and com-
paring it with the Scripture, finding no footfteps
therein of fuch a fort of Witch, have thereupon
defperately concluded ; that tho the Scripture is
full in it, that a Witch fhould not live ; yet that
it has not at all defcribed the crime, nor means
whereby the culpable might be detected.

And hence they are fallen fo far as to reckon
it neceffary to make ufe of thofe Diabolical and
Bloody ways, always heretofore practiced for their
Difcovery.   As finding that the Rules given to
detect other crimes, are wholly ufelefs for the
Difcovery of fuch.

This is that which has produced that deluge of
Blood mentioned, and muft certainly do fo again,
the fame belief remaining.

And who can wonder, if Chriftians that are fo

eaſily prevailed with to lay aſide their Swords as
uſeleſs, and ſo have loſt their Strength (if with
Samſon) they are led blindfold into an Idol Temple, to make ſport for Enemies and Infidels, and
to do abominable actions, not only not Chriſtian,
but againſt even the light of Nature and Reaſon.
And now Reverend Fathers, you who are appointed as Guides to the People, and whoſe Lips
ſhould preſerve Knowledge; who are ſet as Shepherds, and as Watchmen, this matter appertains
to. you. I did write to you formerly upon this
head, and acquainted you with my Sentiments,
requeſting that, if I erred, you would be pleaſed
to ſhew it me by Scripture; but from your
ſilence, I gather that you approve thereof. For
I may reaſonably preſume, that you would have
ſeen it your duty to have in[51]formed me better,
if you had been ſenſible of any Error. But if in
this matter you have acquitted yourſelves, becoming the Titles you are dignified with, you have
cauſe of rejoicing in the midſt of the calamities
that afflict a ſinning world.

Particularly, if you have taught the People to
fear God, and truſt in him, and not to fear a
Witch or a Devil. That the Devil has no power
to afflict any with Diſeaſes, or loſs of Cattle, *&c.*
without a Commiſſion from the moſt high. That
he is ſo filled with malice, that whatever Commiſſion he may have againſt any, he will not fail
to execute it. That no mortal ever was, or can
be able to Commiſſionate him, or to lengthen his

Chain in the leaft, and that he who can Commiffionate him is God ; and that the Scriptures of
truth not only affign the punifhment of a Witch ;
but give fufficient Rules to detect them by, and
that (according to Mr. *Gauls* fourth head,) a
Witch is one that hates and oppofes the word,
work, and worfhip of God, and feeks by a fign to
feduce therefrom. That they who are guilty
according to that head, are guilty of Witchcraft,
and by the Law given by *Mofes*, were to be put
to Death. If you have taught the People the
neceffity of Charity, and the evil of entertaining
fo much as a jealoufie againft their Neighbours
for fuch crimes upon the Devils fuggeftions to a
perfon pretending to a Spectral (or Diabolical)
fight ; who utter their Oracles from Malice, fren-
fie, or a Satanical Delufion ; that to be inquifitive
of fuch, whofe Spectres they fee, or who it is that
afflicts ? In order to put the accufed perfons life
in queftion, is a wickednefs beyond what *Saul*
was guilty of in going to the Witch. That to
confult with the dead, by the help of fuch as
pretend to this Spectral fight, and fo to get Information againft the life of any perfon, is the worft
fort of Necromancy. That the pretending to
drive away Spectres, *i. e.* Devils, with the hand,
or by ftriking thefe to wound a perfon at a diftance, cannot be without Witchcraft, as pretending
to affign in order to deceive in matters of fo
high a Nature. That 'tis Ridiculous to think by
making laws againft feeding, imploying, or re-

W

warding of evil Spirits, thereby to get rid of them. That their natures require not sucking to support it.

That it is a horrid Injury and Barbarity to search those parts, which even Nature itself commands the concealing of, to find some Excrescence to be called a Tet for those to suck; which yet is said sometimes to appear as a Fleabite. Finally if you have taught the People what to believe and practice, as to the probation of the Accused, by their saying, or not saying the Lord's Prayer; and as to praying that the Afflicted may be able to accuse; And have not shunned in these matters to declare the whole mind of God; you have then well acquitted yourselves (in time of General Defection) as faithful Watchmen. But if instead [52] of this, you have some by word and writing propagated; others recommended such writings, and abetted the false Notions, which are so prevalent in this Apostate Age, it is high time to consider it. If when Authority found themselves almost nonplust in such prosecutions, and sent to you for your Advice what they ought to do,

Cases of Conscience, and you have then thanked them
ult. for what they had already done (and thereby encouraged them to proceed in those very by Paths already fallen into) it so much the [more] nearly concerns you, *Ezek.* xxxiii. 2, to 8.

To conclude, this whole People are invited

and commanded to humble their Souls before
God, as for other caufes, fo for the

Vid. *The Procla-* Errors that may have been fallen into
mation for a Faft, in thefe profecutions on either hand,
to be the 14 *Inft. as* and to pray that God would teach
fet forth by Autho- us what we know not, and help us
rity. wherein we have done amifs, that
we may do fo no more.

This more immediately concerns yourfelves,
for 'tis not fuppofed to be intended, that God
would fhew us thefe things by Infpiration. But
that fuch who are called to it, fhould fhew the
mind of God in thefe things on both hands;
i. e. whether there has been any Error in Excefs
or Deficiency, or neither in the one nor the other.
And if you do not thus far ferve the publick you
need not complain of great Sufferings and un-
righteous Difcouragements; if Peo-

Vid. *The Declara-* ple do not applaude your conduct, as
tion, as drawn by you might otherways have expected.
the Deputies with But if you altogether hold your peace
the Affiftance of the at fuch a time as this is; your filence
Minifters; but re- at leaft feemingly will fpeak this
ceiv'd a Noncon- Language; that you are not con-
currence. cerned tho' Men afcribe the power
and providence of the Almighty to
the worft of his Creatures. That if other Ages
or Countries improve the Doctrines and Examples given them, either to the taking away of the
Life or Reputations of Innocents you are well
fatisfied. Which that there may be no fhadow

of a Reafon to believe but that your conduct
herein may remove all fuch Jealoufies; and that
God be with you in declaring his whole mind to
the People, is the earneft defire and prayer of,
Reverend Sirs,

Yours to my utmoft,

R. C.

Mr. *Benjamin Wadfworth.*[73]

Reverend Sir,

AFTER that dreadful and fevere Perfecution
of fuch a Multitude of People, under the
notion of Witches, which in the day thereof, was
the foreft tryal and affliction that ever befel this
Country. And after [53] many of the principal
Actors had declared their fears and jealoufies, that
they had greatly erred in thofe Profecutions.
And after a Solemn day of Fafting had been
kept, with Prayers that God would fhew us what

---

[73] Mr. Wadfworth was Minifter
of the Firft Church in Bofton from
1696 to 1725, when he became
Prefident of Harvard College. He
was Son of Capt. Samuel Wadfworth of Milton, who fell in the
bloody Fight at Sudbury, April the
21ft, 1676. And here it may be
noted that Prefident Wadfworth,
praifeworthily and in filial Duty,
erected a Monument to his father's
Memory, at Sudbury, on the Site
of the fierce Conflict, in which he
ended his Life; but from fome Caufe
eafily explained, fixed the Date of
his father's Death on April 18th;

See *N. E. Hift. and Gen. Reg.* for
1853, p. 221, where the Caufe of
the Error is explained. There has
been a feeble Attempt to maintain
the old Date, becaufe it happened
ignorantly to be placed upon a new
Monument which replaced the old
One in 1852. This Attempt has
been admitted into the Regifter for
1866, page 135-141, as unaccountably as the Date on the New
Monument.

Prefident Wadfworth, though a
Believer in Witchcraft, did not en-
courage the Proceedings and Profecutions.

we knew not; *viz.* what errors might therein have been fallen into, *&c.* And after moft People were convinc'd of the Evil of fome, if not of moft of thofe Actions. At fuch a time as this it might have been juftly expected that the Minifters would make it their work to Explain the Scriptures to the People; and from thence to have fhown them, the evil and danger of thofe falfe Notions, which not only gave fome occafion; but in a blind Zeal hurried them into thofe unwarrantable practices, fo to prevent a falling into the like for the future.

But inftead of this, for a Minifter of the Gofpel (Paftor of the old Meeting [74]) to abet fuch Notions; and to ftir up the Magiftrates to fuch Profecutions, and this without any cautions given, is what is truly amazing, and of moft dangerous confequence.

It is a truth, Witchcraft is, in the Text then infifted on, reckon'd up as a manifeft work of the Flefh. *Viz. Gal.* v. 19. But it is as true, that in recounting thofe other Works (which are indeed Manifeft Flefhly Works) the Magiftrate was not ftirred up againft thofe others; but as if the reft were either not to be taken notice of by him, or as if all Zeal againft Murder, Adulteries, *&c.* was fwallowed up, and over-fhadowed by this againft Witchcraft.

---

[74] The Author undoubtedly refers to Dr. Mather the Younger, though his Meaning is left rather obfcure. The *Old Meeting* may be fuppofed to mean that of the oldeft Church; but of that, Mr. Wadfworth himfelf was the Minifter.

The defcription that was then given, was that they were fuch as made a Covenant with the Devil, and fold themfelves to the evil Angels. It feems faulty, that when fuch Minifter is inquired of, and requefted to give the Reafons, or Grounds in Scripture of fuch Defcription; for fuch Minifter to affert that it is the Inquirers work to difprove it. And his faying further, in anfwer that there are many things true, that are not afferted in Scripture; feems to fpeak this Language, *viz.* that the Law of God is imperfect, in not defcribing this Crime of Witchcraft, though it be therein made Capital.

Thefe perfect Oracles inform us, concerning *Ahab*, that he fold himfelf to work Wickednefs; which may fignifie to us, that great height of Wickednefs he had arrived at; which yet might be, without his being properly, or juftly accounted a Witch; any more than thofe that are faid to have made a Covenant with Death, and with Hell, *&c.* Can it be thought that all thofe, or fuch as are there fpoken of, are Witches, and ought to fuffer as Witches?

As the Servants and People of God, have made a Solemn explicit Covenant with him, *Jofh.* xxiv. 25. *Nehem.* ix. 38. *&c.* So no doubt a Covenant has been made by *Heathen Indian* Nations to ferve, and adore the Devil; yet even for this, it were very hard to affix the Character of [54] a Witch upon each of thofe *Heathen* that fo do: And accordingly to Execute them as fuch. It is alſo poſſible, that ſome that have been called Chriſtians, have ſealed a Writing, ſign'd with their own Blood, or otherways, thereby Covenanting to be the Devil's Servants, *&c.* but from far other grounds, or inducements than what ſways with the *Indians;* theſe Heathen hoping to pleaſe him, that ſo he may not harm them. But theſe having been Educated and Confirmed in the Belief, that by vertue of ſuch Covenant, they ſhall have a Knowledge and Power more than Humane, aſ-ſiſting of them; this may have prevail'd with ſome to ſo horrible a wickedneſs; for none can ſeek Evil for Evils ſake; but as the Serpent in his firſt tempting Man, made uſe of the know-ledge of Good and Evil; ſo to teach Men that ſuch effects do uſually follow ſuch Covenant, is properly the work of the Serpent; for without this, what inducement, or temptation could they have to make ſuch a Covenant?

Theſe having thus choſen a falſe God, may well be accounted the worſt ſort of Idolaters. Yet it does not hence follow that in a Scripture ſenſe, they are thereby become Witches, till they have, or rather till they pretend to have aſſiſtances an-ſwerable; and do thereby endeavour to deceive others, which endeavours to deceive, by a ſign may be without any previous Covenant.

But ſuppoſing none of all thoſe ſeveral ſorts of Covenants was intended, it remains that the Cove-nant, that was underſtood to be intended, in that Diſcourſe at Old Meeting, is agreeable to the late dangerous Notion that has fo much prevailed, *viz.* That the Devil appears to the perfons, that they and the Devil make mutual engagements each to other, confirmed by figning to the Devil's Book; and are from hence inabled, not only to know futurities, and things done at diftance; but are alfo thereby impowered to do harm to the Neighbours, to raife Storms, and do things above and againft a courfe of Nature: This being the notion that has occafioned the fhedding fo much Blood in the World, it may be thought to need explaining.

For as Reafon knows nothing of an Afflicting, Covenanting Witch; fo it feems as Forreign from Scripture in general, as it is from the Text then infifted on; which fpeaks of fuch wickedneffes as are manifeftly the works of the flefh: but fuch Communication with Spirits, the flefh doth man-ifeftly dread even as death itfelf. Therefore the ufual Salvation of the Holy Angels to the beft of Men was, fear not; and experience fhews, that the moft wicked, are moft afrighted at the appre-henfions of the appearances of Devils; therefore fuch an explicit Covenanting cannot be a manfeft work of the Flefh.

[55] Yet this is manifeft, that the belief of the Witches power to do the things above mentioned, is an ancient belief of the Heathen. And that from them it was received by the Papifts, as a part of their Faith, who have fince improved upon it, and brought in the notion of a Covenant.

But it feems yet a further improvement lately made by Proteſtants, that ſuch Witches can Commiſſionate Devils to do thoſe miſchiefs, thereby ſetting the Witch in the place of God ; for tho few of the Papiſts are known to be thus abſurd ; yet when ſuch Doctrines have been Preached, and Printed in *New England,* they have met with none to oppoſe ; but many to incourage them.[75] Other conſiderable additions or new improvements have been made here; as the art to knock off inviſible chains with the hand, to drive away Spectres (*i. e.* Devils) by bruſhing, ſpelling words to the Afflicted, *&c.* What has followed upon theſe notions, and upon ſuch improvements, is needleſs here to repeat, it were unaccountable to recount the effuſion of Blood that has been hereby occaſioned, ſuch remaining Scars, and ſuch yet bleeding wounds as are to be found ; which none can wholly pretend ignorance of.

[75] The Defenders of Dr. Mather's *Wonders,* &c., remark : "After that thoſe our Honourable Judges (fearing leaſt wrong Steps might have been taken) had thus ſet apart a Day for ſolemn Humiliation before the Lord, humbly Imploring His Pardon for what might have been done amiſs; for him to repeat that Matter, and ſet it out with imperfect Relations and odious Aggravations, thereby intending to render the Land, and the Judges obnoxious (tho all the Learning that he and wiſer Men than he, pretend unto, is inſufficient to dive to the Bottom of the Matter,) and for him to ſpeak as he does of the Honourable Perſons, as *Men obſtinate in an Error, and involved in the Guilt of the Blood ſhed by Pagans and Papiſts before them:* what ſhall we think of it, but that 'tis inhumane, and fit for none but a *Servant of the worſt Maſter?* One would have thought, that the *Fear of God* (if he has any) ſhould have darted that Scripture into his Mind, Exod. 22. 28. *Thou ſhalt not ſpeak Evil of the Ruler of thy People.*"— *Anſwer to a Scandalous Book,* &c. Paternity of Extract unmiſtakable.

X

And if Blood ſhall be required of that Watchman that ſeeth the Sword a coming, and gives
not the needful warning; how much more of
ſuch as join with the Enemy, to bring in the
Sword to deſtroy them, over whom he was placed
a Watchman.

And if the law of God be perfeɗ, and exceeding broad, as being given forth by the Omnicient
Law-giver; it is exceeding high preſumption and
arrogance, and highly deſtruɗive to the lives of
Innocents, for any to pretend to give another, and
a pretended better deſcription of a crime made
thereby Capital, with new rules to try ſuch offenders by.

*Reverend Sir, the matter being of ſuch high con-
cern requires (and it is again prayed) that you would
be pleaſed to conſider, and give the grounds from
Scripture, or Reaſon of ſuch Definition, or elſe that
you would explode it, as inconſiſtent with both.
From, Reverend Sir, Yours to my utmoſt.*

R. C.

PART III.

An Account of the Differences in SALEM *Village.*

THE Reaſons why we withdraw from Communion with the Church of *Salem* Village,
both as to hearing the word Preached, and from

partaking with them at the Lord's Table, are as followeth.

Why we attend not on publick Prayer, and preaching the word, there are,

|56] *I. The Diſtracting, and Diſturbing tumults, and noiſes made by the perſons under Diabolical Power and deluſions: preventing ſometimes our hearing, underſtanding, and profiting by the word preached. We having after many Trials, and Experiences found no redreſs in this matter, accountea ourſelves under a neceſſity to go where we might hear the word in quiet.*

2. The apprehenſion of danger of ourſelves, being accuſed as the Devil's Inſtruments, to afflict the perſons complaining, we ſeeing thoſe that we have reaſon to eſteem better than ourſelves thus accuſed, blemiſhed, and of their lives bereaved: for ſeeing this, thought it our prudence to withdraw.

3. We found ſo frequent and poſitive preaching up ſome Principles and Practices by Mr. Parris,[76] *referring to the dark and diſmal myſtery of Iniquity working among us, was not profitable; but offenſive.*

4. Neither could we in Conſcience join with Mr. Parris, in many of the Requeſts which he made in Prayer, referring to the trouble then among us and upon us; therefore thought it our moſt ſafe and peaceable way to withdraw.

---

[76] A brief Article on this deluded Man will be ſeen in Dr. Allen's *Amer. Biog. Dictionary.* He will be found further noticed in theſe Pages. He poſſeſſed conſiderable Ability, but was very weak minded.

The Reasons why we hold not Communion with them at the Lord's Table, are because we find ourselves justly aggrieved, and offended with the Officer, who does administer, for the Reasons following.

I. *From his declared and published Principles, referring to our molestations from the Invisible World: Differing from the Opinion of the generality of the Orthodox Ministers of the Country.*

2. *His easie and strong Faith and Belief of the before-mentioned Accusations, made by those called the Afflicted.*

3. *His laying aside that grace (which above all we are to put on,) viz. Charity towards his Neighbours, and especially those of his Church, when there is no apparent reason, but for the contrary.*

4. *His approving and practicing unwarrantable and ungrounded methods, for discovering what he was desirous to know, referring to the bewitched, or possessed persons, as in bringing some to others, and by them pretending to inform himself and others, who were the Devil's instruments to afflict the sick and maimed.*

5. *His unsafe unaccountable Oath, given by him against sundry of the accused.*

6. *His not rendering to the World so fair (if so true) account of what he wrote on Examination of the afflicted.*

7. *Sundry unsafe (if found points of Doctrine delivered in his Preaching) which we find not warrantable (if Christian.)*

8. *His perfifting in thefe Principles, and jufti-
fying his Practice; not rendering any fatisfaction
to us, when regularly defired, but rather offending,
and diffatisfying ourfelves.*

[57] We whofe Names are under written,
heard this Paper read to our Paftor, Mr. *Samuel
Parris*, the 21*ft* of *April*, 1693.

Nathaniel Jigarfon,[76]	*Peter Cloyce*, Seniour.
Edward Pulman,	*Samuel Nurce*,
Aaron Way,	*John Jarboll*,
William Way,	*Thomas Wilkins*.

Mr. Parris's *Acknowledgment.*

FOR as much as it is the undoubted duty of all
Chriftians to purfue Peace, *Pfal.* xxxiv. 14.
even to a reaching of it, if it be poffible, *Amos*
xii. 18, 19. And whereas through the righteous,
Sovereign, and awful Providence of God, the
grand Enemy to all Chriftian Peace, has been of
late tremendoufly let loofe in divers places herea-
bout, and more efpecially among our finful felves,
not only to interrupt that partial peace which we
did fometimes enjoy, but alfo through his wiles
and temptations, and our weaknefs, and corrup-
tions, to make wider breaches, and raife more
bitter Animofities between too many of us. In
which dark and difficult difpenfations, we have

---

[76] Perhaps a typographical Error. Nathaniel *Ingerfon* or *Inger-
foll* is undoubtedly meant. Edward
Pulman is Edward *Putman;* Nurce
is fince *Nourfe;* Jarboll is *Tar-
bell*.

been all or moſt of us of one mind for a time; and afterwards of differing apprehenſions. And at laſt we are but in the dark, upon ſerious thoughts of all; and after many Prayers, I have been moved to preſent to you (my beloved Flock) the following particulars, in way of Contribution towards a regaining of Chriſtian Concord; if ſo be we be not altogether unappeaſeable, irreconcileable, and ſo deſtitute of that good Spirit, which is firſt pure, then peaceable, gentle, and eaſy to be intreated, *James* iii. 17. viz.

1. In that the Lord ordered the late horrid calamity[77] (which afterward plague-like ſpread in many other places) to break out firſt in my Family, I cannot but look upon as a very ſore rebuke, and humbling providence, both to myſelf and mine, and deſire ſome may improve it.

2. In that alſo in my Family were ſome of both parties, *viz.* Accuſers and Accuſed, I look alſo upon as an aggravation of that rebuke, as an addition of Wormwood to the Gall.

3. In the means which were uſed in my Family, though totally unknown to me or mine (except Servants) till afterwards, to raiſe Spirits and Apparitions in no better than a Diabolical way, I do alſo look upon as a further rebuke of Divine Providence. And by all, I do humbly own this day before the Lord and his People, that God has been righteouſly ſpitting in my face, *Numb.*

---

[77] This flatly contradiᴄts thoſe who have charged all to the Devil.

xii. 14. And I defire to lye low under all this reproach, and to lay my hand on my mouth.

[58] 4. As to the management of thefe Myf-teries, as far as concerns myfelf, I am very defi-rous upon further light to own any errors I have therein fallen into, and can come to a difcerning of; in the mean while I do acknowledge upon after-confiderations, that were the fame troubles again, (which the Lord of his rich mercy fore-ver prevent) I fhould not agree with my former apprehenfions in all points. As for Inftance,

1. I queftion not but God fometimes fuffers the Devil, as of late, to afflict in fhape of not only Innocent, but Pious perfons, or fo to delude the Senfes of the afflicted, that they ftrongly con-ceit their hurt is from fuch perfons, when indeed it is not.

2. The improving of one afflicted to inquire by who afflicts the other, I fear may be, and has been unlawfully ufed to Satan's great Advantage.

3. As to my writing, it was put upon me by Authority, and therein I have been very careful to avoid the wronging of any.

4. As to my Oath I never meant it, nor do I know how it can be otherwife conftrued, than as vulgarly, and every one underftood, yea, and upon inquiry it may be found fo worded alfo.

5. As to any paffage in preaching, or praying in the fore hour of diftrefs and darknefs, I always intended but due Juftice on each hand, and that not according to Men but God; who knows all

things moſt perfectly; however through weakneſs, or ſore exerciſe, I might ſometimes, yea and
poſſibly ſundry times unadviſedly expreſs myſelf.

6. As to ſeveral that have confeſſed againſt
themſelves, they being wholly ſtrangers to me,
but yet of good account with better Men than
myſelf, to whom alſo they are well known, I do
not paſs ſo much as a ſecret condemnation upon
them. But rather ſeeing God hath ſo amazingly
lengthened out Satan's Chain, in this moſt formidable outrage, I much more incline to ſide
with the Opinion of thoſe that have grounds to
hope better of them.

7. As to all that have unduly ſuffered in theſe
matters, either in their Perſons or Relations,
through the clouds of human weakneſs, and Satan's wiles and ſophiſtry, I do truly ſympathize
with them, taking it for granted, that ſuch as
know themſelves clear of this great tranſgreſſion,
or that have ſufficient grounds ſo to look upon
their dear Friends, have hereby been under thoſe
ſore tryals and temptations, that not an ordinary
meaſure of true grace would be ſufficient to prevent a bewraying of remaining corruption.

8. I am very much in the mind, and abundantly perſwaded that God for holy ends (though
for what in particular, is beſt known to himſelf)
has ſuffered the Evil Angels to delude us on both
hands; but how far on the one ſide, or the other,
is much above me to ſay, and if we cannot recon-
cile till we come to a full diſcerning of theſe

things, I fear we fhall never come to an agreement, or at fooneft not in this World.

[59] Therefore in fine, the matter being fo dark and perplexed, as that there is no prefent appearance, that all God's Servants fhould be altogether of one mind in all circumftances, touching the fame; I do moft heartily, fervently, and humbly befeech pardon of the merciful God, through the Blood of Chrift for all my· miftakes and trefpaffes in fo weighty a matter. And alfo all your forgivenefs of every offence, in this or other affairs, wherein you fee or conceived that I have erred and offended, profeffing in the prefence of the Almighty God, that what I have done has been as for fubftance as I apprehended was [my] duty, however thro' weaknefs, Ignorance, &c. I may have been miftaken. I alfo thro' grace promifing each of you the like of me; fo again I beg, intreat, and befeech you, that Satan, the Devil, the roaring Lion, the old Dragon, the Enemy of all Righteoufnefs, may no longer be ferved by us, by our Envy and Strifes, where every evil work prevails whilft thefe bear fway, *James* iii. 14, 15, 16. But that all from this day forward may be covered with the mantle of love, and we may on all hands forgive each other heartily, fincerely and thoroughly, as we do hope and pray, that God for Chrift's fake would forgive each of ourfelves, *Mat.* xviii. 21. to the end. *Colof.* iii. 12, 13. *Put on therefore (as the elect of God, holy and beloved) bowels of mercies, kindnefs,*

Y

*humblene∫s of mind, meekne∫s, long-∫uffering; For-
bearing one another, and forgiving one another, if
any man have a quarrel again∫t any, even as Chri∫t
forgave you, ∫o al∫o do ye.* Eph. iv. 31, 32. *Let
all bitterne∫s, and anger, and clamour, and evil-
∫peaking be put away from you with all malice.
And be ye kind one to another, tender-hearted, forgiving one another, even as God for Chri∫t's ∫ake,
hath forgiven you.* Amen. Amen.

Samuel Parris.

Given to the Di∫∫enting Brethren, for their con-
∫ideration of, at their reque∫t. *Nov.* 26, 1694.

*The Elders and Me∫∫engers of the churches
met at* Salem *Village,* April 3, 1695, *to
con∫ider and determine what is to be done,
for the compo∫ure of the pre∫ent unhappy
differences in that place. After ∫olemn
invocation of God in Chri∫t for his di-
re&ion, do unanimou∫ly declare, as followeth,* viz.

1. WE judge that all be it in the late and dark
time of the confu∫ions, wherein Satan
had obtained a more than ordinary liberty, to
be ∫ifting of this Plantation, there were ∫undry unwarrantable, and uncomfortable ∫teps, taken by
Mr. *Samuel Parris,* the Pa∫tor of the Church in
Salem Village, then under the hurrying di∫tra&ions

of amazing Afflictions; yet the said Mr. *Parris,*
by the good hand of God brought unto a better
sense of things, hath so fully expreſt it, that a
Chriſtian charity may and ſhould receive satisfaction therewith.

[60] 2. Inaſmuch as diverſe Chriſtian Brethren, in the Church of *Salem* Village, have been
offended at Mr. *Parris,* for his conduct in the
time of their difficulties, which have diſtreſſed
them; we now adviſe them Charitably to accept
the ſatisfaction which he hath tendered in his
Chriſtian acknowledgment of the Errors therein
committed; yea to endeavour, as far as it is poſſible, the fulleſt reconciliation of their minds unto
Communion with him, in the whole Exerciſe of
his Miniſtry, and with the reſt of the Church,
Matt. vi. 12, 14.   *Luke* xvii. 3.   *James* v. 16.

3. Conſidering the extream tryals and troubles,
which the diſſatisfied Brethren in the Church of
Salem Village have undergone, in the day of ſore
temptation, which hath been upon them; we
cannot but adviſe the Church to treat them with
bowels of much compaſſion, inſtead of all more
critical, or rigorous proceedings againſt them for
the Infirmities diſcovered by them, in ſuch an
heart-breaking day; and if after a patient waiting
for it, the ſaid Brethren cannot ſo far overcome
the uneaſineſs of their Spirits, in the remembrance
of the diſaſters that have hapned, as to ſit under
his Miniſtry; we adviſe the Church with all
tenderneſs to grant them admiſſion to any other

Society of the Faithful, whereunto they may be defired to be difmift. *Gal.* vi. 1, 2. *Pfal.* ciii. 13, 14. *Job* xix. 21.

4. Mr. *Parris* having (as we underftand) with much fidelity and integrity acquitted himfelf, in the main courfe of his Miniftry, fince he hath been Paftor of the Church of *Salem* Village; about his firft call whereunto, we look upon all conteftations now to be both unreafonable and unfeafonable: And our Lord having made him a bleffing to the Souls of not a few, both old and young in this place, we advife that he be accordingly refpected, honour'd and fupported, with all the regards that are due to a painful Minifter of the gofpel.   1 *Thef.* v. 12, 13.   1 *Tim.* v. 17.

5. Having obferved that there is in *Salem* Village, a Spirit full of contention and animofity, too fadly verifying the blemifh which hath heretofore lain upon them: And that fome complaints againft Mr. *Parris* have been either caufelefs, or groundlefs, or unduly aggravated; we do in the name and fear of the Lord folemnly warn them to confider, whether if they continue to devour one another it will not be bitternefs in the latter end, and beware left the Lord be provoked thereby utterly to deprive them of thofe (which they fhould count) their precious and pleafant things, and abandon them to all the defolations of a People that fin away the Mercies of the Gofpel. *James* iii. 16.   *Gal.* v. 15.   2 *Sam.* ii. 26.   *Ifa.* v. 45.   *Mat.* xxi. 43.

6. If the Diſtempers in *Salem* Village ſhould be (which God forbid) ſo. incurable, that Mr. *Parris* after all find that he cannot with any comfort and ſervice continue in his preſent Station, his removal from thence will [61] not expoſe him to any hard Charaſter with us; nor we hope with the reſt of the People of God, among whom we live. *Matt.* x. 14. *Acts* xxii. 18. All which advice we follow, with our Prayers that the God of Peace would bruiſe Satan under our Feet; now the Lord of Peace himſelf give you Peace always by all means.

Joſ. Bridgham,[79]	*John Walley,*	*Samuel Phillips,*
Samuel Chickley,	*Jer. Dummer,*	*James Allen,*
William Tory,	*Neh. Jewitt,*	*Samuel Tory,*
Joſ. Boynton,	*Ephr. Hunt,*	*Samuel Willard,*
Richard Middle-	*Nath. Williams,*	*Edward Paiſon,*
cutt,	*Incr. Mather,*	*Cotton Mather.*

[79] Joſeph Bridgham was probably the Son of Henry, of Dorcheſter, and afterwards of Boſton, born in 1651. He was a Member of the Artillery Company, Repreſentative, and in other Walks a prominent Man. He died about 1709. Samuel *Checkley* was the Miniſter of the New South Church, Boſton. Jeremiah Dummer was the well known Author, the *Defence of the New England Charters.* Nehemiah *Jewett,* I ſuppoſe, was of Ipſwich, a Repreſentative, and, at one Time, Speaker of the Houſe, and died about 1720. James Allen was Miniſter of the Firſt Church, Boſton. Samuel *Torrey* was Miniſter of Weymouth, and died in 1707. William *Torrey* was alſo of Weymouth, and Brother of the Rev. Samuel. Joſeph Boynton was of Rowley. Richard *Middlecott* was of Boſton. John Walley was probably the Major Walley who ſhared the Diſgrace of the ill adviſed and iller executed Expedition againſt Canada, under Sir William Phips. Hunt was another of Phips's Colonels, &c., was of Weymouth, and died 1713. Williams was probably the *Nathaniel* Williams, of Boſton, a Commiſſary in Philip's War. *Samuel* Phillips

To the Reverend Elders of the Three Churches of Chrift, at *Bofton*, with others the Elders and Brethren of other Churches, late of a Council at *Salem* Village.

WE *whofe Names are hereunto Subfcribed, are bold once more to trouble you with our humble Propofals. That whereas there has been long and uncomfortable differences among us, chiefly relating to Mr.* Parris ; *and we having, as we apprehend, attended all probable means for a compofure of our troubles ; and whereas we had hopes of an happy Iffue, by your endeavors among us, but now are utterly fruftrated of our Expectations, and that inftead of uniting, our rent is made worfe, and our breach made wider.*

We humbly Query, *Whether yourfelves being ftreightned of time, might not omit fuch fatisfactory liberty of debating the whole of our Controverfie ; whereby yourfelves had not fo large an opportunity of underftanding the Cafe ; nor the offended fo much reafon to be fatisfied in your advice : We therefore humbly propofe, and give full liberty of proving and defending of what may be charged on either hand,*

was the Minifter of Rowley, perhaps, who died in 1696. *Samuel* Willard, of the Old South, Author of *A Body of Divinity*, and other theological Work, Vice-Prefident of Harvard College, &c.; he died in 1707. See Note *ante.* *Edward* Payfon was Minifter of Rowley, and was Father of feventeen Children, and died 1732.

leaving it to yourfelves to appoint both time and place.

   1. *That if yourfelves pleafe to take the trouble with patience once more to hear the whole Cafe.*

   2. *Or that you will more plainly advife Mr.* Parris, *(the Cafe being fo circumftanced, that he cannot with comfort or profit, to himfelf, or others, abide in the Work of the Miniftry among us) to ceafe his labours, and feek to difpofe himfelf elfewhere, as God in his Providence may direct: and that yourfelves would pleafe to help us in advifing to fuch a choice, wherein we may be more unanimous; which we hope would tend much to a compofure of our differences.*

   3. *Or, that we may without any offence take the liberty of calling fome other proved Minifter of the Gofpel, to Preach the Word of God to us and ours:* [62] *and that we may not be denied our proportionable privilege, in our publick difburfments in the place.*

So leaving the whole case with the Lord and yourfelves, we Subfcribe our Names. Signed by 16 young Men, from 16 upwards; and 52 Houfholders, and 18 Church Members. This was delivered to the Minifters, *May* 3, 1695.[80]

---

[80] Whether the Original manufcript of this Paper is in exiftence I have not learned. The Names of the Signers would be of much intereft at this Time, and the Hiftorian of Salem fhould not ceafe his Labours until it is found, if anywhere preferved.

The Copy of a Paper that was handed about touching thofe Differences.

AS to the conteft between Mr. *Parris* and his Hearers, &c. it may be compofed by a Satisfactory Anfwer, to *Levit.* xx. 6. *And the Soul that turneth after fuch as have familiar Spirits, and after Wizzards, to go a whoring after them, I will even fet my face againft that Soul; and will cut him off from among his People.* 1 Chron. x. 13, 14. *So* Saul *died for his tranfgreffion, which he committed againft the Lord, even againft the word of the Lord, which he kept not, and alfo for afking Counfil of one that had a familiar Spirit to inquire of it. And inquired not of the Lord, therefore he flew him, &c.*[81]

---

[81] One who was as firm a Believer as Dr. Mather in Witch Myfteries, remarks in Juftification of what was done—"That I may fatisfy fuch as are not refolved to the Contrary; that there may be (and are) fuch Operations of the Powers of Darknefs on the Bodies and Minds of Mankind; by Divine Permiffion; and that thofe who fate Judges in thofe Cafes, may by the ferious Confideration of the formidable Afpect and perplexed Circumftances, of that Afflictive Providence; be in fome meafure excufed; or at leaft be lefs cenfured, for paffing Sentence on feveral Perfons, as being the Inftruments of *Satan* in thofe Diabolical Operations, when they were involved in fuch a Dark and Difmal fcene of Providence, in which *Satan* did feem to Spin a finer Thred of Spiritual Wickednefs than in the ordinary methods of Witchcraft; hence the Judges defiring to bear due Teftimony, againft fuch Diabolical Practices, were inclined to admit the validity of fuch a fort of Evidence, as was not fo clearly and directly demonftrable to Human Senfes, as in other Cafes is required or elfe they could not difcover the Myfteries of Witchcraft; I prefume not to impofe upon my *Chriftian* or *Learned* Reader; any opinion of mine, how far *Satan* was an Inftrument in God's Hand, in thofe

Some part of the Determination of the
Elders and Meſſengers of the Churches,
met at *Salem* Village, *April* 3, 1695,
relating to the Differences there.

IF *the Diſtemper in* Salem *Village ſhould be* (which
God forbid) *ſo incurable that Mr.* Parris *after
all, find that he cannot with any comfort and ſervice
continue in this preſent ſtation, his removal from
thence will not expoſe him to any hard Character
with us* (*nor we hope*) *with the reſt of the People of
God, among whom we live,* Mat. x. 14. And whoſo-
ever ſhall not receive you, nor hear your words;
when you depart out of that houſe, or city, ſhake
off the duſt of your feet, *&c.* Acts xxii. 18.
*All which Advice we follow with our Prayers,
that the God of Peace would bruiſe Satan under our
feet, Now the Lord of Peace give you Peace always, by all means,* &c.

Queſt. Whether Mr. *Parris* his going to *Abi-*

---

amazing Afflictions, which were on
many Perſons there, [at Salem]
about that time; but I am certainly
convinced, that the Great GOD was
pleaſed to lengthen his Chain to a
very great Degree, for the hurting
of *Some* and reproaching of *Others*,
as far as he was permitted to do
ſo."—Lawſon, *pages* 93-4.

From this Author's uncertain
view of the Operations of the
Devil (which was the View of a
great majority of the World), it is

not at all ſtrange that ſome among
the very Conſcientious people inquired as to the Difference between
the Malignant and Supreme Power;
that is, if the Supreme controlled
the Malignant, there was no queſtion to whom the Conſequences
were to be charged; and hence
it is in no wiſe to be wondered
at that ſome in their Simplicity
could not underſtand what uſe there
was for any Devil at all, mutch leſs
for Witches.

Z

gail Williams[82] (and others) whom he ſuppoſed to have a Spectral ſight (to be informed who were Witches and who afflicted thoſe pretended ſufferers by Witchcraft) in order to their being queſtioned upon their lives for it, were not a turning after ſuch as had familiar Spirits; and a greater wickedneſs than *Saul* was guilty of (in that he did not intend thereby bodily hurt to any others.)

And whether in a crime of ſuch a high nature, the making a ſlender and general confeſſion, without any propoſals of reparations, or due time of probation, ought ſo far to be accounted ſufficient, · from ſuch a Paſtor to his People.

[63] And whether ſuch as were accuſed, or the ſurviving Friends and Relations of thoſe that were any ways ſufferers, by Accuſations ſo by him proved, are in duty and conſcience bound to continue their reſpect, honour and ſupport to him, in the Miniſtry, after ſuch known departures from the Rule of Gods word, and ·after ſuch dire effects as followed thereupon, under the penalty *of the duſt ſhaken from his feet*, teſtifying againſt them, even ſo as to render them in a worſe caſe than thoſe of *Sodom* and *Gomorrah*.

82 Mr. Lawſon ſays ſhe was "about twelve Years of Age."— *Brief and True Nar.*, P. 3. Much more concerning her will be found.

To the Honourable Wait Winthrop,[83] Eliſha Cook,[84] *and* Samuel Sewall, *Eſquires, Arbitrators indifferently choſen, between Mr.* Samuel Parris, *and the inhabitants of* Salem *Village.*

THE Remonſtrances of ſeveral aggrieved perſons in the ſaid Village, with further reaſons why they conceive they ought not to hear Mr. *Parris,* nor to own him as a Miniſter of the Goſpel, nor to contribute any ſupport to him as ſuch, for ſeveral Years paſt; humbly offered as fit for conſideration.

We humbly conceive that having in *April* 1693, given our Reaſons why we could not join with Mr. *Parris* in Prayer, Preaching, or Sacraments. If theſe Reaſons are found ſufficient for our withdrawing, (and we cannot yet find but they are) Then we conceive ourſelves virtually diſcharged, not only in Conſcience, but alſo in Law; which requires maintenance to be given to ſuch as are Orthodox, and blameleſs. The ſaid Mr. *Parris* having been teaching ſuch dangerous Errors, and preached ſuch ſcandalous Immoralities, as ought

---

[83] *Wait Still* was his full Name. He was Son of Gov. John Winthrop, of Connecticut; died in Boſton about 1717.

[84] Mr. Cook was one of the very diſtinguiſhed Men of the Period under Notice. He wrote his Name *Cooke,* I need only refer to Allen's *Biographical Dictionary* and the *Hiſt. and Antiq's of Boſton* for an Account of him. He agreed with Mr. Calef about the New Charter.

to difcharge any (tho ever fo gifted otherways) from the work of the Miniftry.

Particularly in his Oath againft the lives of feveral, wherein he fwears that the Prifoners with their looks knock down thofe pretended fufferers. We humbly conceive, that he that Swears to more than he is certain of, is equally guilty of Perjury, with him that Swears to what is falfe. And tho they did fall at fuch a time, yet it could not be known that they did it, much lefs could they be certain of it; yet did Swear pofitively againft the lives of fuch, as he could not have any knowledge but they might be Innocent.

His believing the Devil's Accufations, and readily departing from all Charity to perfons, tho of blamelefs and godly lives, upon fuch fuggeftions, his promoting fuch Accufations, as alfo his partiality therein, in ftifling the Accufation of fome, and the fame time vigilantly promoting others; as we conceive are juft caufes for our refufal, &c.

That Mr. *Parris's* going to *Mary Walcut*,[85] or *Abigail Williams*, and directing others to them, to know who afflicted the People in their illneffes; [64] we underftand this to be a dealing with them that have a familiar fpirit, and an implicit denying the providence of God, which alone, as we believe, can fend Afflictions, or caufe Devils to Afflict any; this we alfo conceive fufficient to juftifie fuch refufal.

---

[85] She was a Daughter, I fuppofe, of Jonathan Walcut, by Wife Mary, Daughter of John Sibley. Walcut was an early Salem Family, fome of whom went to Rhode Ifland, where Defcendants are yet found.

. That Mr. *Parris* by thefe Practices and Principles, has been the beginner and procurer of the foreſt Afflictions, not to this Village only, but to this whole Country, that did ever befal them.

We the Subſcribers, in behalf of ourſelves, and of feveral others of the fame mind with us (touching thefe things) having fome of us had our Relations by thefe practices taken off by an untimely Death; others have been impriſoned, and ſuffered in our Perſons, Reputations, and Eſtates; ſubmit the whole to your Honours deciſion, to determine whether we are or ought to be any ways obliged to honour, refpect and ſupport fuch an Inſtrument of our miſeries; praying God to guide your Honours, to act herein, as may be for his Glory, and the future ſettlement of our Village, in Amity and Unity.

> JOHN TARBALL,[86]
> SAMUEL NURSE, ⎱ Attornies for the people
> Jos. PUTNAM, ⎰ of the Village.
> DAN. ANDREW,

Boſton, July 21, 1697.

According to the order of the aforeſaid arbitrators, the faid Mr. *Parris*, had fome of his arrears paid him, as alfo a fum of money for his repairs of the miniſterial houſe of the faid Village, and is difmiſſed therefrom.

---

[86] Tarball and Nurſe are the fame mentioned at Note 77. The others will be noticed onward, in the Account of the Trials.

PART IV.

A Letter of a Gentleman [87] *endeavouring to prove the received Opinions about Witchcraft.*

SIR,

I Told you, I had fome thoughts concerning Witchcraft, and an Intention of conferring with the Gentleman, [88] who has publifhed feveral Treatifes about Witchcraft, and perfons afflicted by them, lately here in *New-England;* but fince you have put thofe three Books into my hands, I find myfelf engaged in a very hard Province, to give you my opinion of them. I plainly forefee, that fhould this fcribling of mine come to [65] publick view, it would difpleafe all Parties, but that

---

[87] The only Mention of the Author of thefe Letters I have met with is contained in the Anfwer to the *More Wonders*, by Dr. Mather, and is in this Paffage : "The *Antifcriptural Doctrines* efpoufed by this Man [Calef] do alfo call for no *further Anfwer ;* for a certain *Scotchman* (one Stuart) of no very great Circumftances, aboard one of our Frigates then in our Harbour, fent him *Two Letters,* which he has been fo filly as to infert in his wretched Volume." This " one Stuart" was, perhaps, Chaplain on board the Man-of-war. The Doctor thinks Mr. Calef was very filly to print the Letters, becaufe they were, in his Judgment, a complete Vindication of Witchcraft. Mr. Calef was willing all fhould be faid on that fide that could be faid. He felt fully convinced that,

" Falfehoods which we fpurn To-day
    Were the Truths of Long-ago ;
Let the dead Bough fall away,
    Frefher fhall the living grow."
                                   WHITTIER.

[88] Doctor Mather.

is the leaft; moreover it is fo far out of my Road
to fet my thoughts to confider a matter on every
fide, which in itfelf is fo abftruce, and every ftep
I advance therein, if I mifs truth (which is a
narrow and undivided line) I muft tumble down
headlong into the Gulph of dangerous error; yet
notwithftanding I have forced myfelf to fend
thefe few lines, if fo be I may clear to you a
truth, you now feem to be offended at, becaufe
of the ill confequences, which (you think) lately
have and again may be drawn from it, by the ill
conduct of fome Men. I am not ignorant that
the pious frauds of the Ancient, and the inbred
fire (I do not call it pride) of many of our
Modern Divines have precipitated them to propagate, and maintain truth as well as falfehood, in
fuch an unfair manner, as has given advantage to
the Enemy, to fufpect the whole Doctrine, thefe
Men have profeft to be nothing but a meer trick.
But it is certain, that as no lover of truth will
juftifie an Illegitimate Corollary, tho drawn from
a true Propofition; fo neither will he reject a
truth, becaufe fome or many Men take unfair
mediums to prove it, or draw falfe confequences
from it: The many Herefies among Chriftians,
muft not give a mortal wound to the Effence of
the Chriftian Religion; neither muft any one
Chriftian Doctrine be exterminated, becaufe Evil
Men make ufe of it, as a Cloak to cover their
own felf-ends; particularly, becaufe fome men
perhaps among all forts of Chriftians, have under

pretence of Witchcraft coloured their own Malice, Pride and Popularity; we muſt not therefore conclude (firſt) that there are no Witches (2.) or that Witches cannot be Convicted by ſuch clear and undeniable proof, as the Law of God requires in the caſe of Death (3.) Or that a Witch ſo Convicted ought not to be put to death.   1. That there are Witches is manfeſt from the precept of *Moſes, Thou ſhalt not ſuffer a Witch to live.* Exod. xxii. 18. for it is certain God would not have given a vain and unintelligible Law, as this muſt be of putting Witches to death, if there are no Witches.   But you object that this doth not anſwer our Caſe, for we have formed another Idea of Witches than what can be gathered from Scriptures; you quote four places, *viz. Deut.* xiii. *Mat.* xxiv. *Acts* xiii. 2. *Tim.* iii. from all which you infer that Witchcraft is a maligning and oppugning the Word, Works and Worſhip of God; and by an extraordinary ſign, ſeeking to ſeduce any from it, and this you readily grant. But then you ſay, What is this to Witches now a days? who are ſaid to have made an explicit Covenant with the Devil, and to be impowered by him, to the doing of things ſtrange in themſelves, and beſides their natural courſe.   This you ſay does not follow, and herein indeed conſiſts the whole Controverſie.   Therefore it is neceſſary, that firſt of all we clear this point, laying aſide thoſe prejudices we may have from the fatal application of this Doctrine, [66] to ſome (who

were in your judgment) really at leaft in Law,
and before Men Innocent. In a word, we are
feeking after truth, and truth fhall and will be
truth, in fpite of Men and Devils. I do not
repeat this caution to foreftall you, to believe the
Doctrine of Witchcraft, as it is above defined,
without inquiring into the reafon and truth of it;
only I defire you to enquire into it, as a thing
doubtful. For no Man can be certain of a Negative, unlefs either the Affirmative imply a contradiction, or he can prove it by certain teftimony,
to neither of which you pretend; only you alledge it cannot be proved by Scripture, *i. e.* you
cannot prove it, nor have feen it proved by any
other you have read on that Subject. I am not
fo vain as to think I can do better than the learned
Authors you have confulted with (though I know
not what they have done, for I had no other
Book but the Bible, to make ufe of on this occafion;) but becaufe I am fatisfied myfelf, I am
willing to communicate my Reafons, which I
divide into Three heads. 1. The appearance of
Angels. 2. The nature of Poffeffion. 3 and the
fcripture notion of Witchcraft. 1. Good Angels
did appear to *Abraham,* and did eat, *Gen.* xv. it
feems he wafh'd their Feet, it is certain he faw
and heard them, therefore there is no impoffibility
in Angels being converfant with men. God is
true, and whatever is contained in Sacred Writ is
true; if we poor fhallow Mortals do not comprehend the manner how, that argues only our

Aa

weaknefs and ignorance in this dark Prifon of
Flefh, wherein we are inclofed, during our abode
in this vale of mifery, but doth not in the leaft
infringe the verity of the Scripture; it is fufficient
that we undoubtedly know they have appeared
unto Men in bodily fhape, and done their Errand
they were fent on from God. Now if good Angels have appeared, why may not bad? Surely
the Devils, becaufe fallen and Evil, have not
therefore loft the Nature of Angels, neither is
there any contradiction in their appearing in a
bodily fhape, now after any more than before
their Fall. But you will fay you muft allow of
the appearances of Good Angels, becaufe of the
Scripture teftimony; but not of bad, feeing there
is no place of Scripture that clearly proves it.
Mat. 4. The words in the Gofpel do as plainly
fignifie the Devils outward appearance to our
Saviour, when he was tempted, as can be exprefs'd, *and when the tempter came to him he faid—
but he anfwered*—the fame form St. *Luke* ufeth
to fignifie the appearance of *Mofes* and *Elias,* in
the transfiguration, *And behold there talked with
him two men:* for what follows, ver. 31, *who appeared* is ufed to fignifie (not their appearance,
but) the manner of their appearance· *in great
Glory.* But you'l urge that 'tis very eafie to be
underftood, that *Mofes* and *Elias* did appear, becaufe they had human bodies; but that it is unintelligible to you, how the Devil being a Spirit
can appear, a Spirit, *i. e.* a fubftance void of all

dimenfions; therefore the words in [67] the
Hiftory muft not be taken in a literal Senfe.
Do not miftake; tho fome Philofophers are of
opinion (which whether true or falfe, is all one
to our prefent Argument) that a Spirits fubftance
is extended, and hath befides length, breadth and
depth, a fourth dimenfion, *viz.* effential fpiffitude;
yet the fame do not fay, that pure fubftance is
perceptible by our bodily fenfes; on the contrary,
they tell us, that Spirits are cloathed with vehi-
cles, *i. e.* they are united to certain portions of
matter, which they inform, move and actuate.
Now this we muft not reject as impoffible, becaufe we cannot comprehend the formal reafon,
how a Spirit acts upon matter : For who can give
the Reafon, that upon the Volition of the human
Soul, the Hand fhould be lifted up, or any ways
moved? for to fay the Contraction of the Muf-
cles is the Mechanick caufe of voluntary motion,
is not to folve the Queftion which recurs, why
upon Volition fhould that Contraction enfue
which caufes that motion? all that I know the
wifeft Man ever faid upon this head, is, that it is
the will of the Creator; who hath ordered fuch a
fpecies of thinking Creatures, by a Catholick Law
to be united to fuch portions of matter, fo and
fo difpofed, or, if you will in the vulgar Phrafe,
to Organiz'd bodies, and that there fhould be
between them and the feveral bodies, they are
united to, a mutual re-action and paffion :   Now
you fee how little we know of the reafon, of that

which is moſt near to us, and moſt certain, *viz.*
The Souls informing the Body, yet you would
think it a bad Argument, if one ſhould, as ſome
have done, include from this our Ignorance, that
there was nothing in us but matter, it is no otherways to deny a Spirits acting a Vehicle. The
plaineſt and moſt certain things when denied are
hardeſt to be proved, therefore the Axiom ſaith
well, *contra principa, &c.* There are ſome certain truths which are rather to be explained to
young beginners than proved, upon which yet all
Science is built, as every whole is more than his
part, and of this ſort I take theſe two following.
1. That there are two ſubſtances, *Corpus* & *Mens,*
Body and Spirit, altogether different, for the Ideas
we have of them are quite diſtinct. 2. That a
Spirit can Actuate, Animate, or inform a certain
portion of matter, and be united to it: from
whence it is very evident, that the Devil united
to a portion of matter (which hereafter I'll call a
Vehicle) may fall under the cognizance of our
.Senſes, and be converſant with us in a bodily
ſhape. Where then is the reaſon or need to run
to a Metaphorical, and forced Interpretation,
when the words are ſo plain, and the literal ſenſe.
implieth no contradiction, nor any greater difficulty than (as has been ſaid) what ariſeth from
the Union of the Soul and Body, which is moſt
certain. Now after all to ſay, God *will not* permit the Devil ſo to appear, is to beg the queſtion
without ſaying any thing to the preceeding Ar-

gument, and it is againſt the ſenſe of almoſt all
mankind; [68] for in all Ages, and all places
there have been many Witneſſes of the appearances of *Dæmons*, all of whom that taught any
thing contrary to the right Worſhip of the true
God, were certainly evil ones: and it were moſt
preſumptuous, barely to aſſert that all theſe witneſſes were always deceived, and it is impoſſible
they could all agree to deceive. 2. We come to
conſider the nature of Poſſeſſion. The Man
poſſeſt, *Luk.* viii. 27. had a Power more than
Natural, for he break the bands, which he could
not have done by his own ſtrength: Now from
whom had he this Power? The Scripture ſaith,
he had Devils along time, and oftentimes it had
caught him, *&c.* he was kept bound with Chains
and in Fetters, and he break the bands, and was
driven of the Devil into the Wilderneſs; this
Power then was immediately from the Devil,
and whatſoever poſſeſſed perſons does, or ſuffers
things beyond his natural power; he is inabled
by the *Dæmon* ſo to do: or to ſpeak more properly, it is the *Dæemon* who acteth the ſame, as is
plain from St. *Mark's* Relation of this paſſage, v.
5. 2. A Man with an unclean Spirit, v. 3. 2.
and no Man could bind him, no, not with Chains,
6. v. but when he ſaw Jeſus afar off he ran and
worſhiped him, and the ſame He. v. 7. ſaid I
adjure thee by God that thou torment me not,
and *v.* 10. My name is *Legion*, for we are many,
v. 11. and he beſought him much, that he would

not fend *them* away out of the Countrey : it is
manifeft from hence, that it was not the poor
Man who was poffeft, but the Devils who poffeffed him, by whom the Chains had been pluck'd
afunder, and the Fetters broken in pieces ; now
here is Divine teftimony, that the Devils have
actuated a Humane body to the doing of things
beyond the Natural ftrength of that Body, as it
was fimply united to its humane Soul ; how much
more then can the Devil actuate any other proportion of fimple Matter, Earth, Air, Fire or
Water ; and make it a fit organ for himfelf to
act in.

But enough of this already, let us rather enquire
how the Devil enters into the body of the poffeſt, to
move it at his pleafure ; this I think he cannot do
as a meer Spirit, or by any never fo ftrict Union
with the Humane Soul, for in that cafe he is only a
tempter or feducer ; and nothing above humane
ftrength can be done : But here there being fome-
thing performed (the bonds broken) by a force which
could not proceed from humane ftrength, it neceffarily
follows that the Devils entered into the poffeft, other-
ways qualified than as a meer Spirit, he did not enter
without fome portion of matter, to which he was
united by the Intermedium whereof he acted upon
and actuated the humane body. Again if it is faid
that the Devil entered as a meer Spirit, and imme-
diately acted upon and moved that body ; it follows
the Devil hath a Vehicle, a certain portion of mat-
ter (that Body) to actuate and difpofe of at will ;

which is abfurd. 1. *Becaufe it afferts what it
feems to deny, viz. the Devils having a Vehicle to
act immediately upon, and to be united to a portion
of matter (as* [69] *has been faid before) is the fame
thing.* 2. *It fights againft the Catholick Law of
the Union of Soul and Body, by which the Omnipotent hath ordained the voluntary motion of a humane
body to depend upon the Will of its humane Soul, and
thofe that are not voluntary to proceed either from
its own Mechanifon, or from material force, hence
we may certainly conclude, that it is by the Inter-
vening of the Devils Vehicle, that he enters into the
Body of the poffeft.   But what if you and I cannot
agree about this Notion of Poffeffion, muft we therefore reject the truth itfelf, and run to a far fetched
and intolerable fenfe of the words : No, our opinions
do not alter the Nature of things, it is certain there
were perfons poffeft, and it is as certain that the
Devil enteed into them, either with or without a
Vehicle, it is all one which part of the contradiction
you take, the confequence is the fame, viz.*

*That the Devil doth act immediately upon matter,
there is another acceptation of the word poffeffion in
Scripture, Acts* xvi. 16, *where one is faid to be
poffeft with a Spirit of Divination,* (πνεῦμα Πύθωνος)
the word commonly ufed to the Prieftefs of Apollo,
*who gave refponfes ; and it feems this Damfel was
fuch an one, for fhe brought her Mafters much Money, or gain by foothfaying.   Now if the Hiftory of
them be true that they were dementea, and knew
not themfelves what they uttered,* donec erant Deo

plenæ, (*as they word it*) *their cafe is not different, but the fame with the foregoing ; but if they under-ftood what they fpoke, then had they familiar Spirits, whereof there is frequent mention made in the* Old Teftament, *and one good* King *is commended for hav-ing cut off them that had fuch, therefore I think the meaning of the word was very obvious in his time, neither was it ever controverted, being joyned with any other name than fpirit Familiar, one of our own Family, that is oft, every day converfant with us, and almoft ever ready upon call to attend us. But the confideration of them, who have familiar Spirits falleth under the head of Witchcraft, which we are to confider in the third place.* 3. *Witchcraft, to inquire into the Scripture Notion of it, and compare whether it be the fame with that above defined ; the Cabaliftick learning would be of great ufe in this fearch, and afford us much light ; there is little doubt but that there are many great truths not commonly known.* (Non eft Religio ubi omnia patent.) *And our Saviour exprefly cautions his Difciples that they do not throw their Pearl be-fore Swine ; therefore it is no wonder that fome Doctrines, tho' unqueftionably true are not fo fully defcribed, becaufe the Authors who treat of them are afraid, left evil Men fhould be the more depraved by being informed ; but I am in no fuch fear ; nor can I give you any other thoughts but what are ob-vious to any Man, from the plain fenfe of the Scrip ture. Our definition we'l divide into two Propofi-tions, and handle them feverally.* 1. *Propofition.*

The Witch is impower'd by the Devil to do things strange in themselves, and beside their natural courfe. 2. Prop. The manner how the Witch is impowered to do thofe ftrange things, is by Explicit Com-[70] paſt, or Covenant with the Devil. For clearing of *the firft, we will confider the four places above cited, wherein a Witch is called a falfe Prophet, a falfe Chrift, a Sorcerer, a refifter of the truth, and is faid to fhew figns to feduce the People to feek after other Gods: whence let us note, 3 things.* 1. *That thofe terms Witch, falfe Chrift, falfe Prophet, and Sorcerer, are all Synonimous; i. e. fignifie the fame thing.* 2. *That a Witch doth do things ftrange in themfelves, and beyond their Natural courfe: for it were moft ridiculous, to alledge that our bleffed Saviour, when he faid,* there fhall arife falfe Chrifts, and fhall fhew great figns and wonders, in fo much that (if it were poffible) they fhould deceive the very Elect *meant that cunning cheats fhould arife and fhew Legerdemain tricks; the words will in no wife bear it, and I believe you are from interpreting them, fo it is manifeft, they fignifie not a feign'd, but a real doing of things, beyond their Natural courfe; therefore the Sorceries of* Elimas[89] *and* Simon *were not fimple delufions, but real effects that could not have been produced by Phyfical caufes in the ordinary courfe of nature.* 3. *That the end of the Witches fhewing thefe figns, is to feduce the People to feek after other Gods, from which premifes*

---

[89] See *Remarkable Providences,* 128, by Dr. I. Mather.

I infer, that the Witches have the power of doing thofe wonders, or ftrange things immediately from the Devil: they are without the reach of Nature, and therefore above humane power, and no meer Man can effect them; the Witch then who does them muft have the power of doing them from another; but who is the other? God will not give his teftimony to a lye, and to fay God did at any time impower a Witch to work wonders to gain belief to the Doctrine of Devils were with one breath to deftroy root and branch of all revealed Religion; no, it cannot be, it is only God's permiffion, who proveth his People, whether they love him with all their heart, and with all their Soul. Therefore the Witch has a power of doing Wonders, or ftrange things immediately from the Devil. 2. Propofit. we'll fubdivide into thefe two. 1. That there is an exprefs Covenant between the Witch and the Devil. 2. That 'tis not reafonable to fuppofe this Covenant to be tranfacted mentally. 1. The Devil cannot communicate this power, by never fo ftrict a Union with the Soul of the Witch; for in that cafe he is only a tempter, and nothing above humane power can be done, as has been already proved; therefore the Devil who improves the Witch to do things above humane power, muft either appear in an External fhape, and inftruct him how, and upon what terms he will inable him to do thofe Wonders; or elfe he muft enter into the body of the Witch and poffefs it. The Demoniacs in the Gofpel are fuch whom the Devils invade, by main force, their Soul having no further command

*of their bodies, which are subjected to the Will of the
Devils; whose end is to wound and torment those
miserable Creatures, to throw them into the fire, and
into the water; but the Witch, who likewise is possessed, is not treated in such an outrageous manner,
his* Dæmon *is tame and familiar unto him, and suf-
fers him for* [71] *a time to live quietly, without any
further molestation, then prompting him to do his
utmost endeavour to withdraw Men from God; he is
not bereaved of his Senses as the poor lunatick, but is
conscious of all he does, and willeth all his crimes, he
receiveth power from the Devil to do wonders, and
doth them to serve the Devils turn. Therefore there
must be a Covenant, an express Covenant between the
Devil and him, viz. that he shall obey the Devil and
serve him, and that the Devil shall both enable him
so to do, and also reward him for so doing; for if
there is no contract between them, How comes the
Witch to know he has a supernatural power? or how
can he so peremptorily pretend to do that which is so
much above his natural power, not knowing he has a
supernatural one inabling him to do the same: There
can be no doubt but there was a very intimate com-
merce between Satan and him; who is call'd by* St.
Paul *thou child of the Devil* (not as other unholy
men) *but in an especial manner, as being the Enemy
of all righteousness, who would not cease to pervert
the right ways of the Lord, it is not to be supposed
that he enter'd into this so near a Relation with Satan, with which he is stigmatized, that others may
beware of him, without his own knowledge and con-*

fent; and is not this a Covenant, an exprefs Cove-
nant on his part to ferve the Devil inceffantly, and
on the Devils to impower him to act his Sorceries
wherewith he bewitched the People; now I think, I
have from Scripture fully fatisfied you of the truth
of what I offered, in a Difcourfe at ―― but fince
you have told me an Explicit Covenant with the
Devil, fignifying the Devil's appearing in a bodily
fhape to the Witch, and their figning an exprefs
Covenant, which you fay cannot be proved from
Scripture. It were moft unreafonable to imagine
that the ceremonies of this hellifh myftery are parti-
cularly fet down in the word of God; therefore we
muft gather by Analogy and Reafon the manner how
this exprefs Covenant is tranfacted: and to that
end I'le fet down thefe following Confiderations.

1. Under the Law God did ordain his People
in all their matters to have recourfe immediately
to himfelf, and depend upon him for Counfil,
which they were ready to obey, with full affur-
ance of aid and protection from him againft their
Enemies; this the Devil imitateth by setting up
of Oracles among the Heathen, to which all
the Kings, Nations, and mighty Conquerors,
upon Earth did come, and paid their humbleft
adoration to the God (as the Devil blafphemoufly
call'd himfelf) of the Temple, in which they
were imploring his direction and affiftance in
their doubtful and profperous affairs. Again,
God inftituted Sacrifices to put Men in mind of
their duty to their Creator, to whom they owe

all things, even themfelves ; but the Devil is not contented with the bare imitation hereof; the acknowledgment and worfhip he receiveth from the deluded World is not enough, tho' they offer up unto him innumerable Hecatombs, unlefs they caufe their Children to pafs through the [72] fire unto him, to whom no facrifice is fo well pleafing as that of humane blood.   And there is no reafon to think, that now under the Œconomy of the Gofpel, the Devil hath left off to vie with God, and thereby to enfnare Men.   No, it is rather to be feared that his Kingdom doth now more prevail, for by how much the light is greater ; fo much greater is their condemnation, who do not receive it : it is reafonable to fuppofe that (seeing the Son of God, when he came to tranfact with Men, the wonderful Covenant of their Redemption, took upon him their Nature, and was perfect Man) the Devil likewife doth counterfeit the fame, in appearing in an humane fhape to them, who receive him, and confederate themfelves with him, and become his Vaffals.

2. Confider, It is not probable that thofe falfe Apoftles mention'd, 2 *Cor*. xi. 13. erred only in Ceremonies or Circumftances, or that their Errors, tho' great, did proceed rather from their Ignorance, than from the perverfenefs of their minds. 1 *Cor*. iii. 15.   For, for fuch we may have charity and hope, that God will be merciful unto them, if they fincerely do the beft they know, tho' they diffent in fome, nay many things,

from the practices and belief of the Chriftian
Church; but thofe St. *Paul* threatens with a
heavy curfe, that their end fhall be according to
their works; therefore it feems they immediately
ftruck at the very root and being of the Chriftian
Religion, and were the fame with them fpoken
of, 2 *Tim.* iii. 6. but with this difference, that
they did not refift, but beholding the Miracles
and Signs which were done by the true Apoftle
of our Lord, wondered and believed alfo, and
were Baptized; yet being Sorcerers they were
unwilling to lofe that great efteem they had obtained; as it is related of *Simon*, who had bewitched the People of *Samaria*, giving out that
he himfelf was fome great one, to whom they all
gave heed, from the leaft to the greateft, faying,
this Man is the great Power of God, therefore
he could not brook that *Peter* or *John* fhould
have a greater Power than himfelf; but offered
them Money, that on whomfoever he laid hands,
he (that perfon) fhould receive the Holy Ghoft;
which fhews him, who thus defigned to make
Merchandize of the B. Spirit, tho' Baptized, to
have been no true believer, but ftill a Sorcerer in
the Gall of bitternefs, and in the bond of Iniquity; fuch were thofe deceitful workers, who
not being able barefaced to refift, did put on
Chriftianity as a Mafk, that they might under-
mine the truth, and introduce the Doctrines of
Devils. *Samaria* and *Paphos*, were not the only
two places where the Devil had fuch Agents,

there was no part of the Earth where his Kingdom was not Eftablifhed, and where he had not
his Emiffaries before the preaching of the Gofpel; and fince the Text telleth us he hath his
Minifters, who do imitate their Mafter, by being
transformed into the Apoftles of Chrift, as he
himfelf is transformed into an [73] Angel of
light: whofe defign in being thus transformed,
cannot be to impofe upon the Almighty; for
whatever fhape he appears in, he cannot hide his
uglinefs from the Eyes of him who is Omnif-
cent, therefore he appeareth thus in the fhape of
an Angel of light, either to tempt and feduce the
bleffed Spirits to rebel againft God, or to enfnare
wicked Men, who by their hainous crimes (being
lovers of themfelves, covetous, boafters, proud
blafphemers were before difpofed to be fit In-
ftrumets to ferve him and to enter into league
with him. Surely I, who am ignorant of the
Laws by which the Intellectual World is gov-
ern'd, dare not affirm that it is impoffible for Satan fo to appear, as to hide his deformities from
the good Angels, and under that vail to tempt
them: But certain I am that it is more confonant
to Reafon, to think that the Apoftles intention
here was to teach that the Devil appear'd as a
glorified Angel unto Men to gain Minifters,
whom he might imbue with the Poyfon of his
Black-Art, and (when he had gotten full poffeffion of them) inftruct them by his own Example
to transform themfelves into the Apoftles of

Chrift, that under that Vizard they might with the greater Advantage promote his ends, and join with him in doing the utmoft defpite to the Spirit of Grace.

3. Confideration, It is againft the Nature of this Covenant, that it fhould be confummated by a mental Colloquy, between the Devil and the Witch. I know not how many Articles it con-fifts of, but it is certain from what has been al-ready proved, that the renouncing of Chrift to be the Son of God, and owning the Devil to be, and worfhipping him as God, are the two chief, to which our Saviour who was accufed of cafting out Devils by Beelzebub (*i. e.*) of being confed-erated with Beelzebub, was tempted to confent : *If thou be the Son of God command that thefe ftones be made bread:* And again, *throw thy felf down from hence, for it is written, he will give his Angels charge over thee; and again all thefe things will I give thee, if thou wilt fall down and worfhip me :* Whence it is evident that here the Devil La-boured to infinuate into our Lord, either to do things rafh and unwarrantable, or to fufpect his Sonfhip, revolt from God his father, and worfhip Satan, that he might obtain the glory of the World. Now it has been already faid, that when Jefus was tempted, the Devil appeared unto him in a bodily fhape; therefore it is agreeable to Reafon, that he doth appear in the fame manner to all them, whom he alfo tempteth to worfhip him ; moreover the form of renouncing a Cove-

nant ought to bear refemblance to the form of entring into the fame Covenant; therefore Men who are received into the Myftical Body of Chrift by God's Minifter, who in God's ftead exprefsly covenanteth with and then Adminiftereth the Sacrament of Baptifm unto them, muft in the like manner go out of, or renounce the faid Covenant; and of them there are [74] two forts, one who through the perverfenefs of their own hearts, the lucre of the world, the fear of Men more than of God, abjure their Saviour, turn Apoftates, Turks, or Pagans; The other fort is of them who do contract with the Devil to be his Subjects, in the imitation of whom, it is not to be fuppofed that the Devil will omit any material Circumftances, which tend both to bring them into and confirm them in his Service. To effect which his outward appearance, when he receives his Catechumens is of greater force than any mental contract, for many wicked men who have denied God and Chrift not only in their practice, but alfo blafphemoufly in profeffion, yet have repented, and at laft obtained fome hope of mercy; I dare not fay it is impoffible for a Witch to repent and find mercy, the fecrets of the Almighty are too high for me; but it is certain, thefe wretches are ftrangely hardned, by what paffes between them and the Devil, in a bodily fhape, particularly their worfhipping him, which neceffarily implies his outward appearance unto them; for no man can apete Evil as Evil, becaufe

Cc

the Law of felf-prefervation deeply rooted in all
men, determineth their wills to purfue that which
feems good, and fly from that which feems evil
unto them, but the inbred notions that every man
has of the Devil, is that he is an Enemy and deftroyer
of mankind, therefore every man hath a Natural
averfion from him, and confequently cannot formally worfhip him as fuch, becaufe the objeft
of worfhip muft be efteemed to be propitious
and placable by the worfhippers, otherwife if fear
alone be the adequate caufe of Adoration, it follows that the Devils and damned in Hell do
worfhip God, which is contrary to Scripture,
which faith they blafphemed, becaufe of their
pains, whence it follows that they who worfhip
the Devil muft have changed the innate Idea that
they had of him, *viz.* that he is an implacable
Worrier of Men, and take him to be benign at leaft
to his own; but this change cannot be wrought
by any fuggeftion of Satan unto the minds of
Men, whom indeed he mentally tempteth to
Luft, Pride and Malice; but it is his greateft
Artifice to caufe his Infinuations to arife in the
hearts of Men, as their own natural thoughts,
and if confcience difcovers their Author and oppofes them, then he varnifhes them over with
the fpecious colours of pleafure, honour and
glory; and fo reprefents them as really good, to
be willed and defired by the Soul, which judgeth
of all things without according to the Ideas fhe
hath of them; but becaufe moft objefts have

two, and some many faces, and she not always
attends, therefore she often errs in her choice,
neverthelefs it is impoffible for her to apete an
object, whofe fimple Idea is Evil; but the Idea
we have of the Devil is fuch, for we cannot reprefent him in our minds any otherwife than the
great· deftroyer of Men, therefore no mental
temptation can make us believe this our grand
Enemy to be [75] ever Exorable by, or in any
meafure favourable to us, whence it evidently
follows, that the Devil to work this change of
opinion his worfhippers have of him, muft appear unto them in a bodily fhape, and impofe
upon them, whom becaufe of their great Corruption and Sinfulnefs, God hath wholly left and
given up [to] ftrong delufions that they fhould
believe a lye, and the Father of lyes; who now
appearing in a humane fhape, telleth them that
he is no fuch Monfter, as he has been reprefented
to them by his Enemy, who calls himfelf God,
which Title of right belongs to him, and that
he (if they contract to be his Servants) will both
amply reward them by giving them power to do
many things very fuitable to their abominable depraved Nature, that the Chriftians, whatever opinion they may pretend to have of their God, cannot
fo much as pretend to, and alfo that he will protect
and defend them againft him, whom heretofore
they have miftaken for the Almighty, and his pretended Son Chrift, whom they muft abjure ere
they can be received by or expect any benefit from

him. Upon no other confideration is it poffible for any man to worfhip the Devil; for the Atheifts, who deny the being of a God, do likewife deny the exiftence of any Spirit good or bad; therefore their drinking the Devils health, even upon their knees (tho' a moft horrid Crime) cannot be conftrued any part of worfhip paid to him, whom they affert to be a Chimera, a meer figment of Statefmen to keep the vulgar in awe. Now I have evinced to you that there are Witches, that the Witch receiveth power from the Devil to do ftrange things, that there is an exprefs Covenant between the Devil and the Witch, that this Covenant cannot be tranfacted mentally, but that the Devil muft appear in a bodily fhape to the Witch; therefore I conclude, that a Witch in the Scripture is fuch, who has made an Explicit Covenant with the Devil, and is impowered by him to do things ftrange in themfelves, and befide their natural courfe.

2. I perfwade myfelf you do not expect from me any Effay concerning the methods, how Witches may or ought to be convinced; I wifh that thofe Gentlemen, whofe Eminent ftation both inables them to perform it, and likewife makes it their duty fo to do, may take this Province upon them, and handle it fo fully as to fatisfie you herein. I once intended to have provided fome materials for this Work, by defining four principal things relating to Witchcraft, viz. 1. Witch-fits. 2. The Imps that are faid to attend

on the Witch. 3. The tranfportation of the
Witch through the Air. 4. Laftly, the invifibi-
lity of the Witch; but upon fecond thoughts
that it was foreign from my purpofe, who am not
concerned to compofe a juft Treatife of Witchcraft, which would require more vacant time,
than my prefent Circumftances will allow, only I
did promife you to give you my Opinion privately; therefore I'le [76] venture to make ufe
of an Argument, which fheweth neither Art nor
Learning in the Author, and it is this, that feeing
there are Witches, and that the Law of God
doth command them to be put to death; therefore there muft be means to convict them, by
clear and certain Proof, otherwife the Law were
in vain; for no Man can be juftly condemned,
who is not fairly convicted by full and certain
Evidence.

III. In the laft place we are to inquire whether
a Witch ought to be put to death or no? you
Anfwer in the *Negative;* becaufe you fay that that
Law, thou fhalt not fuffer a Witch to live, is *Ju-*
dicial, and extendeth only to the People of the
Jews; but our Saviour, or his Apoftles have not
delivered any where any fuch command, therefore
they ought to be fuffered to live, this indeed
feems fomewhat plaufible at firft view, but upon
through Examination hath no weight in it at all
for thefe Reafons, 1. All Penal Laws receive
their Sanction from him or them, who have the
Sovereign -Power in any ftate, as thou fhalt not

commit Adultery, is a Moral-law, and obligatory over the Confciences of Men in all places and Ages; but the Adulterers fhall be put to death is a judicial law, and in force only in that ftate, where it is enacted by the Sovereign.   2. The Government of the *Jews* was a Theocracy, and God himfelf did condefcend to be their King, not only as he is King of Kings; for in that fenfe he is, always was, and ever will be fupreme Lord, and Governour of all his Creatures; but in an efpecial manner to give them Laws for the Government of their State, and to protect them againft their Enemies; in one word to be immediately their Sovereign.   3. Our Saviour's Kingdom was not of this World, he was no Judge to divide fo much as an Inheritance between two Brethren; nay, he himfelf fubmitted patiently to the unjuft Sentence of the Governour of the Country in which he lived; therefore both the rewards and punifhments annexed to his Laws are Spiritual, and then fhall have their full accomplifhment, when the Son of Man at the laft day fhall pronounce, *Come unto me ye bleffed, and depart ye curfed into Everlafting fire.*   4. That Soveraigns, who have received the Gofpel of our Lord, have not therefore loft their Power of enacting Laws for the ruling and preferving their People, and punifhing Malefactors even with Death; fo that the Criminal is as juftly condemned to die by our Municipal, as he was heretofore by the Judicial Law among the Jews: How much more then

ought our Law to advert againſt the higheſt of
all Criminals, thoſe execrable Men and Women,
who tho yet alive, have liſted themſelves under
Satan's banner, and explicitly Sworn Allegiance
to him, to fight againſt God and Chriſt; indeed
all unholy Men afford great matter to the Devils
of Blaſpheming, but theſe wretches have confed-
erated themſelves with the Devils, to blaſpheme
and deſtroy all they can; and do you think that
theſe common [77] Enemies of God and Mankind ought to be ſuffered to live in a Chriſtian
Common wealth, eſpecially conſidering that we
have a Preſident of putting them to death from
God himſelf, when he acted as King over his
own peculiar People. But methinks I hear you
ſaying, all this doth not ſatisfie me, for I am ſure
nothing can be added to the Devils malice, and if
he could, he certainly would appear and frighten
all Men out of their wits. I anſwer, 1. We
muſt not reject a truth, becauſe we cannot reſolve
all the Queſtions that may be propoſed about it;
otherwiſe all our Science muſt be turned into
Scepticiſm, for we have not a comprehenſive
knowledge of any one thing. 2. When you ſay,
that if the Devil could, he would appear and
frighten all Men; the Lawful conſequence is not
that he cannot appear at all, for we have undoubtedly proved the contrary; but that we are
Ignorant of the bounds that the Almighty hath
ſet to him, whoſe malice indeed, if he were not
reſtrain'd, is ſo great as to deſtroy all Men; but

the goodneſs of our God is greater, who hath given us means to eſcape his fury, if we will give earneſt heed to the Goſpel of our Saviour, which only is able to comfort us againſt the ſad and miſerable condition of our preſent ſtate, for not only the Devils, but likewiſe all do conſpire againſt us to work our ruine. The deluge came and ſwept away all the race (ſave eight perſons) of mankind: the Fire will in time devour what the Water has left, and all this cometh to paſs becauſe of Sin; but we who have received the Lord Jeſus, look for new Heavens, and a new Earth, wherein dwelleth Righteouſneſs. Therefore he, if we purifie ourſelves as he is pure, will ſave us (for when he appears we ſhall be made like unto him; to whom be Glory for ever, *Amen*) from the great deſtruction that muſt come upon all the World, and the Inhabitants thereof. Farewell.

March, 8*th* 169¾.

Boſton, *March* 20, 1693.
Worthy Sir,

THE *great pains you have taken for my Information and Satisfaction in thoſe controverted points relating to Witchcraft, whether it attain the end or not, cannot require leſs than ſuitable acknowledgments and gratitude, eſpecially conſidering you had no particular obligation of office to it, and when others, whoſe proper Province it was had declined it. It is a great truth,* [*that the many Hereſies among*

*the Chriſtians (nor the lying Miracles, or Witch-
crafts uſed by ſome to induce to the worſhip of
Images, &c.) muſt not give a Mortal wound to
Chriſtianity or Truth;] but the great queſtion in
theſe con[78]troverted points ſtill is, what is truth.
And in this ſearch being agreed in the Judge or
Rule, there is great hopes of the Iſſue. That there
are Witches is plain from that Rule of Truth, the
Scriptures, which commands their puniſhment by
Death. But what that Witchcraft is, or wherein
it does conſiſt is the whole difficulty. That head cited
from Mr. Gaule,[90] and ſo well proved thereby (not
denied by any) makes the work yet ſhorter ; ſo that it
is agreed to conſiſt in a Malignity, &c. and ſeeking
by a ſign to ſeduce, &c. not excluding any other ſorts
or branches, when as well proved by that infallible
Rule. That good Angels have appeared, is certain,
tho that inſtance of thoſe to Abraham may admit of
a various conſtruction ; ſome Divines ſuppoſing them
to be the Trinity, others that they were Men-meſ-
ſengers, as Judges ii. 1. and others that they were
Angels; but tho this as I ſaid might admit of a
debate, yet I ſee no queſtion of the Angel Gabriel's
appearance, particularly to the B. Virgin ; for tho
the Angels are Spirits, and ſo not perceptible by our
bodily Eyes without the appointment of the moſt high,
yet he who made all things by his word in the Crea-
tion, can with a word ſpeak things into Being. And
whether the Angels did aſſume matter (or a Vehicle)*

---

[90] See *Volume* I, *Pages* 39-41.

Dd

and by that appear to the bodily Eye; or whether by the same word there were an Idea fram'd in the mind, which needed no Vehicle to reprefent them to the Intellects, is with the All-wife, and not for me to difpute. If we poor fhallow Mortals do not comprehend the manner how, that argues only our weaknefs. Two other times did this glorious Angel appear. Dan. viii. 16. Dan. ix. 21. *The firft of thefe times was in Vifion, as by the text and context will appear. The fecond was the fame as at the firft; which being confidered, as it will afcertain that Angels have appear'd; fo that 'tis at the will of the Sender how they fhall appear, whether to the bodily Eye, or Intellect only.* Mat. i. 20. *The appearance of the Angel to Jofeph was in a Dream, and yet a real appearance; fo was there a real appearance to the Apoftle, but whether in the body or out of the body he could not tell; and that they are fent and come not of their own motion.* Luke i. 26. *And in the fixth Month the Angel Gabriel was fent from God.* Dan. ix. 23. *At the beginning of thy fupplication the commandment came forth, and I am come,* v. 21. *Being caufed to fly fwiftly, &c. but from thefe places may be fet down as undoubted truths or conclufions,*

1. *That the glorious Angels have their Miffion and Commiffion from the moft high.*

2. *That without this they cannot appear to mankind. And from thefe two will neceffarily flow a third.*

3. *That if the glorious Angels have not that*

*power to go till commiſſioned, or to appear to Mortals,
then not the fallen Angels; who are held in Chains
of darkneſs, to the Judgment of the great day.
Therefore to argue, that becauſe the good Angels
have appeared, the evil may or can, is to me as if —*
[79] *becauſe the dead have been raiſed to life by Holy
Prophets, therefore Men, wicked Men can raiſe the
dead. As the ſufferings, ſo the temptations of our
Saviour were (in degree) beyond thoſe common to
Man; he being the ſecond Adam, or publick head,
the ſtrongeſt aſſaults were now improved; and we
read that he was tempted, that he might be able to
ſuccour thoſe that are tempted, as alſo that he was
led of the Spirit into the Wilderneſs, that he might be
tempted, &c. But how the tempter appeared to him
who was God Omniſcient; whether to the bodily Eye
or to the Intellect, is as far beyond my cognizance as
for a blind Man to judge of Colours. But from the
whole ſet down this fourth concluſion,*

4. *That when the Almighty free Agent has a
work to bring about for his own glory, or Man's
good; he can Imploy not only Bleſſed Angels, but the
evil ones in it, as* 2 *Cor.* xii. 7. And leſt I ſhould be
exalted above meaſure, there was given to me a
thorn in the fleſh, the Meſſenger of Satan to
buffet me. 1. Sam. 10. xiv, xv, xxiii. *An evil
Spirit from the Lord troubled him. It is a great truth,
we underſtand little, very little, and that in common
things, how much leſs then in ſpirituals, ſuch as are
above humane cognizance. But tho' upon the ſtricteſt
Scrutiny in ſome natural things, we can only diſcover*

*our own Ignorance, yet we muſt not hence deny what we
do know, or ſuffer a 'Rape to be committed upon our
Reaſon and Senſes in the Dark; and ſay that the
Devil by his ordinary Power can aɛt a Vehicle (i. e.)
ſome matter diſtinɛt from himſelf, who is wholly a
Spirit, and yet this matter not to be felt nor heard,
and at the ſame time to be ſeen; or may be felt, and
not heard nor ſeen, &c. ſeems to me to be a Chimera,
invented at firſt to puzzle the belief of reaſonable
Creatures, and ſince Calculated to a Roman Latitude,
to uphold the Doɛtrine of Tranſubſtantiation; who
teach, that under the Accidents of Bread, is contained
the Body of our Saviour, his humane Body, as long, and
as broad, &c. for here the* **P**ower *of the Almighty
muſt not be confined to be leſs than the Devil's, and
'tis he that has ſaid,* hoc eſt meum Corpus. *As to
the conſent of almoſt all Ages, I meddle not now with
it, but come to the fifth Concluſion.*

5. *That when the Divine Being will imploy the
Agency of Evil Spirits for any ſervice, 'tis with him
the manner how they ſhall exhibit themſelves, whether to the bodily Eye, or Intelleɛt only; and whether
it ſhall be more or leſs formidable — To deny theſe
three laſt were to make the Devil an Independent
Power and conſequently a God. As to the nature
of poſſeſſions by Evil Spirits, for the better under-
ſtanding of it, it may be needful to compare it with
its contraries; and to inſtance in* Samſon, *of whom
it was foretold, that he ſhould begin to deliver* Iſrael,
and how was he inabled to this work? Judges xiii.
25. *The Spirit of the Lord began to move him*

at times in the Camp, &c. ch. xv. 13, 14. v. and they bound him with two new cords, and brought him up from the rock, and when they came to Lehi, [80] the Philiftines fhouted againft him, and the Spirit of the Lord came mightily upon him, and the cords that were upon his Arms became as Flax, that was burnt with fire, and his bands loofed from his hands, *&c. I might inftance further, but this may fuffice to fhow that he had more than a natural ftrength, as alfo whence his ftrength was, viz. he was impowered by the Spirit from God. And now will any fay, that it was not* Samfon, *but the Spirit that did thefe things, or that there being things done, bonds broken, &c. by a force that could not proceed from human ftrength, and that therefore the Spirit entered into him otherwife qualified than as meer Spirit ; or that the Spirit entered not without fome Portion of Matter, and by the Intermediation thereof aĉted* Samfon's *body. If any fay this and more too, this doth not alter the truth, which remains, viz. that the Spirit of God did inable* Samfon *to the doing of things beyond his Natural ftrength. And now what remains but upon parity of Reafon, to apply this to the cafe of Poffeffion, which may be fumm'd up in this fixth Conclufion.*

6. *That God for wife ends, only known to himfelf, may and has impowered Devils to Poffefs and ftrangely to aĉt humane Bodies, even to the doing of things beyond the Natural ftrength of that body. And for any to tell of a Vehicle, or matter ufed in*

it, I muſt obſerve that General Rule, Colos. ii. 8.
Beware leſt any ſpoil you through Philoſophy and
vain deceit, after the tradition of Men, after the
Rudiments of the World, and not after Chriſt.
*To come next to that of Witchcraft, and here taking
that cited head of Mr.* Gaul, *to be uncontroverted,
ſet it as a ſeventh Concluſion.*

7. *That Witchcraft conſiſts in a maligning and
oppugning the Word, Work and Worſhip of God,
and ſeeking by any extraordinary ſign to ſeduce any
from it.* Deut. xiii. 12. Matt. xxiv. 24. *Acts* xiii.
8. 10. 2 Tim. iii. 8. *Do but mark well the places,
and for this very property of thus oppoſing and perverting, they are all there concluded arrant and abſolute
Witches ; and it will be eaſily granted, that the ſame
that is call'd Witch, is call'd a falſe Chriſt, a falſe
Prophet, and a Sorcerer, and that the terms are
Synonimous ; and that what the Witches aim at is, to
ſeduce the People to ſeek after other Gods. But
here the Queſtion will be, whether the Witch do really
do things ſtrange in themſelves, and beyond their
natural courſe, and all this by a Power immediately
from the Devil. In this inquiry, as we have nothing to do with unwritten verities, ſo but little with
Cabaliſtick Learning, which might perhaps but lead
us more aſtray, as in the Inſtance of their charging
our Saviour with caſting out Devils by Beelzebub, his
Anſwer is, if Satan be divided againſt himſelf, his
Kingdom hath an end: But ſeeing all are agreed,
ſet this eighth Concluſion.*

8. *That God will not give his teſtimony to a lye.*

To fay that God did at any time impower a Witch to work Wonders, to gain belief to the Doctrine of Devils, were with one breath to deftroy root and branch of all revealed Re[81]*ligion. And hence 'tis clear the Witch has no fuch wonder-working power from God; and muft we then conclude fhe has fuch a Miraculous Power from the Devil; if fo, then it follows that either God gives the Devil leave to impower the Witch to make ufe of this Seal, in order to deceive, or elfe that the Devil has this Power independent of himfelf;*[91] *to affert the firft of thefe were in effect to fay, that tho God will not give his teftimony to a lye, yet that he may impower the Devil to fet to God's own Seal, in order to deceive; and what were this but to overthrow all revealed Religion. The laft if afferted muft be to own the Devil to be an unconquered Enemy, and confequently a Sovereign Deity, and deferving much thanks, that he exerts his Power no more. Therefore in this Dilemma it is Wifdom for fhallow Mortals to have recourfe to their only guide, and impartially to inquire, whether the Witches really have fuch a Miraculous or Wonder-working Power? And 'tis remarkable that the Apoftle,* Gal. v. 20. *reckons up Withcraft among the Works of the flefh, which were it indeed a Wonder-working Power, received immediately from the Devil, and wholly beyond the Power of Nature; it were very improper to place it with* Drunkennnefs, Murthers, Adulteries, &c. *all mani-*

91 See concluding Part of *Note* 81.

feſt fleſhly works. 'Tis alſo remarkable, that Witchcraft is generally in Scripture joined with ſpiritual
Whordom, i. e. Idolatry. This thence will plainly
appear to be the ſame, only pretending to a ſign, in
order to deceive, ſeems to be yet a further degree, and
in this ſenſe Manaſſah and Jezebel, 2 Chron. xxxiii.
6. 2 Kings ix. 22. uſed Witchcraft and Whore-
doms, Nahum iii. 4. The Idolatrous City is called
Miſtreſs of Witchcrafts. But to inſtance in one place
inſtead of many, that 2 Theſ. ii. from the 3 to the 12
v. particularly 9 and 10 v. Even him whoſe coming
is after the working of Satan, with all power and
ſigns, and lying wonders, and with all deceivable-
neſs. And for this cauſe God ſhall ſend them
ſtrong deluſions that they ſhould believe a lye,
that they all might be damned, who believe not
the truth, &c. This, that then was ſpoken in the
Propheſie of that man of Sin, that was to appear,
how abundantly does Hiſtory teſtifie the fulfilment of
it ; particularly to ſeduce to the Worſhip of Images :
Have not the Images been made to move? to ſmile,
&c. too tedious were it to mention the hundredth
part of what undoubted Hiſtory doth abundantly
teſtifie. And hence do ſet down this nineth Concluſion.

9. That the Man of Sin, or Seducer, &c. makes
uſe of lying wonders to the end to deceive, and that
God in Righteous Judgment, may ſend ſtrong deluſions that they ſhould believe a lye, that they
might be damn'd, who believe not the truth, &c.

'Tis certain that the Devil is a proud Being,

and would be thought to have a Power equal to the Almighty; and it cannot but be very grateful to him to fee Mortals charging one another of doing fuch works by the Devil's Power, as in truth is the proper prerogative of the Almighty, Omnipotent Being. The [82] *next head fhould have been about an Explicit Covenant, between the* Witch *and the* Devil, &c. *But in this, the whole of it, I cannot perfwade myfelf but you muft be fenfible of an apparent leaning to Education (or tradition) the Scriptures being wholly filent in it; and fuppofing this to fall in as a dependent on what went before fhall fay the lefs to it; for if the Devil has no fuch Power to communicate, upon fuch compact, then the whole is a fiction; tho I cannot but acknowledge you have faid fo much to uphold that Doctrine, that I know not how any could have done more; however, as I faid, I find not myfelf ingaged (unlefs Scripture proof were offered) to meddle with it. For as you have in fuch cafes your Reafon for your guide, fo I muft be allowed to ufe that little that I have, do only fay that as God is a Spirit, fo he muft be worfhip'd in fpirit and truth. So alfo that the Devil is a Spirit, and that his rule is in the hearts of the Children of Difobedience, and that an Explicit Covenant of one Nature or another can have little force, any further than as the heart is engaged in it. And fo I pafs to the laft, viz. Whether a* Witch *ought to be put to death. And without accumulation of the offence do Judge, that where the Law of any Countrey is to punifh by death fuch as feduce and*

Ee

tempt to the worſhip of ſtrange Gods (or idols, or Statues) by as good Authority may they (no doubt) puniſh theſe as Capital Offenders, who are diſtinguiſhed by that one remove, viz. to their ſeducing is added a ſign, i. e. they pretend to a ſign in order to ſeduce. And thus worthy Sir, I have freely given you my thoughts upon yours, which you ſo much obliged me with the ſight of, and upon the whole, tho I cannot in the general but commend your Caution in not aſſerting many things contended for by others; yet muſt ſay, that in my eſteem there is retain'd ſo much as will ſecure all the reſt; (to inſtance) if a Spirit has a Vehicle, i. e. ſome portion of matter which it acts, &c. hence as neceſſarily may be inferred that Doctrine of Incubus *and* Succubus, *and why not alſo that of Procreation by Spirits both good and bad? Thus was* Alexander *the* Great, *the* Brittiſh Merlin,[92] *and* Martin Luther, *and many others ſaid to be begotten. Again if the Witch has ſuch a Wonder-working Power, why not to afflict? will not the Devil thus far gratiſie her? And have none this Miraculous Power, but the Covenanting Witch? then the offence lyes in the Cove-*

---

[92] If not a mythical Character, he is ſurrounded with much Myſtery. There, however, ſeems to have been, at ſome remote Period, a Man named *Ambroſe Merlin,* living in Carmarthenſhire, in Wales; and it will pay the Reader well to turn to Thomas Fuller, and ſee what he ſays about him in his *Worthies,* Vol. III, 524. Among other things he ſays: "His Extraction is very Incredible, reported to have an Incubus to his Father, pretending to a Pedigree older than Adam, even from the Serpent himſelf. But a learned Pen demonſtrateth the Impoſſibility of ſuch Conjunctions. And let us not load Satan with groundleſs Sins, whom I believe the Father of Lies, but no Father of Baſtards." A witty Conceit, but ruinous to the Theory of Witchcraft.

nant, then 'tis not only hard, but Impoſſible to find a
Witch by ſuch Evidence as the Law of God re-
quires; for it will not be ſuppoſed that they call
Witneſs to this Covenant; therefore it will here be
neceſſary to admit of ſuch as the nature of ſuch
Covenant will bear (as Mr. Gaul *hath it in his 5th*
head, i. e.) the teſtimony of the afflicted, with their
Spectral ſight, to tell who afflicts themſelves or
others; the experiment of ſaying the Lords Prayer,
falling at the ſight, and riſing at the touch, ſearch-
ing for Tets (i. e. Excreſcencies of Nature) ſtrange
and foreign ſtories of the Death of ſome Cattle, or
over-ſetting ſome Cart; and what can Juries have
better to guide them to find out this Covenant by.

[83] *'Tis matter of lamentation, and let it be for*
a lamentation, to conſider how theſe things have
open'd the Floodgates of Malice, Revenge, Unchar-
itableneſs, and Bloodſhed, what Multitudes have been
ſwept away by this Torrent.

In Germany, *Countries depopulated; In* Scotland
no leſs than 4000 *have ſaid to have ſuffered by Fire*
and Halter at one heat.[93]

Thus we may ſay with the Prophet, Iſa. lix. 10.
We grope for the Wall like the blind, and we
grope as if we had no Eyes: we ſtumble at
Noon-day as in the Night, we are in deſolate
places as dead Men: *and this by ſeeking to be wiſe*
above what is written, in framing to ourſelves ſuch
crimes and ſuch Ordels (or ways of Tryal) as are

[93] See Vol. I, *Introduction,* Page   were but few Years before thoſe in
xv.   The Executions in Scotland   New England.

wholly foreign from the direction of our only guide,
which should be a light to our feet, and a Lanthorn
to our paths; but instead of this, if we have not
followed the direction we have followed the Example
of Pagan *and* Papal Rome, *thereby rendering us*
contemptable, and base before all People, according
as we have not kept his ways, but have been partial
in his Law.

And now that we may in all our fentiments
and ways, have regard to his teftimonies, and give
to the Almighty the glory due to his Name, is
the earneft defire and Prayer of, Sir,
Yours to Command,　　　R. C.

A second Letter of a Gentleman,[94] *endea-*
vouring to prove the received Opinions
about Witchcraft.

SIR,

SINCE your defign of giving Copies of our
Papers (if not to the publick at leaft) out of
your hands, I find myfelf obliged to make a Reply to your Anfwer, left filence fhould be conftrued an Affent to the pofitions whereby (I
think) truth would be fcandaliz'd. I remember
that fome have taught that it is not certain there
is any fuch thing really in being as matter; becaufe the Ideas which we have of our own, and
all other bodies, may be caufed to arife in us by

---

[94] The fame Gentleman mentioned in *Note* 83, *Page* 64.

God, without the real exiftence of the objects
they reprefent. But this opinion is not only abfurd and falfe, but likewife Atheiftical, deftroy-
ing the veracity of the Almighty, whom it afferts
to have determin'd us by a fatal neceffity to believe things to be, which are not; and I wonder
that you fhould allude unto it, becaufe that Angels have appeared in a Dream, in a vifion; for
we dream alfo of Trees, Birds, &c. are there
therefore no fuch things in nature, becaufe we
fometimes Dream to fee and hear them, when we
are. afleep? St. *Paul* in his Vifion was fo far
from believing the Objects that were reprefented
to him, to come by the intermedium of his
Senfes, that he declares, he [84] does not know
whether he was in the body, or out of the body;
therefore the Inftance is in no wife proper. For
Abraham and the B. Virgin did fee and hear; and
if there were not fuch things really, as were reprefented to them by their Senfes, they were deluded, by being made to believe they faw and
heard what was not. There is none who denieth
God caufing thoughts to arife in Mens minds:
but thence to infer he maketh Objects which are
not, by forming their Ideas in our minds, to
appear to us through the Miniftry of our Senfes
as though they were, is a piece not only of vain,
but very dangerous Philofophy. It is true, the
good Angels will not appear without the appointment of God, they will not do any one Action,
but according to the laws he has prefcribed to

them. But you fay they cannot (which does not follow from your premifes) fuppofing their not appearing to proceed from the defeet of their power, and not the rectitude of their will, which fallacy has deceived you into a third Conclufion. For the fallen Angels are not fo held under Chains of darknefs ; but that they can and do go to [and] fro on the earth feeking whom they may devour. Before their fall they could have appeared if fent, and would not then do any thing without a Divine Command But now they have rebell'd againft God, and do all they can to defpife him, therefore their not appearing now (if it were true they never did, they never fhall appear) muft proceed from a reftraint they are under, which is accidental, not Effential to their nature ; fo that the true Conclufion is, the fallen Angels, while they are under forcible reftraint from God to the contrary cannot appear. But what this (being cleared from the Ambiguity you exprefs it in) maketh to the purpofe I know not, unlefs God had promifed for a determinate time to detain them under this reftraint. I do not underftand what you intend by the dead being raifed by Holy Men; the moft natural inference is, that in imitation of them wicked men by their Inchantments calling on a *Dæmon* to appear in the fhape of the dead, will pretend that they alfo can raife the dead. The *Romanifts* are much obliged to you for making Tranfub-ftantiation (fo much contended for by them) to be

of as old a date as the appearance of Devils, and
that the one implieth no more contradiction than
the other : If fo we do well to think ferioufly
whether we are not guilty of great fin in fepa-
rating from them ; for certainly whatever private
Mens Notions in this Age may be, yet it is
matter of great moment, that all Antiquity (the
Saducees the Elder Brethren of our Hobbifts[94]
excepted) hath believed the appearance of Evil
Spirits and their Illufions. I fhould be too offi-
cious if I offered to explain, how matter, real
matter may fall under the cognifance of one of
our fenfes, and not the reft. It is for you to fhew
the impoffibility thereof, if you will build any
thing upon your Affertion, to prove which your
firft Argument is (it feems to me) a Chimera,
which [85] is not enough, when there are many
to whom it feems to be a truth : Your fecond is
very dangerous, and highly derogatory of the
honour of God, between whom and the Devil
you make comparifon more than once as the
power of the Almighty muft not be confined to
be lefs than the Devils. And again, to deny
thefe three laft were to make the Devil an Independent Power and confequently a God. Thefe
expreffions (which cannot but be very pleafing to
the Devil, who vainly boafts himfelf to be a Be-

---

94 Thomas Hobbes, a Native of
Malmfbury in Wiltfhire, England,
born in 1588, and died in 1679.
He has been ftigmatized as an Unbe-
liever in Divine Revelation ; was a
Man of extenfive learning, publifhed Works on Philofophy, and
tranflated Homer.

ing without dependance) are altogether groundlefs, and very unmeet to proceed from a Chriftian:
Confider what you are a doing, to eftablifh a Doctrine (the contrary whereof the greateft part of
mankind does believe) you run upon fuch preci-
pices, as if you are miftaken, and that is not
impoffible, muft totally deftroy all Religion,
Natural and Revealed; for fuppofe it were generally believed according to you, that the Devil
cannot appear, becaufe if he could he muft be a
God, independent, an unconquer'd enemy, and
he doth appear to us as we hear he hath to multitudes, both of the paft and prefent ages: In
fuch a cafe what remains for us to do; but to fall
down and worfhip him. Upon the head of
poffeffion, you have recourfe to that inftance of
Samfon, who was impowered by God, to the
doing of things beyond the Natural ftrength of
common Men, and thence you fay, we may leaft
learn the Nature of Poffeffion by evil Spirits,
this comparifon is indeed very odious, and I had
rather think you have fallen into it unawares;
for what greater Blafphemy than that God and
the Devil do act the bodies, which the one and
the other do poffefs in the fame manner; if the
hypothefis I laid down had not pleafed you, yet
you ought not (for fear of being deceiv'd by vain
Philofophy, to have run fo horrible an extream,
as to affimulate God's manner of working to the
Devils, which neceffarily implies, that either
their Powers are equal, or at leaft that they do

not differ in kind but in degree only; than which
nothing can be more impious or abfurd; for the
moft poffibly perfect Creature, is infinitely diftant
from the Creator, and there can be no Comparifon between them. On the head of Witchcraft,
you acknowledge the Witch has not his Wonder-working Power from God; but then you
fay, the Devil has no fuch power to give; for if
he had, he muft be —— This way of reafoning
as I noted before, is very dangerous, and I think
ought not to be ufed; befides there is a great
fallacy in your Dilemma; which becaufe I per-
ceive, you lay the whole weight of the matter
upon it, I will evince unto you. The Devil tho
fuperlatively Arrogant and Proud, neverthelefs
depends on the firft caufe for his being, and all
his Powers, without whofe Influx he or any
other Creature cannot fubfift a moment, but
muft either return to their primitive Nothing, or
be continually preferved by the fame Power, by
the which they were at firft produced; therefore
the [86] Beings and Powers of all Creatures
(becaufe they immediately flow from God) are
good, and confequently the fimple Actions, as
they proceed from thofe Powers, are in their own
nature likewife good, the Evil proceeding only
from the Rebellious will of the Creature, wherefore 'tis no Paradox, but a certain truth, that the
fame action in refpect to the firft caufe is good,
but in refpect of the fecond is Evil; for inftance,
the act of Copulation is in itfelf good, inftituted

Ff

by God, and may be willed and defired by the
Soul, which finneth not for exerting the fimple
act; but for exerting it contrary to the Laws
prefcribe'd by God: as in Wedlock and Adultery there is the fame fpecial natural Action,
which confider'd fimply, as flowing from a
Power given to Man by God is certainly good;
but confidered with relation to the rebellious
will of the Adulterer (who lieth with his Neighbours Wife, whom he is forbad to touch) is a
very great Evil. We may fay the fame of all
humane Actions, the Executioner and the Murtherer do the fame natural Act of ftriking and
killing: The difference confifts in the rectitude
of the ones and depravation of the others will.
Thefe things premifed, what more reafon have
we to conclude that the Devil (becaufe he fhews
figns and wonders to gain belief to lyes, which is
very contrary to the will of God) muft be therefore
an Independent Power; than that the Adulterer,
the Murtherer, or any other finner (becaufe their
Actions being Evil, of which God cannot be the
caufe) muft be Independent beings: The deceit
of the laft is very palpable, and I doubt not you
will readily acknowledge it, for it is obvious
from what has been faid to the meaneft Capacity, to diftinguifh between the Action itfelf,
which is good, and flows from God, and the
Circumftances of the Action, the choice whereof
proceeds from the Iniquity of the Will, wherein
doth folely confift the Sin; the parallel is fo ex-

act, that I cannot fee the leaft fhadow of reafon, why we ought not in like manner to diftinguifh whatever effect is produced by the Devil; to whom (as to Man) God having given Powers, and a Will to Rule them Powers, is truly and properly the caufe of all the Actions (in a Natural, but not Moral Senfe) that flow from the Powers he has given. Therefore the Wonder-working Power of the Devil, and the effects thereof, confidered as Acts of one of God's Creatures, are not Evil but Good ; the ufing that Power (which proceeds from the Rebellion of Satan) to bear teftimony to a lye, is that one, which conftitutes the Evil thereof.

And now I have done with your Argument, wherein you have indeed fhewn great fkill and dexterity in turning to your Advantage, what being fairly ftated makes againft you, as the Appearance of Angels, &c. obferving nicely the rules of Art, and particularly that grand one of concealing, nay diffembling the fame Art, as when you quote that Scripture [87] concerning vain Philofophy (of which tho altogether foreign from the matter in hand yet) you intend to ferve yourfelf with the Unthinking, who meafure the Senfe of words by their Jingle, not knowing how to weigh the things they fignifie, and truly herein your end is very Artificial ; for you intend both to throw dirt at them that differ from you, and at the fame time to cover yourfelf with fuch a fubtle web, through which you may fee, and

not be feen. What follows, is rather a Rhetorical
Lecture, fuch as the Patriots of Sects (who commonly Explain the Holy Scriptures according to
their own Dogma's, and fo obtrude humane Invention for the pure word of God) ufe with their
Auditors, to recommend any Principle they have
a mind to eftablifh, than an Impartial and through
difquifition of a controverted point; wherefore I
do not think myfelf obliged to take any further
notice of it; efpecially feeing truth, which for
the moft part is little regarded in fuch florid Difcourfes, and not any prejudice of Education, Intereft, or Party, did fet me about this fubject. I
have never been ufed to Complement in points of
Controverfy, therefore I hope you'l not be angry,
becaufe I have given you my thoughts naked and
plain. I have not the leaft motion in my mind
of accufing you of any formal defign to injure
Religion; I only obferve unto you, that your
over eager contention to maintain your Principle,
has hurried you to affert many things of much
greater danger, both in themfelves and their confequences, than thofe you would feem to avoid;
which do amount to no more than that, Men
being (in the ordinary courfe of Providence) the
Depofitories of both Divine and Humane Laws,
may (inftead of ufing them to preferve) pervert
them to deftroy; which indeed is very lament-
able.

But it is the inevitable confequent of our depraved nature, and cannot be wholly remedied,

till Sin, and the grand Author of Sin, the Devil,
be entirely conquered, and God be all in all; to
whom, with the Son, and Holy Ghoſt, be glory
for ever, *Amen.*

  Sir, your Affectionate Friend to ſerve you.
Boſton, July 25, 1694.

        Boſton, Auguſt 17, 1694.
Worthy Sir,

YOURS of *July* 25, being in ſome ſort ſur-
 priſing to me, I could do no leſs than ſay
ſomewhat, as well to vindicate myſelf from thoſe
many Reflections, miſtakes and hard cenſures
therein; as alſo to vindicate what I conceive to
be Important truth, and to that end find it needful
to repeat ſome part of mine, *Viz.* Concluſion.

 [88] 1. That the glorious Angels have their
Miſſion and Commiſſion from the moſt High.

 2. That without this they cannot appear to
mankind.

 3. That if the glorious Angels have not that
power to go till commiſſion'd, or to appear to
Mortals, then not the fallen Angels, who are held
in Chains of Darkneſs to the Judgment of the
great Day.

 4. That when the Almighty free Agent has a
work to bring about for his own glory, or Mans
good, he can employ not only the Bleſſed Angels,
but evil ones in it.

 5. That when the Divine Being will imploy
the Agency of Evil Spirits for any ſervice, 'tis

‣ with him the manner how they fhall exhibit
themfelves, whether to the bodily Eye, or Intellect only, or whether it fhall be more or lefs formidable.

To deny thefe three laft, were to make the
Devil an Independent Power, and confequently a
God.

The bare recital of thefe is fufficient to vindicate me from that reitterated charge, of denying
all appearances of Angels or Devils.

That the good Angels cannot appear without
Miffion and Commiffion from the moft high, is
you fay more than follows from the premifes;
but if you like not fuch Negative deduction,
though fo natural, it concerns you (if you will
affert this Power to be in their Natures, and their
non appearance only to proceed from the rectitude of their wills, and that without fuch Commiffion they have a Power to appear to Mortals,
and upon this to build fo prodigious a Structure,
&c.) very clearly to prove it by Scripture, for
Chriftians have good reafon to take the Apoftles
warning (if fome Philofophers have taught that
Man is nothing but matter. And others that 'tis
not certain there is any Matter at all) *to take heed
leaft they fhould be fpoiled through vain Philofophy,
&c.* but that this fhould be alluded to by fuch as
never heard of either. Notion, or that it was afferted that thofe real appearances to *Jofeph,* and
to the Apoftle, was through the Miniftry of the
Senfes, is as vain as fuch Philofophy. As to the

Dead being raifed, had I ufed Art or Rhetorick
enough to explain my meaning to you, I needed
not now to rejoin.   That 'tis as good an Argument to fay, that becaufe Holy Prophets have
raifed the dead, therefore wicked Men have a
Power to raife the dead: As 'tis to fay, becaufe
good Angels have appeared, therefore the Evil
have a Power to appear; for who can doubt, but
if the Almighty fhall Commiffionate a wicked
Man to it, he alfo fhall raife the dead, as is intimated, *Mat.* vii. 22.   *And in thy name done many
wonderful Works.*   As to comparifons being odious, particularly that concerning *Samfon*, I think
it needful here to add thefe Scriptures further to
confirm the fourth Conclufion.   2 *Sam.* xxiv. 1.
compared with 1 *Chron.* xxi. 1.   *In one 'tis God
moved, &c. and in the o*[89]*ther Satan provoked*
David *to number the People.*   2 Chron. xviii. 21.
*And the Lord faid, thou fhalt intice him, and thou
fhalt alfo prevail, go out and do even fo;* all which,
with many more that might be produc'd, as they
will fhew the truth of the Conclufion; fo that
'tis no odious comparifon to fay, that as the Almighty can make ufe of Good, fo alfo of Evil
Spirits, for the accomplifhing of his own wife
ends, and can impower either without the help
of a Vehicle.   For poffeffions muft be numbred
among Gods afflictive difpenfations, who alfo orders all the Circumftances thereof.   But if any
object God is not the Author of Evil, &c. you
have furnifh'd me with a very learned Anfwer, by

diftinguifhing between the Act and the Evil of the Act, and to which 'tis adapt, but will no wife fute where it is placed, till it be firft proved that the Devil hath of himfelf fuch Power not only of appearing at pleafure, but of working Miracles, and to the Almighty referved only the power of reftraining; for till this be proved the Dilemma muft remain ftable. He that afferts that—Becaufe good Angels have appeared, that therefore the fallen Angels have a Power of themfelves to appear to Mortals; And that they cannot be employed by the Almighty; nor that he does not order the manner and Circumftances of fuch appearance, what doth he lefs than make the Devil an Independent Power, and confequently a God! So he that afferts that the Devil hath a Power of himfelf, and Independent to work Wonders, and Miracles, and to impower Witches to do like in order to deceive, &c. What doth he lefs than own him to be an unconquered Enemy, and confequently a Sovereign Deity![96] and who is it that is culpable? he that afcribes fuch Attributes to the Evil one, or he that afferts that the fo doing gives him (or afcribes to him) fuch Power as is the prerogative of him only who is Almighty? and here Sir, it highly concerns you to confider your foundations, what proof from

---

[96] Finding themfelves in this Dilemma (many of the Believers in Witchcraft never having thought of it, it would feem,) the Advocates muft have been fadly puzzled. Nor is it eafy to fee how, by turning to Locke, Le Clerc, or Cudworth, they are helped at all.

Scripture is to be found for your Affertions, and who it is you are contending for. For hitherto nothing like a proof hath been offer'd from Scripture, which abounds fo with the contrary, that he that runs may read, *As fhall there be evil in the City, and the Lord hath not done it? who is he that faith, and it cameth to pafs when the Lord commandeth it not.* Who among the Gods of the Heathen (of which the Devil is one) can give Rain, *&c.*

But I fhall not be tedious in multiplying proofs, to that which all feem to own. For as to that ftale plea of Univerfality, do fay that I have read of one, if not feveral, general Councels, that have not only difapproved, but Anathematiz'd them that have afcribed fuch Power to the Devils. And feveral National Proteftant Churches at this day in their Exhortation before the Sacrament (among other Enormous Crimes) admonifh all that believe any fuch Power in the Witch, *&c.* to withdraw as unmeet to partake at the Lord's Table.

[90] And I believe Chriftians in general, if they were afked, would own that what Powers the Devil may at any time have to appear, to afflict, deftroy, or caufe tempefts, *&c.* muft be by Power or Commiffion from the Sovereign Being. And that having fuch a Commiffion, not only Hail, but Frogs, Lice, or Flies fhall be impowered to plague a great King and Kingdom. And if fo, this Sandy Structure of the Devils appearance,

Gg

and working Wonders at pleasure, and of Impowering Witches to afflict, &c. (for to this narrow Crisis is that whole Doctrine reduc'd) the whole disappears at the first shaking.[97]

Thus worthy Sir, I have given you my sentiments, and the grounds thereof, as plainly and as concise as I was able, tho 'tis indeed a subject that calls for the ablest Pens to discuss, acknowledging myself to be insufficient for these things; however I think I have done but my duty for the glory of God, the Sovereign Being; and have purposely avoided such a reply as some parts of yours required.

And pray that not only you and I, but all mankind may give to the Almighty the glory due unto his name. From, Sir, Yours to Command,

R. C.

Witchcraft is manifestly a Work of the Flesh.

[97] Le Clerc has one sensible Remark, among many weak ones, about the Existence of Witches. He says: "Those Opinions or Diseases of the Brain which Witches have, who think they go to Feasts and Dancings, upon their talking of it to others, that are of a timorous Disposition and weak Brains, bring others into the same Fits of Fury, and, like a Contagion, spread far and near, infesting many Heads; though it is observable those Diseases are more frequent amongst the Inhabitants of Mountains and solitary Places, than amongst those that live in Cities." It must occur to the judicious Reader, that Mons. Le Clerc took a roundabout Way to tell him that Witchcraft flourished best among ignorant People. See *A Compleat History of Magick, Sorcery, and Witchcraft*, London, 1715, 2 Vols. 12mo.

[END OF VOL. II.]